Endorsements

In *The Poet's Treasure*, the final installment of her futuristic trilogy, *Within the Walls*, Stephanie Bennett again tackles the tensions that exist in an American culture gone awry. The citizens have been told by the government the earth is toxic, and thus life has been reduced to existing within the walls of their domiciles, working, and receiving food rations every week— provided in a food hopper. But most of all, this culture is void of relationships. Emilya and her husband are caught between possibly contributing to a better world, or exiting the system to pursue life in fellowship with others. In reading this trilogy, you will be confronted with the serious issues regarding the impact of technology on human community. I encourage you to step into the *Within the Walls* narrative and be challenged to consider what life is really about!

JON ZENS, author of *No Will of My Own: How Patriarchy Smothers Female Dignity and Personhood*

In a world of people who are completely connected to each other through their OSLM devices, Emilya discovers just how disconnected humans have become from the world around them, each other, and God! This brilliant installment dares the reader to unplug from their smart devices and take a look at the world with fresh eyes.

MARC GOLDBERG, Director of Campus Store, Palm Beach Atlantic University

The Poet's Treasure is a compelling read about the inner turmoil we all face between the community our hearts crave and the technology that too often undermines it, especially when it seeks to control us rather than serve us. Stephanie Bennett offers up a satisfying end to her *Within the Walls* trilogy, an incisive story sorts through the most difficult issues of our age.

WAYNE JACOBSEN, author of *Finding Church, He Loves Me*, and co-author of *The Shack*

The Poet's Treasure

Book 3 in the
***Within the Walls* trilogy**

by Stephanie Bennett

Wild Flower Press, Inc.
Leland, North Carolina

The Poet's Treasure
Book 3 in the Within the Walls trilogy

Published by Wild Flower Press, Inc.
P.O. Box 2532
Leland, NC 28451
Website: www.wildflowerpress.biz

Print book version
ISBN-13: 978-0-9909616-4-2

Library of Congress Control Number: 2015959465

Published and Printed in the United States of America

Acknowledgments

I would like to thank:

Former student, brother, and friend, Marc Goldberg, whose strong, inquisitive mind and thoughtful ways always touch my heart.

Morissa, my gym buddy who labors with me weekly through at least 100 reps of bicep curls and squats, and inspires me to keep pressing on no matter how late I come to class! She labored through the rough draft of the book, providing insight and feedback that was invaluable.

Wayne, a brother whose generous heart always makes time for his friends.

Those who took special care to cheer me on: cousins Robert and Pat, Janelle at Shoppe561, and my chief cheerleader—a true inspiration—my sister Ruthie.

Jon, chief encourager among all my friends. (Thank you for your relentless kindness and active concern for brethren near and far. I love that you have such a strong commitment to helping women see themselves as God sees them—capable, strong, worthy to speak Truth.)

My cherished friend from the Motherland, Chris J., whose artwork and initial photograph captured my imagination and has inspired all three book covers.

Julie and Sandy, two precious friends, both such creative souls who have held up my arms and supported my own creative efforts through three books! They don't know it, but these two friends have even inspired some of Emi's beachy poetry.

Jackie, Deb, Maria, Terry, and all the women who are part of my community. You gals help keep me sane!

The highest regard and appreciation for publisher extraordinaire, Mrs. Craig, publisher of Wild Flower Press, who works tirelessly to produce compelling, intelligent fiction and . . . won't let me get away with a thing. I love you, girl!

Finally, the guy who provides the steady backbeat to my life—Earl "the Hammer" Bennett—whose 'big ears' listen with compassion and creativity to all my ideas and helps me sift through them. Thanks, especially, for simply letting me be me.

Dedication

This is dedicated to all the Emilyas who search for meaning in this crazy, mixed up, beautiful world. There is hope. There is truth. There is love, and it isn't found in a vacuum.

Day 1—The Book

The Crash.
The Falling.
The transmogrification.
Molecules disintegrating;
Flesh morphing into metal
Then graphite
Then air.
Where?
Where does the body go
    when the soul dies
    and the life flies
    out of being?
Where do the questions end
    when the self awakens to
    more than its own
    lonely existence?
Alive
    and kicking,
    she is inside me;
But who she is
    will not be known
    until the song is sewn
    through the fabric
    of her loves.
And I,
Oh dear—am one.

###

Writing makes me feel so safe.

I've no illusions of being too terribly good at it, but man does it calm my nerves. It's hard to explain, but even as paper and pens have become so expensive and scarce, I'm so glad I can still get them. At least that's one benefit of keeping my position at TraveLite Global. It's been a bit of a rocky transition back into my role there, but as VP of Marketing the fat paycheck makes it well worthwhile.

It's not just the money, though. My family's legacy as innovators and early adopters of the new media also contends for part of what inspires me to continue. I definitely continue to feel a responsibility. *That hasn't changed.* However, since I've been back from FRANCO, I really do feel for them—everyone, that is, who has never seen a jot or tittle of anything but the narrow slice of life they experience here in City Centre. I sure hope that my contribution to their drab lives provides a modicum of relief from the utter monotony of it all. I mean, yeah, we've all got everything we need to survive within the walls of our individual flats, but frankly, if I didn't have the LAB as a work destination to change things up a bit, I think I'd go crazy. It's hard to imagine so much of the population doesn't even have that.

Work isn't perfect though. There's already a bit of pushback around the department, but I'm confident that all the new little kinks I've encountered there will work themselves out.

"Hey you—how 'bout a cuppa lavender rose?"

It was yesterday morning and Viddie called to me from the kitchen in his rugged, but nicely upbeat voice. I like to catalog our conversations as much as possible.

"The chamomile came in this week's food supply shipment."

"Please, yes! Thank you, dear, but I'm in the mood for something a little heartier. Can I have the roobious today?"

Ahhh—I am so clearly pampered these days. What a guy! Who'da believed that sharing space with someone else and living in such close quarters could be better than being alone? It's been quite eye-opening, this marriage that we have. That man is the absolute brightest spot in my life. In spite of the intermittent flickers of frustration I have to deal with from the LAB, I'm comforted in knowing he's here, and that we're sharing this life together. In fact, it's hard to imagine ever going back to living alone in this flat again. *FLAT!* Oh yeah, that about describes my entire life before Belvedere Florencia. Flat, unencumbered, and . . . unconsciously miserable.

It's because of him—mainly—that I'm trying to adapt to his . . . *um* . . . what should I call it—his functional imperatives? *Ha!* Actually, it's just his way of being in the world, or I guess, more precisely, the way he chooses to live, and so he's asked me to avoid using my tek when I'm away from the office so that we can be more in sync. It's pretty much the only thing he's requested of me since he left FRANCO, so I have complied. I disengage from my enhanced memory system whenever I'm not at the LAB. Unfortunately, the more I attempt to opt out of that overly-immersive but oh-so-necessary communication tool everyone calls the OLSM—the more I realize this membrane is part of me . . . *it's how I function.* And the more I attempt this feat, the more I am faced with the harsh realization that my brain is just not at its best without it.

It's a strange development because my trusty PZ/1000, that device that we all wear, embedded in the cuticle of our forefinger, is my very own creation. Yup. I'm famous for it, and it's made connection to the Ongoing Life-Sustaining Membrane much easier this past fifteen or so years. I remember when I first came up with it—it was kind of a fluke. I was just a teenager, and Grand'Mere brought my rough schematic to the LAB. They freaked, because it seemed so natural and just made the OLSM more seamless. In any case, it's especially ironic that now, after all these years, the very tek I helped create is something I am challenged to put down. And it's especially hard because it's something I've used to tap into information ever since I was old enough to read! The OLSM has always kept me working at peak performance (such a fantastic feature of contemporary technological wonder) but now, much as I try to use my own gray matter, I find I still need my internal archives.

I've been pondering so many things lately, and as Vidd came back with my roobious he caught me in the middle of a daydream. I couldn't help laughing as he intoned my mother again . . . ah, that affectation . . . it's so her, and he does it so well.

"Here, oh fair one, is your beverage. Wouldst thou prefer one lump of sweetener or perhaps a bit more?"

"Ahhh . . . yes, thank you, love." I tried to mimic the accent. Wasn't happening. Ha! *Mmmm.* The fragrance of my spicy red roobious wafted up to my nostrils with the intense aroma of rose petals, artisanal honey and ginger. As I took the steamy cup from his hands I shot him a grateful smile. He is so good about this little afternoon ritual. Oh how I enjoy having our tea time together.

"Smells good, doesn't it *mi amor*?"

Ever since we tied the knot at ADMIN's Office of the Magistrate he's taken to calling me that. Reminds me, of course, of Grand'Mere, but now that we're a good eight months married, it's become his own pet name for me. My Italian guy, mixing up the French, Spanish and English—ha, what fun he is!

So, back to my notes here in my trusty art book.

This journal is the one and only place I can go to with my thoughts where I feel completely assured that what I'm thinking cannot be hacked by anyone. No cloud, no network, no OLSM, no P/Z 1000–*ah*, writing—it is so totally old school. I mean, I guess someone could burglarize us here at the flat, but heck—people barely come out of their houses these days except for the few work commuters on the road—I seriously doubt that anyone's gonna rob us.

Yeah, this little book provides a strange sort of free space for my cluttered head. Funny, how I sort of mindlessly threw it in the backpack when I left FRANCO in such a moment of torment. There's no way that I was cognizant of just how important it would become, but I'm so glad I've got it. Occasionally I'll pull Russa's red oak leaf from the back of the book where I kept it from one of our walk/talks to rubble ridge. I was struck by its vibrancy on the day we found it. She picked it up and said something profound (which I don't recall) but then gave it to me. I forgot that I stuck it in there, but it got pressed between the pages and now when I look at that crinkly, brown leaf I am left with a lump in my throat, remembering the simple joy of having a real friend.

Yup. I can't quite get over missing her. I am struck by the magnitude of our friendship, and well, friendship in general. It's something I never experienced before living up there in FRANCO in the middle of the grand woods and lower Pocono Mountains. I spend much time reflecting on the joy of it, but also on the lingering pain when friendship is gone. It's not just that you miss a friend who has died; there's a residing sense of loss that feels . . . well, it feels like an empty drum inside me, and it just echoes and echoes, reverberating into the nothingness. The reality of it is still so much a mystery to me, but one thing I know: although it still hurts so much now that Roos is gone, I wouldn't have traded it for anything.

So lately, every day or so I find myself picking up the pen and jotting down a few words, and it feels like . . . I dunno . . . my own little private domain. It's ironic that I have come to enjoy it so. Unfortunately, I am acutely aware that as I recount the day's activities my scribbling is often less than stellar. *And* coming from a culture that has long stopped demanding rigid grammar or penmanship, I often find myself writing in fragments, using broken metaphors, mixing verb tenses, piecing together sentences with single words—*Ha!*—ask me if I care (I don't). Even as a young child Grand'Mere tried to get me writing a little bit every day, but I always cared more about computation and never took writing seriously. And then—that long hiatus without a pen or paper; gosh, it took quite a bit of time for my hand to acclimate to a writing utensil. Even now, I occasionally get a cramp between my thumb and forefinger.

Clearly, my penmanship improved last year after I started keeping my first journal, but in spite of that, my grammar still suffers. And does it ever! I imagine it must at least be partially due to the fact that I sit down to write at all different times of the day. Sometimes I sit and write as I am in the midst of whatever's happening, while other times I write at night, recalling the events that occurred earlier or even the day before. I am thankful that Marissa had this second blank book made for me, but through it I see that there's much I need to work on. I have a long way to go before I can call myself a decent writer. And that's not all. I need to keep working on using my brain to remember the simple details of life!

For instance, the other day, the challenge of my weakened memory function was made abundantly clear to me when I read my thoughts aloud to my husband. I hadn't fully seen it until then, but we were discussing the sad and unlikely possibility of ever getting back to FRANCO and the importance of making a positive difference right here in the midst of the city. Although he is in agreement, I can tell he doesn't have the same fervor for this endeavor as I do. I'm sure if it were up to him he'd have us run back to FRANCO to cloister ourselves in the mountains and live the remainder of our lives in caves and earth shelters! *Anyway*, the conversation led to a lengthy time of reminiscing.

We began to muse over the beauty and splendor of the mountains, particularly Holly Hill, and he quite matter-of-factly told me that the crates of dried meat that I remembered in that dusty basement there were . . . well, they were simply *not there.* I was positive there were stacks and stacks of jerky right behind the hard cheeses! Given that it was he and my father who made the initial discovery of that well-supplied mountain lodge, he undoubtedly knows the inventory much better than I do, but— *Ugh.* I hate being wrong.

Then there was the other thing. In reminiscing about the breathtakingly-beautiful lilac bushes lining the fence leading up to Holly Hill, he had to adjust my faulty recollection again.

"Nope, they definitely weren't lilacs, hon. Totally different from lilacs. We always made tea out of those heart-shaped leaves; your grandmother would fix it for us anytime there was a sore throat in the camp. They were hollyhocks, baby—I'm sure of it."

Sheesh. Using only organics to remember is a challenge—a challenge indeed. It seems I am in need of some intense brain-training! I've definitely got a bit of catching up to do. Unfortunately, I don't think he realizes just how challenging this is for me. Vidd's always functioned without it and learned to do *everything* without enhancement, but for me . . . *man alive,* when I don't connect, it so dreadfully affects my memory, my ability to get my work done, my knowledge of history, the construction of vid-clips—*everything.* So that's my issue these days . . . that, along with dealing with the changes in my body. As the baby gets closer to coming, my excitement increases along with my size. She'll be born soon, and I'll be delivered of this bulbous mountain of a belly, but my brain? I think it's gonna take much longer to return to a more natural state of memory and frankly, I wonder if I ever will.

In any case, as inconvenient as it is, I know it's important to keep working on functioning without the tek because—for one— Viddie's memory is clearly sharper than mine. But it's a strange and clunky sort of change to switch from using my interior filing system and deep archives to rely more and more on my highly undependable organic mode. Viddie calls it plain-brain. *Ha!* That is actually quite funny—*plain-brain.*

In any case, I'm working on it.

Day 4—The Flirt

"Which one have you chosen for your mantra-of-the-week, Belvedere?"

Her banal, high-pitched voice seemed to swing with the same rhythm her hips followed as she walked. The new plate editor is a stealthy little-bit-of-a-thing and much more interested in my husband than she should be. Stick-straight hair the color of straw falls neatly to her shoulders. Her skin is so pale it's nearly translucent, and her eyes are like watercolors that instantly put me in mind of the ocean when the morning sun is shining on it. I should like her for that reason alone, but I do not. When she showed up in our workspace today she was carrying a trio of fully articulated watchwords framed neatly in artesian polymer vinyl chloride with a visible rub of garnet. One said "Balance." Another, "Stability." The third, "Acquiescence."

Monica Veslie Powers. That's her proper name, and what a strange bird she is! Yesterday she informed us all that she'd like to be called "Mon." Hmmn, *Mon.*

Hey Hey Mon—she sounds like someone out of the JamaicanXtreme Vacation package. Can anyone say, "Wannabe island girl?" *UGH.* The waif sports a tat just under her right ear in a ridiculous curlicue font that reads "MVP." I, for one, have no intention of calling her *Mon.* Rather, I am perfectly intent on calling her Ms. Powers.

It's not that Full Articulation is particularly annoying or anything devious; we've been practicing F.A. with weekly "watchwords" for as long as I can remember. *It's her.* She's got this sneaky, false way about her that makes . . . well, it makes me literally cringe. It's all I can do to keep from letting anyone see it when she's around.

As I was pondering her motivations, the strangest thing happened. Jude appeared before my info-space and he was in something of a rumple. I don't think I've ever seen him dressing so slack, but today his shirt looked like he pulled it up out of the bottom of a charity box. His deep ebony skin is such a strong contrast against the white of his standard issue smock and slacks.

I've at times found him to be somewhat attractive, but today—today, why the man's a mess!

His teeth are brilliant, too—white and glistening as if he's never let coffee or tea touch them. It's just so funny, for as long as I've known him he's worn our government issued garb, but today, well—I wonder what's up. Although, I do remember when I was just like that—so rigidly committed to LAB protocol. Hmmm. I do wonder what's going on with him.

"Here you go." He thrust a small messenger tube with the LAB's engraved acronym in the center and sort of grimaced as his hand released it. "It just came through from ADMIN. He asked me to bring it to you."

Immediately, I sensed something strange about him. And it's odd that Allessandro didn't just message me through the OLSM. Our *Ongoing Life Sustaining Membrane* receptors have been the best, the most natural way to communicate for the last fifteen years. In fact, using the OLSM here is a non-negotiable. It's LAB protocol. *Hmmn*; what's even stranger is that my most faithful colleague didn't message me through it. Why is he here in my workspace?

As I took hold of the tube my attempt to thank him failed, for just as soon as the glass cylinder left his hand, he immediately turned on his heel and began to walk away.

"Jude? Wait."

He stopped instantly, continued facing the walkthrough, and jerked his head back over one shoulder in quite robotic fashion. Everything about this man seemed weird today, and he appeared far too eager to leave.

"*Strength,* Leeya—what is it? Can't you see, I'm busy?"

I took a step back from my drafting glass, quite shocked at the abrupt tone of my normally amiable co-worker. The thing about Jude is he has never displayed anything but a quiet, soft demeanor, and has an almost suffering tone in his voice. I was quick to reply.

"Actually, no, Jude. I can't see how busy you are, but I can see that something is terrifically wrong. What *is the matter* with you?

At this point he was staring at the floor. When I addressed him he turned toward me, lifted his perfectly oval, black, face and looked at me with an awful and quite smug expression. Then he stared at me squarely with just about the ugliest look I have ever seen coming from anyone!

"Please don't play dumb, *Mrs.* Florencia. We all know you're the brilliance behind this team, so be brilliant, would you?!"

In spite of his impertinence and my own inability to figure out what was wrong, a quiet tenderness rose up inside me. Perhaps he's as trapped in his own confusion as I was before I found FRANCO. I took a step toward him with my hand outstretched and he pulled away as if my hand was on fire.

"Please tell me why you are so perturbed. I've never seen you like this!"

My once-favorite co-worker stiffened his shoulders; his entire physique seemed to bristle as I spoke. I watched him carefully. He pressed his lips together as if they were glued.

"*Jude?*" I tried softening my approach even more.

Silence. Nothing but awkward, hissing, silence.

"Jude, what's going on? You're acting like a wounded animal instead of a trusted member of my staff. Are you sick? What . . . what? Have I done something to put you in such a state? Are you getting enough sleep?"

Then, like a blast from a dormant volcano, came an eruption the likes of which I had not seen at least since my mother's raw emotion spewed on me that day back in the mountains when I spoke ill of Liam. Jude's anger was much more intense, his venom, nearly palpable. It almost seemed to spray out of his pores as his forefinger came flinging within five inches of my face. The tumble of words spilled out in a vengeful whisper.

"What, pray tell, do you know about a wounded animal? In fact, you know nothing about the vacation spots you create, *Mrs.* Florencia. And clearly, *you know nothing* about the people you work with, and . . . to top it off, you know *nothing* about how things actually run around here."

Recoiling, I was quite shocked.

"*In fact?* Jude Lasorum—you have got some nerve speaking to me like that! You seem to forget that pretty much anything you know about *how to run things around here* is what you learned from me! *In fact,* you're making no sense at all. Do I really need to remind you that the entire Xtreme Vacation line was my own brainchild? Seems to me you've really got your

FACTS mixed up something terrible. What on EARTH has gotten into you?"

"*Strength, Leeya*! Do you really think that Allessandro wanted you back? Do you know what we had to do to get him to take you back? The digital protocols you created belong to the LAB! Yeah, yeah, yeah—your vision got us going, but do you think the work halted when you waltzed out of here? Heck no!"

"JUDE! What's gotten into you?!?! I've never ever heard you speak with such insult and vitriol. And you of all people know that I did not waltz anywhere! What are . . ."

"Oh don't stop me now, Leeya. When you *waltzed* back in here, you never even gave us a second thought! You never even said 'thank you' for protecting you! And, you . . . you came back into our lives with a husband AND a bab–look at you! YOU never once thought about us."

"Jude, Jude. Now wait just a minute. There is nothing true about what you are saying, nothing at all. I did think of you. I thought about you often—all of you. I never lost sight of coming back. How can you accuse me this way? C'mon, now. I hired you and Zeej myself—chose you out of more than five hundred applicants. Have you lost your memory? I believed in you, Jude. I still do!"

Pausing for a moment, he cleared his throat and shook his head mockingly. His eyes, a bit glassy, were full of nothing but rage.

"Do I really have to tell you, Miss Brilliance? I mean— excuse me—*Mrs. Belvedere* or whatever your crazy foreign name is these days. Come now. At the very least you are the sharpest person in this building—probably in the rest of what's left in this miserable world. Didn't you think we'd notice how much you've changed? Why don't you come outside of your fancy little façade and give us a clue as to what really happened to you for the six months you were away. Mon has seen your weirdness too, and she didn't even know you before your . . . your breakdown."

The tender compassion I felt just moments earlier was quickly draining away. I held my jaw steady so as not to react, but I felt pinned to the corner. My exterior nonchalance began to give way and my entire being felt slightly off kilter. The wobbly feeling was horribly reminiscent of the days before my leave of absence. It never really occurred to me that I should explain where I met Viddie. Do I really owe them an explanation? Ugh—now what to do? In the absence of my response, Jude continued his verbal barrage in a hideous, hissing whisper. "Since your return it's like there's a completely different lead designer on the floor. We have no idea *where* he has come from, *how* you met him, and your . . . your pregnancy— *STRENGTH, Leeya*, what has that man done to you?"

I'd had enough.

"*That man* is my husband, Jude, and you'll do well to respect him. We have done nothing wrong. People fall in love and marry; perhaps not as much as they used to, but love is still something important. I am sorry that you are so . . . so irate. So let's be clear: my marital status has nothing to do with my ability to lead this team or give you direction, and right now I believe you'd best get to the medic and have him give you a sedative."

His weighted breath filled the room with a black silence, but his unwelcome opinion and ugly outburst did not end there.

"Really? *A sedative?* Is that what you're going to offer me after all we've been through? And do not speak to me about love. *You* are clueless! We will get to the bottom of all this nonsense, oh favored one boss lady. You will not get away with whatever it is you think you're doing!"

My jaw seemed to fall to my chest and I had all I could do to keep my mouth from staying agape. No longer could I think of one single word to say to this man. His blatant disrespect and simmering anger was nearly tangible even though the entire rampage never got louder than a slightly elevated whisper. I just stared at him in bewildered frustration. His eyes burrowed into mine and then he turned and walked clear out of my workspace.

Deep breath.

Deep breath.

When I regained composure I realized that we might be in some real trouble. Jude said some scary things. *Why-oh-why would they suspect Viddie of being foreign? What does that even mean? Heck—the entire world as we know it is limited to the thin strip of populated land along the east coast of this continent. And what on earth could he mean about "all that we've been through together?"* What on earth?!?!

Oh dear, I wonder if I really am just being selfish, but right about now all I could think of was getting out of here, getting back to the flat and talking to Viddie about this outlandish day, but the day was not done with me.

Just as I was closing down the external system to head out, I noticed Ms. Powers. Twice in one day—*ugh.* Like a little Roman silhouette, she stood erect and elegant, staring at the preview wall, which lists the names of the highest officers of ADMIN. The glass partition that separates my draft-glass from the others made it easy to see that she was facing the billing department and seemed to be looking into space. Had she been there the whole time? Was she listening to us? It's hard to imagine any reason she'd be away from the design department, let alone up here by me. I winged out of my docking space, opened the glass door, and walked briskly toward Billing. I'm sure it was with a bit of sharpness in my greeting that I addressed her.

"Excuse me?"

"Oh! *Oh my Strength*—Leeya, you startled me." She turned spritely and greeted me with a look of feigned surprise.

"Yes. Excuse *me*; may I help you?"

"Ms. Powers, I'm not sure why you are in the executive wing. Is there something I can do for you here?"

"Oh, please call me Mon, Mrs. Leeya; I've asked you before. Must I insist? I mean no harm. I'll get back there in a few minutes; I just needed to air out my head for a bit. The men in there are so . . . you know, boisterous."

"Excuse me? *The men* . . . meaning Jude, Zeejay and Ion?"

(Did she just address me by my first name?)

Powers nodded with an insipid smile.

"Ms. Powers; excuse me, but these men are anything but boisterous; I've known each of them more than a decade and I don't think any of them could be described as *boisterous.*"

"Oh, I am sorry; *truly.* Perhaps they've never behaved this way *with you,* but I can't even take a break for a quick provisio without one of them—you know—sidling up to me and trying to . . . well, you know."

This woman tries my nerves like nobody else.

"I'm afraid I do not know, Ms. Powers, and if you're having a problem with the work environment, please say so. I'll speak to them immediately. If need be I will engage HR."

"No, no, *no*. Please don't. {giggle giggle} I rather like the attention." She paused and winked—yes, winked at me—and continued with a mealy-mouthed little whine that sounded a bit like a horsefly stuck inside a lampshade. "Sometimes all the attention gets me a little off track, and well, you know, the mission here is so very important *to Allessandro*. Strength—he would fire them all if he knew."

I hardly knew how to respond so I simply attempted to straighten out this woman's twisted perception.

"These men are your superiors here, Ms Powers. They are looking to you to support the current project; I believe today's mission is to complete the haptic links for the Mediterranean Cruise package. Haptics is Zeejay's department. Need I remind you, you are assisting him *with work?* That is the extent of your engagement here. I trust you will return to your drafting glass and be attentive to his requests for analysis and editing. That is all."

She smiled unconvincingly, nodded, and sauntered out of the executive wing.

I'm not getting a stick of work done today.

Day 6—The Annoyance

Allessandro flashed us a smile that looked more like a sneer and then his image quickly faded. It was pixelating on the wall behind his icon so it's quite possible that I was reading him wrong, but clearly his countenance these days—and overall behavior—is a bit mysterious. There is something amiss and I am not sure about how to get to the bottom of it.

I am especially annoyed by the hair-flicking Ms. Powers and so glad we were out of there early today. Although I don't usually even see her at the LAB, when I do it has never been anything less than cosmically weird. What is especially odd is to finally have another female (two, counting Margene) at TLG, but to have absolutely *nothing* in common with either of them. It's like we're from different planets or something. It seems Zeejay brought her in two months after I left, and while I can't say it hasn't been helpful to have an extra person in the design department, it's terribly frustrating to have someone who continues to bypass my input and go straight to Allessandro. How do I know this? It is three times in three weeks that I have discovered his stamp on my initializing screen letting me know that he has approved or disapproved changes. These are projects that I have not even sent up to him yet!!! Reporting directly to Zeejay, it's her job to traffic the designs and make sure all the files have been delivered, viewed, and time-stamped, but she has somehow missed the fact that I need to see them first!!!

The discussion I had with her about it last week produced no change and things are simply too awkward between Allessandro and I for me to bring it up. Viddie thinks I should just let her know her services are no longer needed. I dunno. Don't want to upset the apple cart this early in my return. We'll see.

In spite of getting out early, our daily trek to the beachfront was thwarted. Again, all because of nit-picky colleagues. And it's not like we dallied. We arrived at the LAB promptly at six, long before sun-up and attempted to put the final draft together for the next level of Xtreme packages, but Zeejay's execution of my latest input threw the entire team into a tizzy and all progress came to a screeching halt. What's worse is that in spite of the mess-up he just continued at his workspace, staring straight ahead, expressionless—as if nothing was wrong. I spoke with him about it and encouraged him to maintain focus, but unfortunately both our feathers got ruffled.

To top it off, this little one is literally doing somersaults inside me today. If I place my hand on my beach-ball belly I can feel her pressing her knee into me as if she's trying to kick her way out of a small wicker basket! It's such a strange sensation to have another human being living inside of me. A whole other human being! AAAAHHHH! Crazy. Wild, wonderful . . . but weird, too. *I wonder what she looks like.* Hopefully, it'll just be another three weeks or so before she makes her appearance. *Ugh—I wish she'd come today!*

Day 7—The Funk

Why do Viddie and I misunderstand each other so much lately? All the walks and talks we had in the mountains before we were married never led us into the deep weeds of agitation like these last couple of weeks. There have been at least two or three times we disagreed . . . heartily. I don't like it!

When I brought up the rifts I had with Jude and Zeejay we got all tangled up in yet another discussion about the difference between the culture of City Centre and that of FRANCO. I'm not exactly sure why or how a simple conversation about his upbringing could go so terribly wrong. I find it rather confusing. It makes no sense that my opinion should get his ire up. And I just don't understand why it matters that we have different backgrounds and don't fully jive with the nuances of each other's respective childhoods.

In any case, in spite of the love I know we have for one another, our communication seems more complicated than it has to be. If we could just keep our conversation to the inner screens we'd surely have less problems, but then again . . . actually being together does bring a closeness that I've never had with anybody but him. Oh, why-oh-why do I keep going back and forth about all these things? I don't feel especially confused, but when I go back and read what I've written I keep seeing such conflict. Ugh, I'm such a waffler!

Happily, we did work out our differences before we fell asleep last night. We kissed and dozed off in each other's arms; that is, until this little one started kicking in the middle of the night. UGH. This week the medic told me baby girl dropped and was nearly ready to make her arrival. I do hope it's soon!

When morning came I found Viddie had already packed our beach gear into the car. It was late—late for me, at least, so as soon as the sun came up we headed straight down to the ocean and were there before the LAB ever even entered my mind. I do love the couple of days a week that he comes to work with me, but even more, oh how I love the beach days. Beach days are the best days!

Thankfully, I ran back inside for my winter coat before we got going. The day was bright and cold—the chilliest day in April thus far, and the beach only makes it colder. Oh my, just thinking about the bitter days of February when we bundled up and braved it through the blustery weather just to get some fresh air and a look at the ocean—well, how can I even think of 60 degrees as cold? Perspective, ha! When I came back out and lumbered into the car he was waiting for me, holding up my gloves.

"Looking for these?" That smile of his was enough to warm my heart without them, but I snatched them from his hands and gave him a quick smooch. The car warmed up fast and we made it down to Old Bath in no time flat.

As he always does, Vidd pulled up to the steps to let me off before he parked. I pointed the ignition fob toward the '70 to unlock the door, and he grabbed my hand and pulled me back from the door.

"Not so fast, milady." He held his other hand over his left eye and raised the same eyebrow in just the same way that LJ does when he gets ready to start a chorus or say something profound. His voice took on our friend's deep intonation too, and when I heard him say milady, a lump formed immediately in my throat. Could he really know how much I miss them all too?

I know he thought he was being funny, but when my eyes suddenly filled up, he let go of my hand and wrapped both arms around me.

"Baby, what? What did I say? What's wrong?"

Swallowing hard, I fought back the tears and couldn't quite bring myself to look at him. If anyone should be sad about missing FRANCO it should be Viddie, not me. Having spent his entire life there, his loss is clearly much greater than mine, but I do love those folks. Everyone from Harold-in-the-Camper, LJ, Liberty, Fiorella, even my mother and father—I miss them all. A ripple of guilt twisted my stomach and the baby shifted her weight from one side of my body to the other. Several quiet tears escaped over my bottom lid and splashed onto my coat collar.

He gently touched my chin and steered my face toward his. "Emi, seriously, Love. Did I say something wrong?"

Slowly shaking my head, I was unable to look up. It's hard to articulate what I myself barely understand, but Viddie—with his usual tender and sweet sensibilities—was exhibiting considerable patience.

"You know I'd give you the moon and the stars, my love. Whatever you want—I'll do it. But you've got to talk to me. Feelings are meant to be shared. Don't shut them up inside you."

His whispered affection tore open my heart as his lips brushed against my temple and I could no longer hold back the flood that was gathering just beneath my eyelids.

"You . . . you sounded just like him," I eked out a few words through the quiet sobs.

He looked bewildered as he squeezed closer to me, and a question mark seemed to hang on his face. Managing to choke out a few more words I tried to explain the tangled mess of conflict I felt inside me.

"I don't know how you do it, but your impressions of everyone there are . . . so real. It's surreal. And whether it's the tone . . . or . . . or their mannerisms or just that special phrase you turn so well, you put me right back there, right there in the midst of FRANCO on a Friday night at Stone Camp, and—oh Vidd—I miss them. I miss them all so much. They're my people too!"

In less than a moment his arms completely enfolded me, wrapping me like a blanket. I felt safe as a rush of peace seemed to swallow me up. He held me this way until the last gush from my watery eyes stopped. I hate that I am so weak these days. It feels like my emotions are so . . . all over the place. Medic has been careful to remind me that my hormones are to blame, but man alive I feel like I'm on one of those old fashioned roller coasters from a hundred years ago.

The sniffles slowed as I leaned my head on his shoulder. Comforting silence ensued for a few moments, wrapping around us like the bright sun after a day of rain. When words came, I was encouraged that he seemed to understand just exactly what I felt.

"They are your people, baby."

Pulling away for just a moment, I wanted to make sure that we weren't going to take a nosedive into another conflict over culture. It definitely seemed we were on the precipice of it. I looked deeply into his warm blue-grey eyes and was reasonably sure that he understood my dilemma. It felt safe to delve further.

"But Vidd—why do I feel so weak? I've opened my heart and mind to an entirely new palate of emotions and it seems to me that it has made me weaker; it doesn't seem quite right."

"C'mere. It's okay. I know you miss them."

"Umm-hmmm. I do. I even miss Marissa's nutty expressions and over-the-top drama."

As I nodded and sniffled he immediately lightened things up.

"Ha, ha, ha. Marisssa. She is a peach, for sure, and you take after her, whether you realize it or not. And baby—it's perfectly natural to feel this way; I do too."

"Oh Vidd . . . it's all so foreign . . . just so foreign to me. I can't get over the difference it makes when you really share life with others. It's an experience of true community that can't be translated by mere words. If you've never had it, you wouldn't really know how important and truly amazing it is to share such a sense of kinship. When you actually share life together, it's as if they all truly become family."

"Yes they do. They are really family—not just those that are blood relatives, but all of 'em. Part of it is because we need each other to survive. When you need each other so much you come to see yourself as part of each other, it builds a oneness that helps keep us all strong. You learn to love and respect the older ones without seeing them as needy or weak and their ways become just . . . well, I dunno . . . ingrained in ya."

"Yes, and well, I saw it; I lived it, too, and now it's *in* me!"

"Yes, it is, *mi amor*. That's one part of it; there's another reason we're so close that has little to do with being in a similar circumstance. The tie that binds us transcends the cares and concerns of survival. We truly see ourselves as brothers and sisters in Christ, so we don't just act like family, we *are* family. And that, my darling, is the amazing, wonderful thing you feel when you think of FRANCO." He held me closer and kissed my nose.

I looked at him squarely, deftly ignored his last statement, and shook my head. "It's just uncanny how much you actually looked . . . you looked so much like LJ before! How do you do that? There are over forty years between you two and—my goodness—your personalities are nothing alike. But then . . . then . . . when you put your hand over your eye and spoke in that mock English accent you reminded me so clearly of that precious one-eyed minstrel. I just can't believe that we'll . . . we'll never see him again. None of them. We may only be a hundred miles away, but we're worlds apart and for all intents and purposes, completely lost to each other!"

Several more moments of silence ensued and the baby started rolling around my middle. When Viddie finally spoke, his words seemed carefully measured as his hand rested on my belly.

He rubbed my upper abdomen as he spoke, so tenderly and without demands. "Maybe we can . . . take her to meet everyone this summer."

As soon as he mentioned going back to FRANCO, I felt the muscles in my shoulders tighten. Rationality poked holes in my oozing heart and began to take hold of me once again. Gathering all the tenderness I could muster, I answered him quietly.

"I don't see how. I . . . I just don't see how."

His eyes met mine with sadness, though he tried to cloak it. I dried the remaining tears from my eyes with the back of my hand and wiped my nose on my sleeve. I can't stand how disgusting I am lately.

"We've been through this, Vidd. We've pledged to make it work here. We've talked about it countless times before, remember? Keepers of the Traditions—that's us—plus, don't forget, TLG has made it abundantly clear that it will not tolerate our coming and going. They want commitment; it's a requirement of the job."

His eyes mushed to puppy-dog mode as he returned my caring demeanor in like gentleness, nodding his head in the affirmative. His lips, tight with blameless understanding, let me know that my answer was disappointing, but that was the only indication. Not another word was spoken to try and convince me that we should visit our mountain family this summer, but I continued quietly with my unnecessary persuasion anyway.

"Do you remember when ADMIN re-activated my protocols to return to the LAB and they gave me the okay to hire you in to consult? They made it clear that my job must be my all. Remember, remember? I'll never forget the day I submitted your hire memo: I told them I vetted you thoroughly and would vouch for your identity and worth. I told them you understood the protocols. Then I stood at Allessandro's icon for what seemed an eternity until he queued up the forms of assent and intention. The holdup wasn't about you, it was about me. It's true, the very language of the re-instatement made it clear that they were hesitant, but because it was me, they went for it. They *know* me."

"Yeah, yeah, I do remember how easy it was to bring me on, add me to your food plan, and teach me the ropes at the LAB. Crazy, if you ask me. There are so many dichotomies here, Em. It seems free and easy, but the principles and practices don't really line up with your perception of things."

I sat up straight and attempted to bring greater clarity to the subject.

"Now wait a minute. Here's what you don't understand: As much as we all don't talk about it, the authority and dedication I have had all these years puts me in a golden position, but secondly, and maybe even more significantly–we all have relative freedom to do whatever we want here. No one bothers anyone or questions our coming and going. Even our weekly rations—they continue uninterrupted without renewal. The only way they stop is if the door shoot is locked or someone is declared officially deceased."

The sun began to beat down on the car and we still hadn't budged. The sand beckoned me. I was eager to get out of the car and begin our beach day, but I felt like I needed to really bring home this point.

"That's the thing, Vidd. You don't realize how they work. It's not about the community here in City Centre, it's about the level of individual commitment, and when it comes to work, dedication is the watchword. Remember, the 3P's are the very foundation of all we do here. Our government holds us to very high standards. As long as we can prove ourselves to be dedicated workers, loyal to our post, we remain in strong standing. Think of it, hon. I was gone for what, six months in total, and when I returned with you, they immediately added you to my provisions plan and upped our weekly ration, and never even spoke with you directly. That's the level of respect that is held for each individual. They took my word about our relationship and even your worth as a design consultant. For all we lack here, you gotta give 'em that."

He shook his head slowly, still not really getting it. I knew I continued to need patience. After all, he was in my world now and the fact that he sacrificed so much to be here stirs my heart toward compassion. I remember how difficult it was for me to grasp his way of life when I plunged into the integrated life of everybody being in everybody else's business. Tight community is so rich and fulfilling, but it's . . . it certainly is the utter opposite of what's going on here in my world. Even though we'd gone over these things before, I thought a bit more patience was in order, and continued to explain in a measured tone.

"What you have to remember is that our personal freedoms and privacy are highly valued here. It's what makes everything work so seamlessly. It's how we can produce so much and survive on so little. You know, it's all about efficiency, love."

His response wasn't mean, but it was clearly laced with just enough sarcasm to raise my eyebrows and begin to erode that nice pile of patience I had been building.

"Efficiency. Yeah—the all-important value. I know. I know, babe. The LAB must run efficiently so that the government can run efficiently so that everybody gets their very efficient meal bars and everything is done in a timely and *efficient* way. Just don't stop to hold someone's hand, look deeply into their eyes, or check to see if a friend is feeling fine. That is a complete waste of time. I know, I know."

"Viddie! *Stop.* You don't understand. Yes, there's a strong hierarchical chain of command here, but that's in place so that necessary procedures can be streamlined—so we don't waste time with lots of red tape, and that's *because* we care. We care about people."

"Really? I haven't seen much evidence of that. I mean, I think *you may think* that's the purpose, but I haven't observed a whole lot of caring around the office. I know I haven't been there much, but when I do come in with you it seems as though I'm quite invisible. I'm surprised you don't see this. I mean, you all may care about *people,* but not individuals. It's more like 'people' are some sort of abstract group!"

"Well, okay. In terms of personal relationships, I agree. I was just thinking some of the same things as you—they haven't been very welcoming, I know. But there's *never* been a major emphasis on personal relationships. What I'm talking about is the underlying trust that is part of our culture. Nobody really bothers anybody else much. There's a sort of unspoken respect for each other's time, so we live in such a way that maximizes time. Look how easy it was to get you added to the supply chain. And, I know there were a bunch of protocols when you first got hired, but normally we don't even work with forms. I never even had a hire memo or any sort of contract that outlined my terms. When Grand'Mere brought me in, they just started working me."

He interrupted with a deep breath and tried to tell me to stop but I just wanted to fill up the cultural disconnect between us with facts—facts that let him know why I could not possibly entertain the idea of a summer getaway to the mountains.

"So you see, there is no room to go away for any length of time. Between the small, unsaid signals that they've given us, and the explicit ones, it's clear. We don't have a choice."

Thankfully, the April sun, no matter how intense, is never terribly hot, but I felt like I was starting to bake in the car and asked him to open the door. He complied, but looked at me as if he still didn't comprehend what I was talking about. I took one more shot at making it clear.

"Vidd—first off, the fact that your hire memo was held up, even for a short time, and that it arrived on the heels of my own re-instatement let me know that things weren't exactly the same as they have been. That's one thing. Another is the clarity they used in my re-instatement memo. It read, verbatim: Any 'untoward or unseemly behavior' would not be tolerated in the future. I had a sense that they were referring to my time away and then they sent the glassboard to my office, including a copy of the 3Ps."

"I was aware that they never look kindly on sabbaticals or extended leave. Allessandro's bot delivered the message: 'reactivation of the authentication process will no longer be tolerated. Any further leave of absence will result in final termination.' Tell me they weren't sending a clear and intimidating message! I think that the only way I was able to exist under their radar last year was because it was *them* that saddled me with that forced leave of absence. Remember? I told you they thought I was crazy? Do you remember?"

We still hadn't moved from the platform, so he opened his side of the car to let more air in and chuckled softly in acknowledgement. But when he spoke his voice was one of logic and strength and I could tell that his happy demeanor was not that he was lighthearted.

"Oh, I remember alright, but hon, you needn't go through the entire scene again. I am convinced. I understand. Do you want to just get going? It's getting pretty hot in here."

Finally, we gathered our things and started heading down the few rickety stairs to my favorite stoop. After that, the whole tenor of our talk sort of put me off. We're in such different places about these things. I see things my way and he sees things his way. Agreed, City Centre has a long way to go before it becomes a friendly place to live, but he seems to think we are worse off than we are. As we settled into our spot on the sand, he turned to me with an odd statement. If I didn't know better, I'd think he actually hates it here.

"Frankly, Em, some of the ways here strike me as no different than a police state. They are much more regimented than I imagined when you first explained this culture to me. When we were back in FRANCO you talked about City Centre in such cozy terms. For the life of me I never imagined the your sense of home was this. . . this . . . oh man, I don't want to put it down, but it's such a puzzle. Yes, there is . . . there's a cavalier sort-of freedom that you're speaking of, but then in other ways it's as if you're all so *loosely* connected that no one really knows what anyone else is doing. You're right—it's really a bit of a dichotomy."

"Okay, fine. I see where you're going with all this, and I understand why you're puzzled, but I'm sure it's because you don't really understand the culture here yet. First off, this is no police state. In fact, there is probably too much freedom. We do have protocols, yes, and there are a few items on the board that are not up for debate, but all-in-all ADMIN leaves us alone. The government exists merely to feed and clothe the populace and provide a sense of safety and security. That's it."

The ire I felt rising in my gut was quelled just as quickly as it arose when he nodded. I could see through his gentle demeanor that he wasn't interested in fighting with me, but that he really just wanted to understand. I don't know if I really convinced him of anything, but there wasn't an ounce of malice in his face as he looked at me. We agreed to drop it, at least for the moment. But then, tracing a baby-sized circle on my outrageous belly, he did make a good point as he switched gears.

"This is our little girl. She is getting ready to bless us with her presence and our life is going to change. That's what we need to concentrate on, *mi amor.*"

I nodded dutifully. That's one thing I could completely agree with. It's so easy to get snagged into distracting, hurtful, conflict. I don't want to do that, not again. Funny, just as I was getting to a calmer place, he planted another thought in my head.

"Just remember this: you're the first member of the LAB elite *in years* to even have a baby. Seriously, can you think of the last woman who gave birth and worked for the government? That makes you pretty special, if you ask me. So they're just going to have to deal with it. Trust me, it's not going to be as difficult as you think. And . . . one final comment about our ability to come and go as we please. You can't really believe that you have no choice. Seriously? Babe—you have breath. You have volition. You have a life, and as integrated as it is into this . . . this organization, you are not them. Plus, you are the VP of Marketing, and part of the legacy of the whole place, at that! You've got cache. I mean, think about it; just think about it."

His voice, resonating with peace and calm, did manage to put a dent in my doubts concerning my responsibilities to the LAB, but not much more than a dent. Cradling me once again with his arm crooked around my side, we snuggled for a moment then made our way down to the water's edge.

Day 9—The Writing

We made it to the beach today later than we'd planned, but at least we got here! I'm sitting on our favorite stoop, just beyond the small platform and raggedy old graphite stairs that lead from the gravel down to the beach. As usual it was worth the push to get out of the office this morning, but . . . I don't want to think about work today. Nope. Done for the day.

It's breezy today; the sand's whirling around a bit, but it's still delightful—a nice, warm day of sunshine and the fragrance of spring! Viddie has gone for a jog along the stretch of sand we call Old Bath—a place that Marissa and Liam both told him about long before he came to live with me in City Centre. Funny the way things turn out. He never imagined that he'd ever even see the mighty Atlantic, let alone go for a daily run on the very beach where my parents met and fell in love. I am absolutely sure that if it were not for the fact that I came back here, Viddie would have been content to stay in FRANCO all the days of his life. Such a homebody.

Sitting here so close to the ocean's edge, I can't help but ponder what the landscape might have been like when my parents walked along the sand. I think this stoop is made out of an old telephone pole—*it must be ancient*! Oh, it's such fun to write in real time. I like this best.

Lately Viddie's been talking about finding a way to check out the empty flat next door. No one has ever taken up occupancy since LJ and his wife lived there, but now that I've met the former resident, I can't say the thought has not crossed my mind. However, for Vidd, the connection is ten times stronger and the temptation to see if there are any traces of his friend's younger self is definitely on the rise. He's mentioned it more than once. What he doesn't understand are the social protocols here. He has no idea how outrageous an idea it is to invade someone's privacy—even if that someone is long gone. Personally, I find it kind of ironic. For a people who are so free about using tek to weave in and out of each other's minds, the importance of staying out of each other's physical space seems a tad odd. This is yet another example of the strange but definitive changes I am observing in myself.

All the years I lived in that flat by myself it never once occurred to me that I didn't have a neighbor or why I never saw anyone coming or going out of that door. The little bubble of isolation was comfortable—pretty much invisible. Everyone here is pretty much the same—it's the norm. Now . . . well, now the hall just feels so barren. The pale gray walls and dark porcelain tiles feel like a lonely cave every time I head down the corridor to our car. Sometimes I just shake my head and try to get past the multitude of odd feelings and major changes going on in my life; I mean—I'm married; I share my life with this amazing man, and have more going on in my personal space than I ever have, but for the first time in all my thirty years I am just now missing the presence of others around me. *How can that be?* Clearly the richness of life in FRANCO has changed me in ways that are incalculable.

UGH! Baby girl just jabbed me on the other side! C'mon little one—give your mama a break!

Rubbing my side and tracing the action of her little feet . . . or maybe it's her elbows, I dunno. I love to think about what she looks like. Will she have Viddie's gorgeous eyes or get stuck with my longish face? It won't be long now for us to find out. In any case, the rubbing seems to help.

So, while Viddie's talking about investigating LJ's flat anytime I'm ready to poke around in there, I just can't bring myself to do it. It's just—well, we'd have to break in, and although I'm sure he could bash the door in, I can't imagine breaking in. *It's unlawful. Verboten.* Yeah—it's doubtful that anyone would take notice, but *if we did get* caught—oh my—the possible repercussions. It's so antithetical to social protocols. I don't even want to think about it.

Look at him, so close to the water's edge. A specimen, *indeed.*

Mmmm. There he goes again. "Hi Honey!"

I wave from the stoop as he passes me for a third time. One day I may join him in the jog, but today I am quite content to just sit and breathe this delicious, salty air.

A couple of seabirds soar above me in tandem. *Hmmm,* I wonder what species they are?

MMMMMmmmm. Just listening to the lapping water and wiggling my toes through the wavy, shell-covered sand helps me let go of the tension that I feel at work. When I take a deep breath of air and then let it out super slowly it renews my energy. I actually feel stronger at the end of the day, and it's—ah— sooooo needed lately. It may just be that the extra tension is due to the transition of having a consultant accompany me to the LAB a couple times a week. Even though Viddie is quite helpful with design ideas, I can feel everybody's eyes on us, and it's creepy!

Anyway, it's *such* a pleasure to drink in the fading sun as it casts its shadow against the water. I so love the way the light saunters down the sky behind us. The shadow it casts on the water is just perfect. It brings out words and images from inside me that I never knew were there.

> *Shore,*
> *sure,*
> *—surely*
> *the sun in all its radiance*
> *capturing my sight—refusing to let go*
> *walks away with a piece of my heart's forever*
> *gold,*
> *it glows,*
> *grows,*
> *goes down,*
> *sinking only to rise*
> *Again*
> *Tomorrow*
> *Mesmerizing.*

Mmmmm.

More and more I find myself writing verse. *How crazy is that?*

Algorithms are cleaner and sharper, but words are more challenging. I like the challenge. I know it's probably garbage in the scope of real poetry, but it's kind of funny how it just bubbles up out of me these days. Funnier still when I think about how Libby always called me a writer all because I didn't let that first art book out of my sight. *Ha!* How could it be that a child knows more about me than I do? *Mmmm. I do wonder how that little girl is doing*—really, how they all are doing up there at the FRANCO complex. Liberty's a year older now, probably10. I'll bet she's grown at least an inch or two. Sweet girl.

The sun is coming to its peak right about now. I can hardly help but raise my face to its rays, closing my eyes and just letting all that glorious vitamin D soak in for a few minutes. *Mmmmm.*

What a funny guy, my hubs. *Now look at him!* He's rushing full throttle into the water and stopping just short of getting wet—as if the waves were a person and he's playing tag. Why do I love this guy so much? *Ahhhhh.* He's gonna freeze on the way back to the flat. Crazy! I don't know how could I love anyone as much as I do him? He is just . . . well, he's such an amazing man . . . and much more of a rebel than I realized when we were back in FRANCO. I mean, I'm curious too, but he really wants to investigate LJ and Sharon's flat. No doubt, we both wonder if there are any remnants of their life together before they set off for the mountains, but curiosity or not, it's just not a wise thing to do. For one, it we got caught, it would be as though we were mocking the Golden Triangle and secondly—we could get into real trouble with ADMIN for breaching the protocols. I just don't know that I am ready to take that much of a risk.

I mean, it's true—day-to-day life here in the city is generally relaxed, but we are quite strict about maintaining the privacy of each domicile. There are very strict regulations on social propriety here. I don't think my mountain man realizes that yet. *Ha!* I mean—It's even considered impolite to stop in on someone for a short visit—oh, so very different than the rich and easy-going connections that are commonplace in that large family-style community of his.

So, I dunno. *I really don't know.* No doubt, I'd like to see what's inside, but surely there's nothing of worth in the flat, anyway. I mean, our one-eyed minstrel friend left City Centre over twenty years ago now and when I think about how careful they all were about not leaving a trace of evidence as to where they were headed, it just doesn't seem worthwhile to take the risk. But the next time *he* brings it up, well . . . I guess we'll just have to see.

Mmmmmm. Deep breath. Deep, deep, breath. This ocean today is almost intoxicating. It is this scene that I picture in my mind's eye while I am at the LAB and it is the very thing that helps me endure Ms. Powers and all the other weirdness at work. Thank you, thank you . . . universe for such beauty!

Another thing I've been thinking about lately is how much I wanted to be back at my own little flat and the risks I took to get here. *Man alive*—now that I've settled in, I'm struck by my own reckless impropriety. I mean, I didn't even think what might happen to me if ADMIN picked up my ping or what could happen to all the people living in FRANCO! And, much to my own chagrin, I'm realizing that the LAB is a little less wonderful than I pictured it.

"Oh, hello little lady bug. I remember your kind from the lush green of the hilly mountains last July. I love it that you are so harmless and hospitable."

Ha ha. That little polka dot insect just landed on my forearm and rested there for a few seconds as if it was coming by just to say hello. *Ha ha ha.* Could I really have lived thirty years on this planet and I'm just now seeing a real live lady bug in City Centre for the very first time?

Day 11—The Change

The tension that I'm feeling about work has to do with more than just the weirdness of the personnel. I'm feeling it particularly when it comes to getting enough alone time with Viddie. It's one of the reasons our morning drive has become such a sweet treat. Whether it's just an in-depth pre-work heart-to-heart or *mattina*—his word for our morning snuggle—we get to lengthen our private time before I have to connect with others and tap into my OLSM. And even though it's such a short trip to the office, it's nice. So yesterday, on our way to the LAB, *mattina* did double duty. As usual, we cozied up, but our time was also taken up with some work-related brainstorms. It happened quite suddenly when I had a revelation about the number of cars on the skyway. I do think about the strangest things sometimes.

I was reclining on the lounge of my—*our*—trusty '70, and my eyes were drawn to a crumbled yellow and blue wrapper from one of my fave cappuccino provisio bars that was stuck under the seat. When I stretched down to reach it I was in full view of the tiny sliver of a window panel to my right. Now, I never look out the window-slit, but yesterday, the way my body contorted to grab that wrapper made it possible to see the oncoming traffic and I couldn't help noticing that during the entire 15 minute drive only about five cars passed us. Five cars in a world with 30 million people? It struck me as strange. I couldn't wrap my head around the scarcity of people and tried to imagine how different it might have been a hundred years before. When we got to the LAB lot we hung back for a few minutes to talk because my mind had become utterly engrossed in an idea for a new XtremeVaca series. Thoughts began to buzz around my brain like a bee in a raspberry bush. Then he burst into my daydreams with a question.

"What's cooking, milady? I know that look when I see it." Viddie took his hand off the door and sat up straight.

I scrunched my nose and lips together and am sure my face projected all the excitement and doubt that I was feeling about sharing my new idea.

"Well . . ." I started out slowly. "I'm thinking about that patch of road we just passed and . . . well . . ."

"And?" Not quite ready to be my sounding board, I could tell he wanted the information in a quick soundbite, and wasn't terribly keen on hearing the story I was gearing up to tell him. Viddie likes to get in the office and out as quickly as possible. I could see he was already well into work mode. His hand went back on the door handle; I couldn't help but chuckle.

"*And,*" I continued, "I was just wondering what it might have looked like a couple of hundred years ago or even a hundred years ago. Those roads beneath the skyway—do you think they were dirt or cobblestone before they were covered in asphalt? I mean, surely, folks travelled back and forth this way long before there were highways, right?"

He let out a friendly chuckle.

"*That's* what you're thinking about?"

By now he sat up fully from his previous lounging position and smiled with a wide and open grin, realizing that he was in for a full-on convo. I gave him a playful little slug in the arm as he checked himself out in the mirror above our heads.

"Yes, that is exactly what I am thinking about. Are you going to listen to me, Mr. Charming?"

A compliant nod and his hand off the door urged me on. I blinked, blew him a kiss, and continued.

"So, first I want to think about how they dressed and how busy the skyways were—I mean, the old highways, of course. I'm thinking about a time before our skyways were built so far above the streets. Maybe, what? A hundred years ago?"

He straightened his bow tie and seemed preoccupied by the tiny bit of bright blue lipstick I left on his cheek. "Wait—what do you mean like . . . in the *1970s?*"

"Here, let me get that for you. You can hardly see it, Vidd. *There*—it's gone. Now please pay attention to me, would you? *You really crack me up!* Are you the same guy I met with a hoe in his hand, digging up potatoes behind Grand'Mere's earth shelter in those bluesy, folksy overalls just . . . *hmmmm* . . . just twelve mere months ago? My goodness, you are just a tad preoccupied with your clothes, now, aren't you? Did you hear what I said? Yes, the 1970s –I'm talking about a hundred years ago—and also maybe a hundred and fifty. It was all horses and wagons back then, right?"

"We met nearly fourteen months ago, as a matter of fact, my love, and c'mon, you know you're more the history buff than I am. In fact, isn't that why they pay you the big bucks?" He lunged toward me for a kiss.

"Stop teasing me! Why are you teasing me so lately? *C'mon Vidd.* You're much better at remembering what you read in those history books that your mother used to teach you—much better than I am. Stop and think about it. *What were they like?"*

The whine in my voice had come to a pitch, but even though I was aware of how unbecoming the tone, I could do nothing to eliminate the urgency I felt at that moment. I get that way—stuck on something and I can't get off.

"Hon, I don't have the world of knowledge at my command the way you do either. Why don't you tap into your archives when we get inside?"

"*C'mon Vidd*—you've been insisting that I limit my tek use to only what is absolutely necessary each day. You know very well that anything I do or think *or say* once I connect to my OLSM is open to everyone else who is tapped into the network."

I pointed toward the complex and craned my neck around toward his face.

"*Anybody* in there can gain access to what I'm doing or even thinking the minute I press my P/Z in. Do you really want them to know that we're trying to re-trace history and introduce early American values into the population?"

He sat up straighter again and turned me toward him. "So, that's what we're doing, eh? Introducing alternative values? Yeah, I guess you're right. ADMIN's not going to be thrilled about that bit, I'm sure. By the way, this is the first you're admitting such a thing, Emi. Gotta say, I'm surprised. Not unhappy, just surprised."

The periwinkle bowtie I ordered for him from HQ central was crooked again. He doesn't know how to tie it, and I never had experience tying one either. I chuckled a bit in my attempt to straighten it out before trying to move our conversation along toward something productive.

"Well, so—help me, wouldja? I know you can call up some info from that finely tuned and high functioning hippocampus of yours."

He pulled the ribbon away from his neck and feigned choking. A good-natured round of laughter ensued along with a few more hugs. I leaned back again against his chest and thought we should maybe just work from the car today. *Ha!*

"You over-estimate my knowledge capital, Em. 'Course I'm happy to share the little I do know about those days. First, let me just say that the skyways were definitely not around in the 1970s. And, I listened to enough stories about everybody's grandparents who had colorful memories of the early 20th century and although there were still many dirt and gravel roads throughout the country, at that time the horse-and-buggy type transport was long gone. The highways were beginning to zigzag throughout the landscape, but they were definitely not skyways, hon."

"*Mmmm.* Okay. Well, you actually know people who have recollections of that time, so I'll take your word for it." Tell me more. What sort of stories do you remember?" *These convos are the best! I love gaining his insight from the stories he's heard!*

"Oh yeah, Emi, I've sure got some. The oral histories were the best! Harold-at-the-Camper used to tell us about his great-grandfather's farm out in Oklahoma when the cattle and chickens still roamed free and they'd saddle up a horse just as easily as get in their gas-guzzling cars. *Ha!* I remember the one he told us about the time his paw-paw (that's what they called his great granddad) drove his John Deere—I guess, what? It's a tractor or truck of sorts—onto highway 201 and backed up traffic for eighteen miles!"

"Eighteen miles? *Whoa!* There were that many cars on the road? That sounds preposterous. Are you taking me seriously, hon? *Really.* I've got tons of anecdotal information about earlier days, but you know we've got to get the facts to create a virtual vacation worth its price. I know you've got access to real knowledge of history and I . . . I want it. You better not be jiving with me."

Our progress was immediately interrupted by an explosive tickle-fest, the kind of behavior that completely obliterates any modicum of seriousness. When we finally stopped laughing and caught a breather, his tie was once again undone and he was the first to pipe up.

"Wanna know what I think? I think you're just procrastinating the start of the day. *I* think you'd rather sit in this car with me and chat the morning away and . . . maybe . . ."

"Stop!" I pushed him back and turned my shoulder. Before a moment passed, his hand was on my back rubbing it, and kissing my neck.

"I am sorry. I am bad, so bad. I really will listen to you. C'mon. Turn around. Look at me. We can talk just a bit more about history before we go in. Forgive me?"

"Fine. Well, sure. Of course." I pulled myself together and erased any evidence of a smile, softening my shoulders and attitude before I continued.

"You're right, my knowledge of history is fairly solid, but you've read much more than I have and in far greater detail, and I just thought you might have a better idea of what the actual road might have looked like back then. You see, I . . . I . . . I have a few ideas percolating for a new virtual vacation in early America."

"*Early* America, eh?" He answered with the quizzical look that tells me he's got more to say.

"Yes. Early America. You know, the time when horse and buggies were what they used to get around."

"Ah—so it's horses and buggies you want. *Hmmm.* Well, you'll have to go a bit further back than a hundred or a hundred and fifty years. The actual birth of the United States of America happened in the 18th century, a fact I'm sure has not escaped your attention—but yes—most definitely, horse-drawn buggies and wagons were the transportation of *that* day. Folks walked quite a bit too, which is what we should be doing right about now, yes?"

Viddie's hand was back on the door but I knew I needed a few more minutes to hash this thing out.

"Wait, *wait.* Not yet. They can wait. Hon, *listen*—this is the thing: Of course I know that I'm talking about a period earlier than the 1970s, but I have a few ideas that are blending together. They need to be parsed out. First, yes—I'm fascinated with the transportation in the 18th and 19th centuries, but I'm also thinking about a time that's more recent. The people in the 20th century all generally travelled the same routes we travel today. I know they used the old roads and ours are considerably elevated, but we pretty much see the same landscape as they did, don't we? I mean, I never actually thought about it exactly this way before, but help me figure this out for a moment, would you? Please?" I blew him a little kiss followed by my signature wink—the one he's just crazy about.

His hand cradled my face as he came in close. "Only if you give me an extra *bacio*!"

I was glad he bounced back from our little tiff. This man's happy demeanor and light-hearted personality never fail to make me smile. I do love him so.

"Okay, okay. Just one. *Mmmm.* Ugh. Wait, the baby's in the way. Okay." *SMOOCH*!

Ha ha ha . . . it was hard not to giggle again. Man alive, he really does make me feel like a girl again!

"Okay, okay. Now. Think how crowded those highways were. I remember viewing some random images in my Ed Files; the Garden State Parkway was what they called it before the Devastation—it's the roadway just 200 feet beneath us—maybe, what? Or is it 200 yards? I dunno—but we see it every time we drive into work, and a hundred years ago it was like a car park—or what did they call it, a parking lot? I've seen images. I remember I once viewed an image of people stuck for hours trying to come down here from New York and Pennsy during the summer months when the beaches were still the main attraction. Those roads were packed with cars like sardines in a can! Can you even imagine?"

With that, he chuckled out loud. "Who *are* you Anne of Green Gables, and what did you do with my Emi-girl?"

"*Whaaat?*" While I'm sure a smile curled up on the corners of my mouth, I had no idea what this man was talking about. "Annie *who*?"

He held my hand and rubbed the top of it with his thumb. Smiling, my mountain-loving man shook his head without affect.

"Not Annie; *Anne.* Anne of Green Gables. She is a character in a book my mother read every night to sis, and in our small quarters I heard the story whether I liked it or not!"

"So, you're calling me a character that . . . you never liked?"

My puckered lips and quizzical expression sent him reeling just a bit. *I do love to tease him!*

"Oh baby, no. No. *No.*" He jolted a bit forward and scrunched his face closer to mine. "Anne Shirley is a charming character. In fact, I love Anne; *I mean,* I always loved hearing about her. But one of the things about her is that she loves to talk and she goes into great detail about whatever idea or thought is brewing in that beautiful little mind of hers. It's one of the things that makes her *Anne.* I'm just saying that lately you've been reminding me a bit of her with the breadth and the . . . the magnitude of your creative ideas, and . . . and that last little monologue—*ha!* Honey, it sounded just like one of her beautiful brainstorms. And it's not that I never liked her, it's just that I've never known you to be so . . ."

"So what? Go on . . . spit it out." By now I was smiling too, because clearly the man stepped on a landmine and I was having a jolly good time watching him try to dance around the verbal mess he had tangled himself into. I cleared my throat and urged him further.

"Go on . . ."

With his rough hand now cradling the side of my face, Mr. Smokey Eyes kissed my forehead and continued: "So . . . intense about a subject, okay? And . . . I love it. I love YOU. I love everything about you, Emi. You can never doubt that."

"*Mmmm.* That is very good because I love you too, Belvedere Florencia." I planted a kiss on his mouth and lingered for a moment before inching us back to the subject at hand.

"Are you ready to get back to business? C'mon, Vidd. What do you know about the folks who lived back then? Can you help me imagine their lives?"

His sly grin dazzles me. Sometimes . . . *sometimes* it is just so clear that he is a foreign inhabitant of 21st century city life. This husband of mine comes up with phrases and people and ways to do things that are . . . well, they are just out of this world, out of *my* world. It's times like this, though, that his detailed arrangement of interesting facts are really helpful.

"Well, I guess, yes—I *can* imagine—but I can't say that it's taken up much space in my brain. You're the dreamer, Emi. You're the girl with the vision. Why don't you tell me what you think they were like?"

"Perfect. That's exactly what I want to do, actually. I think they were over-emotional workaholics who didn't think about anything of major import like sustainability, efficiency, or the most rudimentary, self-evident aspects of the human body."

"Well, it's not like you have an opinion 'bout that, do you?"

I just stared and held my ground, shrugging my shoulders. That's just the way I feel. I've read a good deal about postindustrial culture and the way America functioned in the past, and it just seems very clear. He wasn't in compete agreement.

Viddie chewed on his lower lip as he spoke, and seemed to be tentative in his response. "I'm afraid I can't buy it totally, though. You aren't basing those ideas on actual facts. And it's ironic that what you're pointing out about their failings is right in line with the blindness of the age we currently find ourselves in. Can we focus in on the things we really know—what's documented?"

I decided not to challenge what he said and even though I wasn't connected to my D.A., I pulled from as much as I could remember from my Early Ed files. At least we were getting somewhere. I decided to follow his lead and continued to muse.

"Okay then, let's look at the things we know. We do know a bit about that time because much of what folks across the country archived after the Devastation was saved at remote repositories in New York and Washington. You know, those zones were part of the very few safe spots that remained intact after that terrible time. So we'll have to request the archival info and that could take a bit of time; of course we want to make sure that we represent those days authentically, but I do hope we find some interesting images. My hope is to discover that they lived lives that were—I dunno—flavorful . . . colorful . . . anything but boring. You know, because boring will never work for the vaca pak. And . . . and . . . well, I wonder what they thought about, Viddie. They must have had very different concerns than we do, right? Do you ever wonder about their thoughts? How do you think they coped with work? Their whole lives seemed to be consumed with work, so we won't be able to avoid including a bit of their work lives. And the landscape . . ."

"There you go again Anne . . . I mean *Emi—ha ha ha!* Seriously though, I actually do think about people who lived in the past, especially how they let the world swirl out of control, but like I said, *you*, my dear, are the main wonderer in our family. It's part of what stirs that creative spirit—part of what makes your mind so beautiful."

"And my work so valuable?" I gave him a quick wink hoping he wouldn't be too hard on me. I could see those eyes getting darker but wasn't in the mood for another lecture about humility.

"And—yes—your work is so valuable. Yes, my sweet woman, and *you* are so valuable. But even if you never did another stitch of work, you would still be of the utmost importance because you are a person and . . ."

A strange glitch in his voice made me turn my attention from preoccupation with the old, provisio wrapper that was half hidden under the front deck. I looked squarely at him and waited. The pause seemed serious, but he responded with a crooked little smile and eyeballs staring squarely into my own.

"*And*? . . . I am a person, and?"

With an expression that is as rare as a rabbit on the skyway, Viddie scrunched up his nose in awkward bunchiness, the way he always does when he's getting ready to say something surprising or challenging. I remember the same look the day he revealed the treasures of Holly Hill as well as the moment I learned our parents talked about us *getting together* long before we were anything more than walking friends.

"What? *What is it, Vidd?* C'mon—give it up."

Taking my right hand in his, he leaned over and kissed me lightly on the nose.

"Because. . . . Because *you are a person* and because God loves you."

Plunk.

Wow.

What am I supposed to do with that?

He knows very well that I barely believe that humans have a soul, let alone in a God who created us. I had no choice but to abruptly change the direction of our conversation.

"Okay, well. *Okay.* We accomplished much. This seems like a good time to wrap up today's history fest and revisit the olden days at another time, don't you agree? C'mon now—we've been in this car for at least an hour."

"You're not kidding. Are you done? Are you really done talking about the past? I can't believe I'm eager to get in there and start working. You are quite a handful, *mi amor*. There is never a dull moment with you. Yes, yes—let's go."

I smiled wryly, straightened his bow tie, and then quickly untied it again, letting the silky cloth dangle loosely from my hand. Then, just as quickly as I set it loose, I balled up the bow in my other hand and hid it behind my back. How oddly fun to watch him fluster a bit, and goodness knows, we needed the air to lighten up a bit.

"*This* is a handful, dear."

After one last tangle of tickles and kisses, he took a deep breath and placed his hand on the door.

"Let's not forget your tie, handsome."

"He rolled his eyes playfully, turned his back toward me so I could help him with it. Everybody needs a teeny bit of color to make ADMIN's uniform white dress code pop. I'm glad he doesn't mind my slightly flamboyant choice for his flair.

What a wonderful morning.

Day 12—The Jog

Swak!

"*Ugh* . . . these black flies might not be noxious, but they are surely annoying. They're almost nasty enough to make me want to leave! How come they're not biting you?"

"Warning: Incoming kiss—*SWAK!*—is this any better?"

His smooch landed smack in the middle of my shoulder and he began sucking on it like a nasty mosquito until I literally pushed him off.

"Oh *you*. I'm gonna swat *you* in a moment if you don't behave!"

"Your skin is just too irresistible for them, *mi amor,* and me too. See? What can I say?"

His teasing tone is difficult enough to resist, but when he comes after me in feigned pursuit and shoots me that sweet little twisted smile of his, I just . . . well, who could have imagined that any man could have this effect on me? He melts me more quickly than today's intense spring sun!

We sat on the bottom step near the bulkhead and watched each thunderous clap of water hit the shore. It was mesmerizing—watching the waves crashing upon the beach, drawing back into the water and then starting all over again.

I do so love the way the light beads up across the serene gray-blue of the ocean in the morning, especially when the sky is cloudless, like today; it looks just like I imagine finely cut diamonds might look if they were floating across the water.

"I'm going for my run. I want to get it in before the rain comes. You okay here?"

I scrunched my nose and shook my head inquisitively. "The sun is shining as brightly as ever, Vidd. *What are you talking about?*"

He smiled and used his chin to motion behind me.

"Take a look at that. It's definitely going to rain, but probably not for a half hour or so."

A quick glance behind my left shoulder revealed one bulbous, coal-gray cumulous cloud that looked so out of place I almost laughed.

"Well, it's hiding back there behind me. Where did it come from anyway? Hmmm. Maybe it'll rain, but maybe it'll pass. You never know with weather, right?"

He planted a kiss on my forehead and gently touched my stomach with his forefinger and then his lips. "Ya ya ya. I'm off! See you soon, baby."

I waved at him with a smile and glanced again at the sky behind me. Yikes. That *does* look foreboding. The sun was beaming brightly down upon the water but the sky did look a little menacing. It'd be nice to capture that unpredictable element of nature in our new VacaPackages. It'll give the experience greater reality. My head is so ensconced in these designs lately. It's both maddening and terribly exciting at the same time!

These latest XtremeVaca Packages have been a bit more complex than in the past, involving quite a bit more research. I've had to make myself more available on site at the LAB—and dealing with the crew hasn't been easy these days. It makes our time down here at the beach all the more needed.

Lately I'm beginning to feel like *I live* at the LAB, and that is not fun. We have been there nearly every day for the past three weeks, for at least four hours every morning!!! What's worse, nearly everyone seems to be gathering on the floor at the same time, so we're constantly in each other's space. It's just too much. I've never seen this much activity on the floor in all the years I've been there. No one should have to work that many hours in the midst of other people. I can't even imagine the horrible, stifling lives of people who lived centuries before and spent 8 or 10 hours a day at an office! My worklife has been cramping our style, even with just a more regular four! I just don't know how we'd handle it if I hadn't been able to bring Viddie on as a design consultant.

I looked up from my writing to scan the horizon and stretched my eyes from one end of the beach to the other. Summer is in the wind. It's a gentle breeze here today and although there's still a chill in the air, I can almost feel the warmth of June. It's just around the corner, and with the warmer weather we'll have a new little member of our family. Ahhhh—can hardly wait! Viddie's red shorts are a tiny pinprick about a half mile up the shoreline. I can see him if I squint.

Why on earth does he like to jog so much? *Egadz*!

Day 13—The Mood

The sunless sky mimics my mood today. Dense cloud cover feels like a dark gray dome over all of City Centre. Oh how it makes me yearn for the mountains. In FRANCO we walked beneath puffy balloons of bright white splendor and wisps of floating air—cloudland was our ballroom. There, even on cold days the sky welcomed the sun with open arms. On damp, brutish days like today the only thing I want to do is curl up and hide. Ugh. It's easy to forget that this part of the country has an ugly schizophrenic season that lasts well into May. Just when I think we are fully plunging into summer, the long, dark hook of winter drags me back inside. Even when the season is dotted with remarkably sunny days that toast up the sand and offer a few gloriously blue, velvety-sky-afternoons filled with the smell of honeysuckle and lilac, there still remains a chance that the very next morning will require full coat and boots. And it sure doesn't help when things get as testy as they have been at the office.

Today's round of resistance at work started with a simple disagreement about the color tone on an old remake. When Jude brought the concern to Allessandro's attention and pointed out that the raspberry bushes might be just a little too perfect, he came back with a zillion changes! We were working on the new DEEP WOODS AMAZON package and had to go back into old foundational files to rework the color. It was a tangled mess! Worst part is, neither Jude nor Allessandro have any idea about the true color. He thought the green we chose was artificial looking but really—when has he ever seen a raspberry bush? To complicate matters, it was Viddie who mingled the pallet hues and suggested the proper green. Now I have to run interference and it's taking me far afield. *Ugh.*

Coming back to the flat to work makes things a bit easier. I realized that I truly do get more accomplished when I'm home. It's probably because the distractions have increased exponentially at the LAB and there are no signs of let up. Like yesterday, for instance, when I came upon that Powers woman. She was standing in front of Allessandro's icon and seemed totally clueless. I mean, everyone knows that his anchored icon is reserved for the only the most extreme needs, and clearly, yesterday she was not in any sort of emergency situation. Then, when she noticed me looking at her she let out a tiny high pitched yelp and straightened her dress. Allessandro's sharp, craven face flashed intermittent looks our way—looks that might be taken for subtle interest if not for the way his brows knit together each time I tried to make eye contact. It's strange—I mean, all Viddie and I were doing was attempting to unravel the flaws in the upcoming version of DEEP WOODS, but Allessandro gazed at us with suspicion and disdain. His demeanor definitely made it seem that something ominous was aloft.

Ugh—Everything I touch at work is giving me a problem lately.

Day 14—The Reminiscing

Watching him as he runs, I smile wryly, still hardly believing that I actually married this stunning specimen of a man, and even more incredulous that I am carrying his child. As happy as I am about this development, it is he who is truly the excited one. Given that the prospect for having babies in his very small, hidden, mountain family is pretty much nil, I'm sure the thought of ever having a child must have evaded him long before I came on the scene. For my part, most of the time I'm just scared—scared about my ability to be a good mother. For starters, I grew up in a world where having a child has become an anomaly. I never even came across many babies and frankly never thought I'd ever have one. Just not on my radar screen. Then when I met Marissa last year and heard that I did not have the ability to get pregnant, well—who would've thought I'd conceive the first month we were married?!? How we'll actually manage with a baby is beyond me, but everything else about this last year has worked itself out, so I believe having a family will work itself out as well.

Ah, FRANCO, when I think of you, the irony of it all is still so strong. Me, once believing that you were a man, how ironic it is to discover that you are actually a sweet, hidden commune existing for the revelation and nurturing of community optimization. FRANCO—I would never have figured out that acronym without finding your people—my people. Sometimes I pinch myself. Is it all real?

We savored the last of our homemade caramels with big sticky smiles, brushing the wayward bits of dirt from our feet, realizing too late that even a tiny bit of sand on our fingers would find its way into our pockets and then onto the candy. Crunch. Oh well, if I could make it out of the deep woods in one piece, I am sure ingesting a few grains of sand is not going to kill me.

The lilting sea, so attentive to its ever-vacant shore, seemed to breathe a welcoming sigh with each rippling wave. I remember watching the ocean from the safety of my car on those bewildering days before I left. Never did I imagine I would actually be standing on the sand—barefoot yet! It's still not quite warm enough to regularly take off our shoes but today the sun is strong and we've had a lovely walk. I plunged my toes into the soft terrain as soon as we got here, pulled out my art book, and immediately started writing.

"C'mere you," Viddie motioned to me with the deliberate raise of his chin and then drew me close to him. His slightly sticky fingers touched my shoulders as he leaned into my face.

"*Ba-cheeo*, just *un poco poco bacia mi amor.*"

"Yes, yes," I laughed aloud as he covered my face with tiny, feather-like kisses. "*Bacia.* You always want *bacia.*"

The sound of my own laughter against the backdrop of our relationship is still fascinating to me, even though some days it continues to be something of an anomaly. Light-heartedness has just never been a part of the *modus operandi* of City Centre living. Yeah. No way. Life at the LAB could never be described as fun. The thought of fun has been almost—well, irreverent. But now—forget it—I'm hooked! I can't even imagine what life would be without a strong dose of humor each day.

"Listen, I know you'd rather stay here and watch the dusk roll in over this most alluring scene, but it's getting a bit chilly and we need to get you back to the flat and get some food in you. By now our weekly fresh vegg and fruit ration is in the door, and I just as soon cook it up quickly and make us a meal. That baby of ours is getting big and—I know you—if I don't remind you to eat, you never will. C'mon, c'mon; take your long last looks."

"I have a coat! Look." With my hands deeply situated in the furry pockets of my faux leather jacket, I looked at him pleadingly.

He patted my burgeoning middle with the affection that is so typical of Belevedere Florencia, a man much older than his years—rugged and so strong, yet always so full of tenderness. This guy—my own personal superman—who followed me out of the wild to set up house in a world as foreign to him as Mars is to moonwalkers; well, I don't know how I got so lucky to become the girl of his dreams, but clearly he is the man of mine. Afternoons like these never fail to stir a spirit of gratefulness in my heart.

A wistful look appeared in his dark eyes, one that I've seen before and is becoming increasingly regular. He's thinking about the baby; I can just tell.

"We will teach her to stand up straight and strong and speak her mind and never back away from what she knows is true," he proclaimed heartily with all the pomp of an old-school politician, and smiled as he again rubbed the huge, rolling landscape of my once-flat abdomen.

I chuckled to myself. What a goof . . . a noble one, at that, but the more I get to know him, the more I realize what I married. Straight up GOOFY!

"*Mmm hmmm.* For sure, but I think we'll have to teach her to eat and walk and put on her clothes before all that, dear."

He planted a quick peck on my lips, nodded, gave me the A-Okay sign accompanied by that fat, pouty smile of his, and then took off down the street to fetch the car.

Once in a while a bit of that Italian temper flares, especially when I push him about adapting to the regulatory imperatives of ADMIN's role in our world. They do have a legitimate role, thank you—but he's "not under the government's rule." That's what he says. So I try. I try to steer clear of those conversations. It doesn't happen much, only when I push him to accept the little things that I take for granted here like signing the yearly census or regular check-ups with the medic. And really, it's not that he's ever been out of control, but I see his ire rise up when the volume of his voice matches his emotion. Not easy to get used to, especially for a girl like me who until last year has had zippo experience with working through conflict.

Even so, the man's acclimated rather well. He's intuitive and works hard at understanding our differences. Truth be told, it's hard to believe he knows me so well even after such a short time that we've been together. The man is correct about most everything including the food; a crunchy 552 would suit me just fine tonight. I'd much rather stay here than give any thought to eating, but he has quite taken to pampering me these days and I reckon I shouldn't complain.

Heck, I lived on Provisio bars for so long that I . . . well, they're not delicious like his mother's warm scones bursting with all that mountain-grown blueberry goodness, but they're really not bad at all and a 552 is the heartiest of all. And well, come to think of it, actually I could go for one of his surprise meals. To be sure, he definitely inherited something of his mother's talent for cooking. I can't believe the menus this man comes up with, all with such limited foodstuff! How fortunate I am to have a husband who knows such things!

These days I find myself just reveling in gratefulness about so many things. This baby—wow—it still seems so unimaginable that I am expecting a little one, and so soon! In fact, I must say that it still baffles my mind. Marissa told me the LAB messed with me in vitro—that I wouldn't ever be able to bear children. In fact, that was part of my parents' outrage with this place. They felt completely violated by not being asked to participate in the medical trial to control the population. I guess I don't blame them, but I'm sure glad that their conclusions about my ability to get pregnant were wrong.

I wiggle my toes and lightly tap my shoes against the cement bulkhead of this lovely beach. *Spiaggia*—that's what my Viddie calls it, and it was just what I needed to get out of my funk.

Life is good.

The late afternoon sun has lifted my mood, but sadly that glorious globe is starting to go down. I guess I should put these old shoes on; it *is* getting a bit chilly.

A quick gaze behind me toward the old great lawn, and I can see him reaching the car. There are no buildings around us here at Old Bath, just a cracked, coal-colored street between the sand and a quarter mile or so of vacant, pebbled lots–probably where they parked their cars when people actually came down here to swim. Sometimes I try and picture the scene down here before the Devastation. In my minds' eye, crowds of tourists mark their territory with heavy blankets, umbrellas plunged into the sand to shade their virgin backs from the sun's intensity; children laughing, kicking balls, and riding waves with tubes. Perhaps there were guitars and singing. I dunno. The vacancy here cannot be reminiscent of the past. Surely others enjoyed this place at least as much as I do.

Funny how the tiny specks of sand on my ankles don't bother me a bit. Sometimes it's still hard to believe that the earth is not utterly toxic. As is typical of our afternoon visits to *spiaggia*, Viddie will bring me a towel when he comes back from the sandlot and I will balk about leaving. Ha! Same drill, every time. Me, clinging to the bulkhead, making excuses about why we should stay, how it's warming up or I'm not hungry; I know I'm stubborn. Surely, today will be no different. Without a doubt, this beachy routine is probably the best part about leaving FRANCO and getting back into the rhythm of work.

Work.

Uhhhh. Maybe not that part.

The idea of work hit me like a ton of granite earlier. Strange, just thinking about the LAB these days sets me a bit on edge, and it was never that way in the past. While once I was most satisfyingly the golden child of our new world, set aloft and so close to the top of ADMIN's rigid hierarchy of command, these days I'm not sure they even remember that it was my genius that integrated the OLSM connection into virtual vacation construction. (Is that haughty? Man alive—I can't help it, it's true!).

Part of the problem is the condescending attitude I sense with almost everyone there. The other thing is what we've got to keep secret. Ever since the six month hiatus from the LAB and immersion in Viddie's rustic lifestyle, it's almost like I've got to don an elaborate mask whenever I step foot in the place. I mean—goodness—I know who I am, and I know who I've become, but keeping it from my team at TraveLite Global is not as easy as I thought it would be. Clearly, however, it's imperative that I do so. If TLG ever finds out that my parents are not dead and that they are living in the mountain community that I discovered while I was away last year—well, it's just too risky. There's no assurance that ADMIN would look kindly on their choices, and although I have no personal evidence of any nefarious government scheme, Marissa and Liam surely wanted to get away for the sake of their own strong convictions. They definitely believe that ADMIN was undermining their freedom. So . . . the whole secrecy aspect of their life choices makes me exceedingly nervous.

When I lay my head on my pillow at night I think about these things. I know I should be thankful to be working at the most prestigious organization in America, and, well, I still am, to some degree. It's just that while I was in FRANCO I think I must have romanticized my job to such a high degree that I made working at the LAB out to be much more than it actually is. Truth be told, I'd much rather be here gazing into the rolling sea or writing in this journal.

Hmmm. . . . Where is he? I don't see the car moving. Hmmm. The sun is so bright behind me I've got to squint a bit, but—wait. What? There he is, just sitting there in it. Viddie, what on earth are you doing?

Turning back to the deep green-gray waves, I relish the bit of bluster they are stirring, and decide to be happy rather than annoyed. Heck—a few extra minutes here is better than a few minutes anywhere else. Knowing Viddie's thoughtful ways, he's most likely hanging back just for that reason.

The fresh, salty air gives me pause from the angst that wanders through my mind. I am grateful as I breathe it in and gaze again at the foamy white caps dancing atop the waves. *Mmmm.* Looking over the steely sea could be my full time job. I feel so free here. It just goes on and on for miles and in the midst of crazy change, those waves just keep comin'. Nothing stops them. *Mmmm.*

Whoops. **WOW**—she's flip-flopping completely. *Baby*—chill out my darling. I can barely breathe. *Whew.* Lately my thoughts about life are stirring as vigorously as this little one is today. Goodness sakes, she sure is rollicking in there! I wonder what she'll look like?

He'll be nudging me into our old '70 momentarily, but I am not ready to go. The beach helps me clear my head and I've so needed it since we've been back. Especially when I think how great it is to be past the tortures of winter 2071.

No doubt, my head was getting really messed up last year. Finding Grand'Mere's letters and solving the mystery of my family's history absolved me of my own self-recrimination as well as all those outlandish accusations of mental instability, etcetera, blah-blah-blah, *ad infinitum. Ugh*, I was SO sick of all those insinuations. So glad it's passed. Anyway, even though nobody at Travelite Global knows a thing about my journey outside the city, it gives me great peace of mind to know that I wasn't nuts. I am, in fact, not nuts!

As our car rolled up on the gravel behind me I only half heard him shut the door.

"Come on now, my baby girl. Time to get going."

Turning briefly toward his welcoming face, I offered my husband little more than pleading eyes and a fleeting, wistful smile and returned to the journal. I want to finish my sentence.

He curled his lips just the way he does when he's trying to be cute and with a good dose of faux self-righteousness, pointed his nose toward the sky, mimicking my mother's affect. I couldn't help but chuckle when with the same lavish lilt of her accent he articulated in perfect British sway, "Shall I attempt to drag you by the hair, my lovely? I can do it; Remember, I've lived in a cave most of my life."

"*Oh you!*" I called to him half-heartedly. "*You're no caveman!* Come on, just a few more minutes, please?"

With that, I took a few steps back from the bulkhead and sat down on the stoop. I was just not ready to walk back up those rickety stairs and head home. He took the seven little steps down to where I was sitting in two quick leaps and, crouching closely behind me, slipped his strong arms around my middle. I could feel his breath on the back of my neck.

Gathering the sleeves of my oversized sweater, I pulled my arms closer to my chest. A chill rippled through me and I nodded my head in affirmation as his lips touched the back of my neck. Warmth washed through every part of me and I could feel a smile emerge on my face. Clearly this unseasonably warm day was starting to fade, but—still—nothing in me was ready to leave.

"You just might have to pull me away, my dear . . . but I hope not by the hair, you silly!" Turning to him I could hardly help but chide. "And listen, while we're at it–I am not your baby girl. *This* is your baby girl." I said it half-jokingly and gave my pot belly a little pat. "You seem to forget young man, that I am quite a bit your senior."

"Really, now? My senior?" His tone was mocking once again, this time his voice falling to the lowest register available to him, and he started to tickle me under my chin.

"You. Are. My. Baby. Girl. And that's that. Get used to it, woman."

"Oh, Viddie. You are too much. I give you an inch and you take a mile."

"Ha! I know where you stole that phrase! Bringin' LJ into the conversation, are we?"

Oh, *dear*. Our beloved guitar-picking minstrel LJ—it's true; FRANCO's words and phrases seem to seep through our conversations like tea into hot water. Whether it's Harold-in-the-camper's long, drawn out version of the word "Weeeell," Fiorella's *"dolce pasti"* or my own mother's cheesy word games spoken in that maddening perfect diction of hers—sometimes they seem so close it feels like we'll bump into one of them around the next corner. But they're not here. No one's around here, ever. People still don't come out of their flats unless they absolutely have to. Hard to believe I lived in this same fear and thought it was "just life" until so recently.

Viddie gently tugged on coat and whispered. "C'mon now, *really*. It's time to go."

I'm sure there was a bit of fire in my eyes as I shot him a quick glance, reminding him that the four o'clock hour is my absolute favorite time of the day down here. *I really can't pull myself away.*

"This is your favorite time of day? *Really????* I did not know that. You really should have said something." Affable sarcasm dripped from his wide mouthy smile as he pulled the blanket around me that we had earlier left in the car. It was nice and toasty.

Sometimes I stare at those rolling waves so long that I feel as though I am actually entering into them. Today, for instance; I feel like I could curl up on the sand and sleep here and become part of the landscape. *Ha!* Throw me a cozy blanket, a couple of chewy provisios and I'll be fine for a couple of days.

I bend down to finally tie my shoes and then, looking up the choppy waters I steal one long, last breath of the salty air and exhale a most satisfying sigh, and then I feel him tugging at my waist.

"Aw, c'mon, Viddie; look—it's so beautiful. Actually, I think I should use the word *magnificent!* Aren't you at all drawn into the flowing undulation and expanse of these waves? Really now—just look at those sweet little sandpipers hopping around like someone spent hours choreographing their movement. Look at them; would you look? Please, just another minute or two."

Pulling the stray hairs away from my face, he turned me around and I was happy to see a note of compliance in his eyes as he joined my long last look.

Looking away from the ocean just long enough to elbow him in the ribs, I countered playfully. "Stop. You're teasing me!"

"Yes, I am," he retorted and began to tickle me into the car.

Day 15—The Discovery

"Hon?"

Looking up from my page I responded to his call from the lounge. "Yes? I'm here on the bed, just scribbling some thoughts down, dear!"

Viddie poked his head through the door with a sparkle in his dark eyes, looking slightly flushed.

"I found something that I think you need to see." He held out his rugged hand.

"Come on over here. You need to see this. C'mere."

Hmmm. Did he finish the baby's cradle? I wonder what's up. The mystery in my husband's voice was intriguing. I put down my pen, rolled off the bed and padded across the hall to follow him.

"Where are we going?"

"You'll see."

"Viddie–*C'mon!* Tell me. This is a 700 square foot flat. There is not much room to go anywhere within these walls. Where are you taking me?" He grabbed my hand and glanced backward at me with a knowing smile."

We stopped short at the vertical cupboard where we keep the shower supplies and sweeper between the water closet and the 2x2 stone slab in the tiny space we call a kitchen. The shelves were dismantled and our small cache of bath towels were strewn everywhere.

"*Yes?*" My patience, growing thin, was soon rewarded when Viddie opened the door to its full breadth.

"*Ta-da!*" His slinky little smile broke into a wide grin as he pulled away the sweeper to reveal a completely empty person-size opening where just this morning when I showered there was a back wall and a well-utilized closet.

"What? What's that? What's going on there? What did you do with the back of the closet, Viddie? What's there?"

By now, his sheepishness was completely gone and raw delight took over.

"Look at this, Emi. You've got to see what is here," he nearly shouted out the words as he squeezed my hand and tugged me forward.

Barely slipping through the door I inched past the side towel rack and followed him through the open space into another closet that was identical to ours. He pushed out another door and walked us right into the very next flat. WHAT?!!?

"Viddie! How did you do this? Where are we? Is this what I think it is?"

"You betcha, *mi amor*. This is LJ's old place. Come on, let's look around!"

I hushed my cranky self immediately and craned my neck around to view the kitchen, which upon a cursory look seemed to be a replica of our own. One large empty bin with the standard slats for provisios standing beside the small counter; check. An old—really old—microwave oven sitting atop a refrigerated drawer; check. Stock graphite tile on the floor and four window slits, each an inch apart, just above the garbage shoot. Wow. Exactly like ours.

The two o'clock sun was strong, shining through the cloudy glass panes, creating a reflection of four narrow rows of light on the wall opposite the closet. Although they'd been gone for over two decades, it looked as if it could well have been that the occupants were simply out. Nothing was out of place, just a little dusty. Nothing was boarded up. No disheveled mess. The sparse kitchen was definitely bare, but it was orderly and wasn't what one might expect after twenty years of inattention. Hmmm. That was probably strategic, to avoid suspicion. When they left it was well planned. Nothing on the walls, no towels in the closet, only an old-fashioned grey and white cooler sitting in the middle of the floor. My eyes were drawn to the lounge. I walked over to the front door and saw that the refrigerated shoot was open, empty, and in locked position, a clear indicator to the Central Food Service that delivery was no longer necessary. Viddie followed me and looked around the room. We both stood in rapt disbelief, me more than him. I queried him as I scoped out the rest of the tiled area.

"That false backing to my towel closet was there the whole time?"

Nodding and shrugging in his own state of wonder, his eyes darted from counter to ceiling scoping every corner of the main room. *"Our* closet, right?"

He shot me a quick smile to let me know the reminder was not intended to annoy me, just a matter of fact.

"Yes, of course: *our* closet. But Vid, where . . . what . . ."

He squeezed my hand and didn't wait for me to finish the question.

"C'mon, E. Let's see what else is here. This is too cool!"

I followed dutifully from the lounge to the washroom to the bedroom. His curiosity led the way and Viddie made no bones about how excited he was about his discovery. He was on his hands and knees under the mattress before I even got through the door. His voice was muffled while the bottom half of his body jutted out from under the bed frame. Watching intently as he wormed his way out from the dusty floor, I was completely wrapped up with the intrigue.

There were a bunch of things in his hands—things I couldn't make out at all. He blew a couple of quick breaths over the items and coughed from the dust.

"What is *that*?" I whispered.

"Why are you whispering?" he laughed as he threw three roles of undeveloped film, a woman's purple hair tie, four copper pennies, and a very dusty collection of negatives in an nicely protective envelope on the unmade bed.

"I . . . I . . . don't know. I don't want anyone to hear us in here, I guess. Viddie, this is dangerous! And—*ew*—look at all that mess on you. Your shirt is covered with dust! Do you see how filthy you are? It looks like all the dirt missing from the rest of the flat congregated under the bed for a party. *Ew*."

He brushed more dust off the envelope and didn't even seem to notice his shirt.

"We've got to check the entire place out, Emi. Let's see what else is here; maybe there are hidden items, like what you found last year in your attic. We'll bring this stuff back to our place and look at it more closely later."

Almost unconsciously I found myself whispering again. "Maybe I should go get my PZ/1000 and engage for a few minutes so we can do a better job of finding out what's here."

Viddie turned in a flash and nearly bowled me over in a tone I didn't like. "Are you *serious*, woman? No way!!! Whatever your tek can do for us in this situation can also be used against us. Who knows if this space is being monitored? Remember the stories of their exodus, the things they told us about how careful they had to be not to be detected? *Woman!* Why were your parents, LJ, and Grand'Mere so darn careful about not leaving a trail? They didn't want to risk being followed. No. *No way.* Let's just use our eyes. Our eyeballs are wonderful instruments of observation. C'mon."

Shame smothered me at that moment. I felt so stupid . . . maybe for the first time in my life! But he was right. What a dumb idea.

I followed dutifully, still incredulous that we were actually in the flat next door without having to break in or risk being seen. Viddie stopped abruptly, and turned toward me. His eyes softened.

A touch of tenderness returned to his voice. "I'm sorry hon. I didn't mean to explode like that. It's just . . . there you were, whispering just two seconds before because you were worried someone might be listening, and yet you could think about connecting to the network? I know you didn't mean it."

My eyes welled a bit and I looked away. With the urgency of our investigation momentarily tamped down, he grabbed both my hands, cocked his head, and smiled sheepishly.

"Truly, I am *sorry*. Will you forgive me? I should not have yelled at you."

Really, he left me quite speechless. What was I to say to that? So, I just nodded and followed . . . with my eyeballs.

Day 16—The Conversation

It got chilly down at the beach again today. The day was damp to begin with, and when the clouds covered the sun, it got cold fast. We settled snuggly into the back seat of the **'70** and the moment we got situated, our conversation started up full throttle. I jumped in first, but not before wrapping myself in the toasty blanket that Viddie's kept in the car all winter.

"Can we talk about the changes in our world again? I love our morning drives. The car is such a cozy, contained space to let our thoughts run wild, and I've been pondering a number of things since our talk the other day."

He kissed my forehead like he always does at the start of our conversations.

"Of course, *mi amor*. But I'd much rather talk about a strategy for dealing with LJ's flat. We've got the envelope with the stuff we found there, and now that we have this really convenient way in, when do you want to go back? We have more investigating to do."

The '70 was already in motion, my feet planted firmly along the soft ledge of the comfy, granite-colored lounge. Hmmm. Our interests were a bit at odds yesterday morning, but we ended up with some pretty interesting developments. I raised my concerns first.

"*Ummm.* I feel like we got in and out and didn't get caught. Let's be satisfied with that, okay? There's nothing there. What more is there to talk about, hon? I was thinking we'd continue our work talk—you know, where we left off."

"Oh. Okay. Just a minute. Before we launch full throttle into *work* talk, I want to note a couple of things about our discovery, *capish*?"

"Ha, ha. Yes, I *capish*, my love. What's up with LJ's flat? What's more to think about, huh?"

"For one, don't you think it's odd that the back of your cupboard came away from the wall so easily? Isn't it a bit strange? It seems to me that LJ must have rigged that long before Grand'Mere left and he must have done it so that you would find it."

"Well, I didn't think of that. I mean, why would he do that?"

"Exactly. Let's think about *why* he might do that. What did he want you to find? Could there be some of those breadcrumbs your grandmother told you they left? I mean, you found enough in your own attic to set you on the road of discovery, but who's to say they did not leave other clues, right?"

I stopped to really think about what he was saying, and although there was certainly logic to it, why on earth wouldn't Grand'Mere or my parents tell me about any further breadcrumbs when I was there? Funny, but I swear he read my mind.

"They probably didn't mention anything to you about other clues because you were there and . . . they expected you to stay."

Gulp. He's good. Real good.

"Yup, you're probably right. So fine. What do think about these trifling little things we found? Do you think there's something there that is worth looking at more closely?"

"No, I mean, I don't know. Em—what if there's more in there that we didn't find. We didn't scope out every inch of the place. Have you thought about his attic? I mean—just think, there may be more gems or clues or . . . artifacts from his generation that could bless you or . . . be useful to you in some way. Plus, you can't really call the stuff we found *trifling* if we haven't thoroughly inspected it. Just sayin'."

"*Hmmm.* You got me. Alright then. We can go back. Let's go back tonight if you want. Now can we talk about the project ideas? We're almost there."

The soft spring sun was just coming up, nearly blinding us through the front windshield. He chuckled and jumped right in.

"Let's see. Where did we leave off? I bet you'd like to talk about the emergence of modern particle theory and your family's part in the examination of the symmetries governing particles and their interactions?"

"Uh . . . not exactly." Now it was my turn to chuckle. Oh how he melts my heart! Particle theory—ha! Not even his area of expertise and yet he can keep up with me. What a great listener.

"Don't laugh. Surely that was happening in science a hundred years ago. I mean, wasn't that the key to making the connections to OSLM—and ultimately the ability to develop virtual vacations?"

"*Viddie.* No. I don't want to talk particle theory. I'm thinking about early America again. No tek talk today, please; yes, it did all start at that time, but particle theory was just the tiniest part of the project. Let's get our heads in 20th century beach life, okay? I don't want to spend even one more minute talking about modern theoretical physics and its symmetries. *Please.* I know it's probably surprising—even to me it is—but I want to stop thinking about the immediate past and take a closer look at what was happening in the world at least a century— maybe two—before all the automation took over. Please, honey. Can we talk about the slow century?

"Okay. Okay. Sorry. I misread you. But, to be honest, I was hoping to impress you with all my tekky, scientific talk. Ha! I should know better than that."

"Yes, sir, you certainly should. I am already so impressed with everything about you—don't be so silly, please."

I didn't mean for it to come out that way and felt a little badly about that part of our conversation because it seemed to saddle a touch of undue shame to him. Reaching over to squeeze his hand, I hoped my earnest look would smooth things over. He piped up fast and met me right where I hoped he would. The historical vaca packages!

"It's just that ever since I've known you, Em, you've been so enthralled with all your tek talk—I thought that's where you were going. I mean, they *did* have tek a hundred years ago. Technology *was* booming mid-20th century, and innovation took a wild tick upward in the crazy-80s and nowhere-90s, especially toward the turn of the century. The economy imploded, huge swaths of the older citizenry were lost in the transition from geo-space to virtual space, not being able to navigate the tek for beans. Some people had fulltime employment just taking care of people's digital devices. That period was poppin' and I know a lot about it because of Harold-in-the-Camper's dad. Man—if he had one story of the late 20th century, he had a hundred, and on Friday nights we'd hear 'em over and over."

"Harold's dad? I don't remember him."

"Naw, you wouldn't. He passed away a few years back. Lots of folks came in their 50s, 60s and 70s and didn't make it through the first few really rugged winters. I don't remember all of 'em, but Grant—that was Harold's dad's name—was quite a guy. And if you think Harold is a character, you should'a seen his dad!"

I do love Viddie's stories—he's got such a different perspective than I do. I egged him on, hoping to hear some more details.

"Yeah, their family trekked into camp together that first year along with their close neighbor friends from Texas—Powell and Wilson; I was just a little kid. They were all pretty hearty, and Grant was a built like an oak tree, so in spite of his upward age we were all sorry to see him pass away. It was in the middle of a really fierce nor'easter that hit the Pocono Mountains one winter. Yeah, sad. I remember it well."

Of course, all this talk of death threw my head into thoughts of my dear Russa—the only true friend (aside from Vidd) that I've ever had. It's still so hard to fathom that she died from a stupid spider bite! Fine that morning; by dinner she was gone. Ugh. It's a scary life up there in those mountains—they're so . . . unprotected.

As I pondered the strange twists of life and death, Viddie kept talking about the old days in FRANCO and mentioned this guy, Powell again. Seems he worked in old tek before he moved to FRANCO and that's how Vidd knew so much about the early part of the century. Powell had a million and one stories about the chaos that was taking place at that time. Our conversation definitely took on a rabbit trail status, but when we finally got back to the meat of our discussion I nearly forgot what we were talking about!!

"Okay, *mi amor*—duly noted: no quarks, chromo-dynamics or talk of the reshaping of protons through organic material. Ha ha—this is really a first for you; you've got to give me that! You, not wanting to talk tek. Ha! Okay then. Now, tell me what you're pondering."

"Whew. [Deep breath] Thank you. Great! But wait, one more thing about this man, Powell. I don't remember anyone ever mentioning him. Why not? Wasn't he a very significant part of the community?"

Viddie scratched the sparse rubble that collects on his jaw every few days and paused to think about my question. He seemed stumped. I smiled at him as he pondered, but doubt that he knew what I was thinking.

"Well, first off, everyone who lives in FRANCO is a significant part. But as far as hearing about Powell, there's a good reason why you didn't. But you do remember Wilson, right?"

He didn't wait for an answer but barreled on after a simple shrug of my shoulders. "Yeah, Wilson was the guy who came around every once in a while last summer, especially when the apples were in. He'd bring the baskets in from the orchard."

"Apples? *Mmmm.* Vaguely. Yeah, I do remember the apples. He was . . . I don't know, kind of a backwards-looking seventy-something with . . . uh . . . did he wear really thick, rustic-looking, blue pants—sort of rugged, frayed . . . ?"

"That's Wils alright. Ha ha. Blue jeans is what we call 'em, baby. They're also called dungarees, but . . . hey—you can call them blue pants if you want. You've got him right, 'cept he's closer to 80, 81, by now, I think. Anyway, his earth-shelter is maybe half a mile or so up the other side of the mountain so we don't see him often. Dude's a lot like Harold-in-the-camper—sort of a loner, but a nice guy."

"But Vidd . . . what does Wilson have to do with Powell? *C'mon hon.* I'm beginning to think you've got us headed down one of your famous rabbit trails again!"

With that he grabbed me gently and smushed his face directly into my left cheek. His breath was warm and wonderful and his close presence gave my heart a little leap. Without a breath between us he laughingly eked out a single word and suddenly morphed into the tickle monster.

"Twin."

"What? What are you . . . ha . . . what . . . haha. Vidd! Stop tickling me. Would you st—I can't breathe!"

After several rounds of feverish laughter, he finally let up and I caught my breath. I leaned back and shook my head.

"Whew—one never can tell when that monster will appear. Out of the blue, right? Ha ha! *Whew.*"

He chortled and sat back on the car's comfy lounge—ah—the one in our car is so much better than the one in the flat. It's nice and wide, too. We'd had lots of fun these last months in that car!

When we settled down he explained that Wilson and Powell were identical twins, but the tale he told was really terrible. It seems they were out together in the storm trying to haul in a deer they just shot. The snow and wind kicked up and although they eventually made it back to Stone Camp, Powell dropped to the ground in the middle of hanging the deer, and he never got up again. Doc said it was a heart attack. This was all only a few years after their friend Grant died.

"That's *awful*. What a dreadful story, Vidd—coming all the way out there only to drop dead like that? Doesn't seem fair."

"Yup. And Wilson never was quite the same. Never again did I see him hunt, and he stopped joining us on Friday nights at Stone Camp. That spring he set up a new earth shelter on the outskirts of the orchard, just beyond Harold's camper, and told us he would take the orchard on as his primary responsibility. He was true to his word and we enjoy apple-everything all year long—mostly 'cause of Wils. So, have you had enough my camp stories? *Ha!* All we need is a campfire and a guitar! Are you ready to resume our brainstorming?"

I smiled weakly, took a deep breath, and turned away in thought. Something about the wildness of that life really hit me hard. After just a moment or two of silence I attempted to return to work-talk and laid out what I envisioned in my mind's eye.

"*Hmmmm.* Here's the thing, Vidd. They were real people—people just like Wilson who lost his brother, and people like us who fell in love and got married. They had babies and joys and sorrows and . . . and I want all of that to somehow be a part of the new packages. Up till now I have not spent much time populating the VacaPackages with people, and when I have they've been thoroughly one-dimensional. But I'm thinking deeply about these folks who lived in the past, and I want to make sure that I include them as people, not props. They are not some de-contextualized images that I can pull up out of my Deep Archives or the WorldSearchAtlas. The people in these settings are—well, they're occupying my thoughts much more than they ever have."

"That's cool, Em, very cool."

Viddie seemed deep in his own thought—maybe all the talk of Wils and Powell is what got him daydreaming.

"*Vidd?* I think part of the reason is that I want to honor people's lives—you know—remember their journeys. I have learned so much about the intrinsic worth of all people. It's a much deeper sense than I had all the rest of my life before finding you . . . and FRANCO. Hon, are you listening? Do you understand what I am envisioning?"

"Oh, I'm listening alright. I hear you and I am tracking, *mi amor* . . . for sure. You're totally right: if we want to create a legitimate experience for today's virtual travelers we'll have to get the people exactly right—what they thought, how they walked, what they ate, where they went, what they liked—everything."

"That's it! You're right. You're getting it. I love that you get me!!! I'll bet we could we incorporate CG images of people journaling or hiking or just sitting under a tree watching a bird—what do you think? Zeejay is so good with imaging techniques. Hey—I wonder if they journaled like I do? Do you think they ever thought about the stars or if they ever thought about people who'd live in the future? You know there were a number of futurist stories and films that populated the media of the day, if I recall. And, also, we've got to . . . ."

"Hon . . . *baby* . . . slow down. I am listening. *I get it.* Yes, I get *you.* You are thinking about people who lived right here in this area a hundred years before us and wondering if they were at all like us. It's an interesting thought. I hear you . . . I really do!"

"Well, yes, a hundred years, but like I've mentioned before, maybe further back too. Right? You know—the ones who lived on this shore and loved it *long* before us—maybe even 200 years ago—when the continent was still bursting with hope and it was a young United States. You know, you know . . . when hope for a future of innovation was strong and people were still visiting from house-to-house and horses and buggies clopped down small, cobble-stoned streets and . . . and . . . you know, when they still used simple paper and pens and . . . and . . . well, when tek didn't rule everything."

He took my hands and held them in his, looking at me squarely.

"Emi, let's make sure we're talking about the same thing. There's such a wide span of time you're bringing into this. If you're talking a hundred years ago every decade brought the kind of change that once took centuries. Remember, the United States was intact up until The Devastation and viable all the way up through our parent's early adulthood. In fact, the continent was still three separate countries all the way up to 2037. It was just before you were born that ADMIN stepped in to help restructure things. I'm sure I don't have to tell you that, but . . . it makes a difference when considering what we might include in these packages. Obviously, we don't need anything from January 2000 on, so . . . what time period are you most interested in? Is it the decades leading up to this century—or are we talking about the 1800s? Or maybe it's the late 1700s? Those are wildly different time frames. Whatever you decide, you've really got to narrow the focus, otherwise the package you're envisioning just won't make any sense."

Throughout the whole rest of the day our conversation continued; At one point I had to back off because he started to dip into one of his rare but explosive tirades and only calmed down when I assured him for the tenth time (at least!) that I definitely was not going to use any of the real names from our FRANCO family for the new vaca package. Man alive—just because I mentioned it jokingly at the start, he would not let me live it down! I don't know what his deal is sometimes. *That temper.* It's rare, but when he gets going, it can flare up without a moment's notice.

As we continued our conversation sometimes we ventured into a tumble of confusion; other times it was way over-the-top-exciting. When we got back home from the beach we kept talking even as we enjoyed our weekly real-meal. Red cabbage, mung bean sprouts, mushrooms, brown rice, and chicken, YUM! We gabbed about it all the way through preparation of the rice and veggies, all the way through clean-up, and even as we settled down into bed.

"Emi? Did you hear me? Don't you think we should narrow the focus?"

Why does he keep trying to *narrow* the focus? There's so much to include!

"Well yeah, I said that, but haven't we already narrowed it enough? Maybe it's *two* early American packages we should work on—one that brings folks back to the more rural life of the 19th century and another that takes them to a 20th century beach. That's it! Two! Let's create two! How 'bout that, hon? Do you like that idea?"

"Love your ideas, Emi–they're always BIG! Can we just talk background a bit more before we get into the details, and then we can make a choice about which one we'll start with, okay?"

"Wait. Didn't you hear me? Why can't we start simultaneously? I'll initialize two files and . . ."

"Sweetheart, slow down. You've got to pace yourself. We'll get both of them going before long, but can we please talk about the vacpacs one at a time? It gets so confusing otherwise. And aren't you exhausted?"

"Hey, did you just call my Xtreme VacaPackages, *VacPacs*? Where'd you get that from? I like it. It's a sort of cool way to abbreviate the whole deal. Maybe we can make five-minute getaways and call them mini VacPacs. *Ha!* I like it hon. Cool!!!"

It had been a long day and Viddie's eyelids were heavy. Our bed is so comfy—not quite as comfortable as the lounge in the car—but I've gotten into the habit of putting my feet up. I love to stretch out before I go to sleep. Not the same for him. We had already been talking there for a quite a while, and I could see that he was fighting sleep.

Facing each other, we blinked at the same moment with twin smiles breaking out over our faces, like it was synchronized. He laid back on his pillow, squeezed my hand and puckered his lips to send me an air kiss. I stared at him and could see his eyes start to close. He still needs more sleep than I do, and I had hours to go before I would sleep.

"Viddie!"

"What, uh . . . yeah? I'm here. I'm listening,"

"Yeah. You're snoring too. I just heard a big snore! Amazing the way you can be asleep and awake at the same time."

"I'm up. *I'm here.* Go ahead."

"Okay, fine. So . . . 20th century beach life first. We could definitely have some fun writing about the sun and the sand, especially with our firsthand knowledge of it all. It'll be interesting to try to get into the 20th century head, though. I always think of them as so very different from us—vastly different—but as I dig more deeply into the archives I'm beginning to get a new picture. What did you say Harold's friend told you about his mother's swimwear and personal appearance? They wore skimpy little strings called bikinis, right? I can't believe they allowed that much sun on their skin! And their style—it's seem so strange, doesn't it? It's hard to imagine they had such bland faces with makeup the same color as their skin, and no stir-o-steen on their temples—*ugh,* they looked like ghosts! It's hard to imagine that this was the same generation that pushed the world into a great new age of TotalTek, yet they were still so ignorant about so many things!"

A giant snore nearly scared me out of my skin. I think the baby may have even heard it! Ha! My darling was off to his dreamworld and our conversation—at least for the moment—was over.

Day 20—The Emotions

Dusk fell and I was sorry to see the day close. What a day it was. Last night's dinner of asparagus, bibb lettuce, brussel sprouts, soy sprinkle, and green onions was the sum of our weekly luxury, and what a delight that ration has become since Viddie's been doing the cooking. The way he puts our fresh foods together in a pan is just mind-boggling.

As we watched the remnants of the late April sun start to fade I ruminated on the way my life seems to be kissed with such intense blessedness lately. That's what he calls it anyway; blessedness. *Mmmmm.* Just being together has added so much meaning to my life. It's the love we share, I know that for sure. What a . . . I don't know—gift it is. I've been pondering the wonder of it all.

Mmmmm.

Of course, until just recently I thought it was a feeling associated with childhood—fairy tales, storybooks and the lot. But there's a . . . I hardly know how to say it, but there's a certain two-in-oneness in the way we've been living, and it's as if . . . well, this *love* is so much more than an emotion. It's rock solid, almost like . . . like a mountain. When his words fall upon my ears I don't just hear him, but I can feel him . . . I sort of lock into what he's feeling and it seems like I can actually *feel* what he is feeling. And, and . . . the emotions that bubble up inside of me are so nuanced—almost as if entirely new colors come bursting onto my field of vision. Yeah, that's *it.* It's like a palate of bright blues and greens and reds. *Sometimes* what I feel nearly overwhelms me. And then I begin to analyze all these *feelings* and I can't help but chuckle. Fact is, it's really rather funny because I am actually happy about this lack of control. Truth be told, *I am happier than I've ever been.* What a life this is; oh how freeing it feels to no longer be fighting the feelings!

Lately, too, I've been remembering those early months of our marriage—*man alive*—this was all so new to me. At first, everything seemed terribly amiss in the way I was thinking about . . . well, *about everything*! The sturdy, stable *rational* me seemed to go into hiding. "Lost" was the best way to describe my state of mind. Part of it was that when I returned from FRANCO I imagined the worst. In my mind's eye I could see my little flat ravaged and pillaged or maybe even boarded up. I was happily surprised, however because absolutely nothing was touched, even my provisio stash was intact.

I should've known because no one touches anything of anyone else's around here. The rule of privacy reigns and is not breeched, not unless there is strong suspicion of someone's unattended death, disappearance, or major wrongdoing. It's gross to think about, but I have a feeling there might even be some decomposed bodies left untouched and untended throughout the city domiciles, especially since the dead are expected to be cremated by the family they've left behind. The protocol is mostly unspoken, but everybody knows we don't speak of the dead. They're just . . . gone. When an order for the weekly freshfood rations stops coming in, the government just removes the name from its population roster, or as in my case, it's put on hold. Sometimes people tire of fresh food or feel that it's a bother to cook. ADMIN has recognized this pattern and just assumes the provisio bars are enough.

Yeah, there's a strange sort of irony that exists among us. I guess part of it is that physicality has been so successfully marginalized in the population that the ADMIN barely bothers with our geo-space. Plus, with everyone so tightly controlled by this crazy toxic-earth mix-up, there's a real lock on everyone's headspace, so little—if any—policing needs to be done. I, for one, do not want to press the issue.

In any case, the emotions are not all feel-good and fluffy. What I didn't expect was that my heart would be in need of such extensive repair. *Talk about depression!* Although everything here at the flat was in the precise spot I left it five and a half months prior, another part of my return was the realization that some of my core beliefs were . . . uh . . . really no more than illusions. Instead of last year's chaos and questions clicking at my heels, when I left FRANCO and was finally back to Addison Avenue I was not confused, but felt torn apart from my very self. It was right then and there—even before Viddie and I discussed it—that awareness of my soul began settling deeply into me.

Now my emotions are much more stable. It's been a good long time since I've fallen apart and I know that much of what keeps me sane and steady is to lasso my thoughts and refuse to give them too much of an audience because I know that ten minutes in any direction could cause me to unravel again. All it takes for me to go emotionally haywire—*really*—is to focus too long on the loss or the deception that my family devised when they staged their deaths, or . . . or . . . the discontinuity between what I now know about life's true beauty and the culture of the LAB; *man,* there are just so many things that can throw me off balance!

Thankfully, having Vidd in my life has been a part of keeping me steady. It wasn't that long ago that he came to find me, but even though I didn't have to deal with being separated from him for very long, the pain I experienced as I fled FRANCO was almost unbearable. I think it was sheer adrenalin that kept me going. And then . . . then . . . from the moment I first saw his exhausted, dirty, *gorgeous* self standing there on my own lonely doorstep I realized that emotions aren't the enemy. From that day forward I have vowed to no longer bow to Rationality and Control. My mind opened up. The thick, caked-on walls of my muddy heart cracked open.

Well . . . at least I try not to bow. Frankly, a day hasn't gone by when I haven't caught myself from falling into the ditch of doubt, attempting to control our life together—to reason everything out and create a formula to follow that will make our marriage invincible. I fail fairly regularly, but Viddie is such a help. He is patient and gentle and–oh so sweet to me—even with that little sharp temper of his that reveals itself on occasion. It's hard to admit because he has no formal training, but that man is so often a step ahead of me. So I am learning to listen, to listen to ideas that are foreign to me, to be open to . . . love.

Starting my writing up again has been so helpful in the process; I think that's why I relish this journal so much. Between the writing and our marathon conversations—I'm adjusting. I'm really dealing with all the change without freaking out like I did last year. Three months ago we sat across from each other in the lounge and had a really long discussion about all this and, well, just about everything that's happened to get us both to this point. Viddie called it a "heart-to-heart." *Ha!* Can you imagine? Thirty years old and I am having "heart-to-hearts!" I feel like a kid again!!!

Anyway—Ever since then we have these mini "heart-to-hearts" where we air stuff out regularly, and talk about all the things we're feeling—our worries, thoughts about the future, the past, what's happening today. Then, of course, in spite of the love, sometimes we fall into strange conflicts. It's like we talk past each other and I feel like I don't even know him at all.

That happened this morning. He came back into the bedroom while I was drinking the B-Tea brew and sat down on the corner of the bed. He glanced at me and then looked toward the ceiling and closed his eyes.

My question was simple . . . or so I thought.

"What's up, dear?"

He shrugged, looked my way again, and didn't say a word.

"You're thinking about FRANCO, aren't you?"

Viddie blinked and the sides of his mouth curled up in a half smile, but his gaze remained far off and his attention on something beyond our bedroom. "I miss my sister."

I wiggled my way off the mattress and joined him at the foot of the bed.

"I know it can't be easy, my love."

Rubbing his forearm gently, I placed my cheek on his strong shoulder. The long, dark, curly hairs on his arm brushed against my neck and tickled me a bit.

"Yeah, you guessed it Emi. Some days it's my sister; other days it's my parents, and then sometimes it's just the whole lot of 'em. I hate the idea that they don't know what happened to me—to us—and I hope the Lord will show them that we are alive and well."

It's never easy talking about FRANCO, what with both of us leaving so abruptly and the unspoken knowledge that we will probably never go back. But I really wish we could talk about it more than we do, otherwise it's like a big black bear in the middle of the meadow with both of us pretending there's nothing there. The thing is, lately he gets so morose about it. Well, maybe not quite morose, but . . . clearly sad. No matter what, I always broach the subject with care and a little trepidation.

Viddie's chest expanded with a deep sigh as he turned to face me. "I don't expect you to understand, Emi. After all, you spent such a short time up there. I'm just thinking about everything . . . everyone who counted on me to . . ."

His voice trailed off, and in spite of his reticence and my own wariness to open my mouth—I knew he needed to talk about it.

"So, you think I don't miss the generous, lovely people, the luscious freedom and remarkable greenery, do you? I mean, six months is six months."

"Hold on, there." He didn't move, but interruption lit up the conversation. At least I got some sort of reaction from him.

"It was five and half, to be exact, Emi. Not even a full half year."

"*Whatever*—it was enough time to see that FRANCO is more than just some primitive camp in the woods. It's a grand place, Viddie, and after living there I realize that life in a closely knit community is a wonderful way to live. I'm insulted that you think I don't understand. I *do* miss it too."

He sat up squarely and looked at me with just the slightest twinge of fierceness in his eyes.

"No I don't think you do, Emi, *not really*. Do you know what it feels like to be so integral to the survival of a group of people that if you don't do your part, people could go hungry and die? Do you know what it is to grow up sleeping on a hammock on summer nights with the stars as your canopy? Or how about winters when you may not see everyone for days at a time because it's too cold to leave the narrow cleft in the rock where you live? Primitive yes; challenging, totally, but in spite of all that, life up there seemed somehow easier."

Although a growing tension began to fill the room I couldn't help but laughing a little out loud. "Oh now, c'mon. *Easier*? You've got to be kidding. That's a hard life in the mountains, Vidd. You don't have to persuade me about how challenging it is; I lived there! I couldn't have survived on my own and I wasn't even there through the winter. What are you talking about—easier?"

"See what I mean?" That strong brown brow that furrowed with intensity just a moment earlier, softened. He inched closer, and taking my hand in his, spoke gently, but with much conviction. "You see, as much as you lived there for *nearly* six months, the rhythm of the woods and changing of the seasons isn't in your bones like it is in mine. You've lived pretty much inside your head your whole life and so nature and fresh air. I'm sorry, but *people* have been something you can take or leave. For me, people aren't incidental—and well, I've lived my life very much in public and I can't pretend it doesn't get to me sometimes. Just sayin'."

I got up to stretch my legs and then decided I needed some support for my back. My pillow has been my best friend these last weeks of my pregnancy, so I sat at the head of the bed again and squeezed the pillow down by my lumbar–*oooo* it felt good. I scrunched up against our plush grey headboard and attempted to sit with my legs crisscrossed. At eight and a half months pregnant it's not an easy feat and I realized quickly that this normally comfortable position was not even a possibility. I could feel myself getting riled up. The exasperation I felt rising was bound to accompany my tone and I was feeling restless anyway, so I stood up again and walked past him to the door. I let out a long, extended breath, and closed my eyes to try and keep from an angry outburst.

"Emi? Look at me. You're upset."

I pondered his attitude for moment before I answered. "You bet I'm upset. You know I can't stand it when you talk to me like that. You treat me like an outsider. *C'mon!* I lived there. Don't get all huffy on your high horse and think you're better than me just because you grew up in a more natural setting! *Seriously.* I don't know why you have to make such a big deal about this. We're here now, and we both have an understanding of a different kind of life. Period."

When he finally moved and started walking toward me I thought he might be coming over to hug. Instead, he looked past me and grabbed hold of the door knob. For a strange split second I thought he was going to leave.

"Viddie, stop." I flung my arm across the doorway. "Would you please say something?"

He stopped short and still said nothing so I continued, unsure of where all this was taking us.

"You know there's more to this subject than what we're actually saying, don't you? It's not just the people of FRANCO, the sloping green of the low hills in the valleys, the plush, pillowy clouds and miracle of gardening that you think I don't understand. You are a Christian; you miss all that singing and stuff. Why not just finally admit it?"

Clearly, he was stunned.

"I've never told you that. Emi. How do you know that about me?" His voice softened as he looked at me with eyes searching the far reaches of my soul. Yup. Those smokey blues took on the familiar puppy-dog look that have the power to melt me like Fiorella's caramel sauce—right down the middle of my soul.

"You're kidding, right? Did you really think I didn't know?"

Day 25—The Baby

The car door closed with a familiar *kerplunk* as Viddie let me off in front of the steps at the edge of Old Bath. He went to park the car and left me here with our beach blanket and water. What a gorgeous day. I can't wait to tear off my shoes and sink my toes into the toasty sand. It's warm, *it's really warm!* I think it's 70 degrees today and the sun is brilliant!

Hmmm . . . what's that fragrance? Not sure. Must be that honeysuckle draped over the wall. It's so . . . *mmmmm* . . . wow, it's intensely alluring. Light and fresh but it's so—I dunno— *captivating. Hmmm.* I can't help but wonder if someone standing in this exact spot fifty years ago was appreciating the same glorious fragrance?

The last few days the baby has been unusually quiet. I wonder if that means she is going to make her entrance into the world a couple of weeks early. The medic tells us that first babies often arrive a bit later than planned, but she's so quiet, I can't help but wonder. It's making the need to choose a name more urgent. I like Saron Joy but Viddie wants something Italian. *Giovanneta* or *Annunziata*—something crazy like that. *Ugh.* He's got a hundred of 'em. Every time I shoot down one of the five syllable names, up comes another. Right now he's been talking about *Concentina.* That's only four syllables; I guess it's getting a little better. The only one I have not rejected is *Sophia.* I think Roos would approve because it means wisdom. He says we should just wait until she's born and as soon as we see her, we'll know. I am hesitant to let him know that I really do like Sophia because I made such a fuss about his other choices. The little competition we seem to have going between us is another thing I've never experienced before—with anyone. It's a little weird and fun at the same time. I'm just not gonna give in too soon.

Lately, I find myself thinking aloud quite a bit. This past few months it's as if my daily writing has jumped off the pen and out of my mouth. This ritual of writing has really taken root, and as I track my activities and feelings throughout the week I'm finding it is much more than cathartic. I *need* to do this, especially this last couple of weeks—my goodness—it is hard to do much else! I'm waddling everywhere!

Mostly when I write it's in the evening, and as I do, I try to remember as much dialogue as possible and I find that it's helping me to depend more on my own brain rather than the tek. Today, I'll write here at the beach, and then I'll probably write again at the flat; once now, and then again before we sleep. It's been especially helpful as I process through the many changes this year has brought. Finding my parents alive after all these years, seeing Grand'Mere again, falling in love, and . . . Russa's death—in all of it, the writing has helped me process. Going back to re-read the conversations we had has helped me savor the richness as well as make some sense of the confusion and pain. Through it, I continue to glean insight and . . . and well, there's much joy from remembering, too. Plus, it helps so much to go back and feel what actually happened. It's also helping my memory function more organically so that I don't have to rely quite as much on my OLSM and Deep Archives. Viddie's encouraging me to avoid that as much as possible.

A quick glance toward the road and I see him shaking out the damp towels from yesterday's time here. Salty, damp; *Mmm,* I'll bet they smell just terrific. One of us should have remembered to bring them in last night.

Day 26—The History

Since I've been back several things have become abundantly clear. One of them is this: I seriously dislike working with Allessandro. I don't know what's up with him. I guess it still bugs me—that crazy off-the-grid all-nighter we spent together.

Biggest.mistake.of.my.life. *What* was I thinking? Thankfully, our dalliance was constrained to the virtual dimension and nothing ever did come of it. But how could I have trusted him with my LS protocols in the first place? *Ugh*—I should never have given him that kind of access. It still surprises me to think we once had such fond regard for each other and that in spite of the organizational jockeying and underlying sexual tension, we actually got along. Ever since he put me on mandatory leave, it's been awkward, but now, now since I've returned from FRANCO, the man's as cold as ice. Even his corporate hologram seems to grimace. It's almost as if there's a shadow surrounding him . . . like he's in some sort of dark bubble.

When I think about it, there's something so surreal about even the memory of that night. What's craziest I think, is that so much sensation can be felt without even touching. I mean, it hardly compares to the real love I now know with Viddie, but since our chief technicians located the user interface in the human hypodermis more than a decade ago we've nearly perfected the synesthetic affect. Once affective computing became internalized it made such a difference in our ability to simulate organic functions of all sorts. *Oh how this stuff still amazes me!* What can I say—I do love my tech.

In any case, am I ever glad that the stupid rendezvous between us was nothing more than a steamy screen affair, but I guess I should let Viddie know about it. I'd want to know if it was the other way around.

Hmmm. Eventually.

Eventually, I will.

Aside from these nettling personnel issues, everything else at Travelite Global is very much the same way it was when I left.

Even though the staff is lacking in passion, the work ethic and underlying values are definitely still intact:

Intense commitment to perfection; check.

Efficiency, supreme value; check.

Strict adherence to ADMIN policy and protocols; check.

No interest in anyone except for what they bring to the team. *Big-time,* check.

It's like we're invisible to each other except for the intermittent times when we confer at the LAB. Even then, most of the discussion happens within our OLSM connections. Before last year, I never imagined we were missing anything. Thought-to-thought communication seemed perfectly satisfactory just last year!

The whole setup saddens me a bit. Somehow I remembered things here differently than they actually are. How often did I dream about the LAB and revel in the important work we do? My goodness, all the stories I told Russa—describing the LAB as family—*ugh.* Clearly, that is not the case. It was never the case!

For so long I held onto my position at the LAB as if it was the only thing worthy of my time and attention, but maybe this idea has really been more of a crutch than anything else. Since I've come back to work I definitely don't feel as much outright happiness as I knew during my months in the mountains, and that's just down right, well . . . that's just *odd.* Not me at all.

Being with Viddie is definitely the absolute joy of my life, and contentment with him is ongoing, but I can't help being dragged down once in a while knowing I work for the same organization that was instrumental in messing up my family. 'Course, the principle players have changed and those bad apples who were in charge 25 years ago have long since gone, but still—my family helped make this corporation strong. One would think that there would be greater collective goodwill coming my way. *One would think* they'd be happy for my happiness—or at least show a bit more support than they have, but even on the first day back—when I brought Viddie in and introduced him *as my husband*—the reaction was lame, at best. I mean—twelve years there! I really thought that someone would at least offer congrats. Zeejay was the most polite. He was the first to speak up the day we walked in.

"Oh. Yeah, yeah. Nice to meet you."

Viddie's broad smile and engaging personality usually light up a room, but you couldn't tell from looking at their faces. Jude just raised those bushy eyebrows of his, nodded, and turned his face back to his drafting glass.

Ion's the new guy. When we were introduced, he scrunched up his face and glanced at us on his way to the waterspout and offered a twisted fist bump into the air. Was that meant for us? Huh? *Who knows?* There was no smile—no nothing!

And Rake? Yeah, no idea what ever happened to him. I am clueless as to where he is or why he's no longer at TLG, and no one is forthcoming with information. Jude mumbled something about letting him go shortly before I returned but no one's giving up the details. Rake never was my favorite, but he was a good worker. Not a great loss, I guess, but I do wonder what happened.

Margene—ah, what a trip this one is. She is another new hire, there on the design department's floor when we first arrived, and—weirdly—I just learned—she is somehow related to the Powers woman. A cousin or something. Initially, I thought it'd be nice to have a few women on the team, especially after all these years of being the only female, so I was encouraged when I discovered they were hired, but oh my, what a couple of oddballs.

Powers has a strange set of eyes. A Gorgeous, lovely shade of blue, but they are dull as the dust on a neglected ceiling fan. And the stealth and chicanery that typifies this woman is worse than her oddity. It's terribly bothersome to watch her career in and out of doorways, swaying to some inaudible music that's going on in her head. Unseemly. So unprofessional. Zeejay assured me that she knows her stuff, and he's always been fairly reliable, so I don't really have a reason to call into question his estimation of her. The cousin, on the other hand—Margene— seems to me to be no more than a nubile empty tekhead.

She and Powers have similar features and mannerisms, but there are a few things that are decidedly different. Their hair, for one. Margene has a short brown bob with bangs that fall in her face. While both she and Powers dress to code, they push it. Margene's face is always appropriate with LAB-approved colors and flair choices, but Powers is an entirely different deal. Not only does she blatantly wear inappropriate flair, she wastes diamond dust like crazy!?!?! It's right there—glossed all across her eyelids every day and Allessandro has never said a word. When I approached him about how he proposed to deal with it he told me that HR had been working on policy changes. I keep expecting a general memo reminder to be generated, but it never comes.

Aside from their appearance, perhaps the strangest part of it all is that neither of them seem to add much to our overall effort there. Margene seems dull, so stiff and blundering, never saying much. And, she is absolutely clueless about the etiquette and functioning of OLSM. It's utterly unclear why Allessandro brought her on. Every time I happen to glance her way she is fumbling with her PZ insert to the point where the thing is visible! She's *always* rubbing her forefinger or working on repairing broken cuticles. It's *so* annoying. *Strength!* I don't believe the woman even knows the difference between a virtual vacation and a real one. Powers may be a tad smarter, but she is just ridiculous. Ugh. Enough about these two weirdos.

One bright spot remains and that's the LAB's long-time Security Guard, Mr. Roland. He did offer a smile at the door when Viddie and I first arrived, and what a comfort that was. His snowy eyebrows match his hair and although his smile is nearly hidden underneath a bushy mustache, it is big, broad, and unpretentious. The moment I introduced Viddie as my husband he just about fell over himself with joy. It's true! Rolly was so surprised that he momentarily lost his balance and stumbled against the building. His chuckle gave us permission to laugh along with him, and then he was quick to congratulate us heartily.

Just as soon as we were alone, Viddie mentioned how much Rolly reminded him of LJ. Funny, but I had the very same thought! I'm guessing the two of them are about the same age, but I dunno . . . I could be wrong. —Makes me wonder if they could possibly have known each other before he made the exodus to FRANCO. A longshot, for sure . . . but a possibility. I mean, twenty years ago LJ had to be . . . what, mid-fifties? We don't ask, of course. That would raise too many questions.

So, while the changes at the LAB are not what I would call *drastic,* there's still this sort of over-arching impression that things are . . . well, not as they were. Clearly, *I* have changed, but something peculiar—not sure what—hangs in the air. It's more like an attitude, but not one that is emanating from just one person (that Powers woman has a gigantic attitude, but that's beside the point). It's just that there are times that I walk into the Travelite Global wing of the LAB and it's so thick I feel as though there is a fog surrounding the place. Then, when I head up to the executive wing, it's even thicker.

Viddie asked me to describe it to him the other day and I couldn't really put my finger on it then, either, but I see it in so many little things. I guess I just expected a little enthusiasm for my return . . . or interest, at least. Anyway, now that my old position is once again firmly intact, I can hardly help but notice how different this environment is from the closely knit community that I experienced with Viddie back in the mountains. At the very least I expected everyone to exhibit some sort of curiosity or interest, but their questions were just as negligible as their expressions. As soon as I introduced Viddie we all just bounced back into work.

It's so weird to think that I used to consider Jude and Zeejay sort of like . . . my brothers. My sense of family—of closeness, in general—has changed so much in just this short year's time.

Day 29—The Ideas

"It's all coming together! Everything we've been talking about for weeks is coming together in my head, hon. Can you feel it, too?"

He smiled and nodded his head slowly, acknowledging all my work thus far. He may not have jumped up and down, but the way his eyes shone—ah, I knew he was with me. My exuberance overwhelms him sometime, but it's hard not to get excited when a design idea moves from scratchy little fragments of thought to full blown integration. I am currently fixated on removing some of the extraneous details and trying to emphasize the simple beauty and elegance of another century.

"Vidd—have a look at this sketch. When I get to the LAB I'll have the team edit out the trivial details; we'll put a history filter-wash on it and we'll be halfway there. Here, have a look!"

I passed the glass-plate over to him, pointing out the landscape detail I included in the mock-up.

"*Wow—it's definitely cool*, Emi, I like what you've done so far, but let's not be too quick to judge our 19th century forbearers for their color choices. I've gotta tell ya, when I first walked into the LAB I had a hard time getting used to the choices your crew have made in the fashion department. Whew-ee!"

"C'mon, Vidd. You know ADMIN makes those decisions for us. There's hasn't been a big retail industry since The Devastation, so the plain white jackets, pants, and shifts just make life easier for everyone. Besides, we do get to choose colors for accessories. That keeps it interesting, you know?"

"Ha ha—interesting, alright! Jude's polka dot bowtie makes him look like a clown, if you ask me, and that Zeejay, with his signature red handkerchief—*man*! When I'm there it makes me feel like we should all be headed to a circus!"

"Oh, Viddie—those are such trivial accents. I wish you wouldn't make such a big deal about City Centre flair. Besides, the accessorizing is an important symbol—it's an outward sign of what sets us apart from the rest of the population, and . . . and, well, that contributes to our own motivation. This is not easy work, you know."

"I know, I know. You are all so intense and focused . . . and you definitely accomplish major feats. *My lands*—when I first saw the initializing software for your team's very first virtual vacation I was in awe. You guys are geniuses. I'm just saying, what we may think is trivial may be an important detail. I mean, can you imagine what future people might say about *us*? Just think about the way we eat."

My attention got sort of stuck on "my lands." I could feel a smile emerge within me as he spoke. That phrase is something I have only ever heard from my grandmother. It was "my lands this," and "my lands that," and just one of the unique expressions that was attached to the many golden sentences that rolled off her tongue. *Ha ha ha!* If I heard it once growing up, I heard it a thousand times, and haven't ever heard it from anyone but her, and now him. When I caught up with what he was saying again and let the daydream of Grand'Mere and my childhood fade, he was still talking about food.

"The fact that you subsist almost completely on provisio is absurd! One meal a week of vegetables and rice—c'mon, Em— you know that's absolutely *crazy*! I should say 'we' now that I am eating them too, but seriously—can you imagine my mother dealing with these flimsy, crunchy bars instead of sitting down as a family and sharing a real meal? Speaking of food, do you see how much weight I've lost since I got here?"

"Oh I see it, alright, but you still look awfully good to me!"

Viddie's face broke out in that famous twinkly-eyed, crooked smile. He was holding a crumbled vanillaFLAV wrapper and making kooky, chewing gesticulations, like he hadn't eaten for a month. We *are* going through these things with a frightening speed now that he's eating them too. He'll eat two or three at a time and still say he's hungry. *Crazy!* Even though Consumer HQ has upped my weekly delivery to include the two of us, sometimes we've run dangerously low. I continued to stroke his under-developed ego, trying to distract him from obliterating our current supply of provisios.

"*Ha ha*—oh baby, has it escaped your notice, or do you realize that we don't have any hulkish looking men here in City Centre. You are still at the top of the heap even though you've lost about . . . what, eight or ten pounds?"

"Yeah. It's closer to fifteen, I think, and I wasn't a hulk to begin with, remember? Speaking of food . . . I really want to do something about our rations. I wish I could hunt here. Even if we had some flour, we could try and make some bread. It would be easy; I saw my mother make it every day."

"*Mmm*, your mother's bread. I have no trouble remembering *that!* Fiorella would have a fit here, wouldn't she? What on earth would she do with so few real ingredients? *Ha ha*—oh dear. I'm sure she'd figure some way to fatten us up with her scones and other delectable foodstuff."

"Oh yeah. Man, do I miss her venison stew and peach scones and raspberry jam and, *oh Emi-girl*—we've got to figure a way to get better stuff to eat. *More* stuff, too. I miss my mother's cooking and I sure want our little one to know some of the same things I knew growing up."

"She will. We will definitely make sure of that, hon. I don't know about the food, but heck, I mean, remembering what's important–isn't that what we're trying to do through the Xtreme nature packages at TLG? I see it as all a part of our . . . our . . . *place* here as Preservers of the Traditions. We're in this together, hon. I promise you I will tell her stories of your parents and your amazing upbringing out there. Sound good?"

"Sounds perfect."

In his usual adorable way, Viddie enclosed me in his arms and wrapped himself around me with, what, a hundred kisses. He gets me, he *really* gets me, but sometimes it feels like he just doesn't get much else here. City Centre culture is utterly different than the simple organic community life in which he was raised. Does he really know that we are just not gonna ever hunt here? Figuring out how to let him down easy is becoming a regular feature of our conversations. *Man alive!* My efforts sometimes feel like they fall on deaf ears, but I try; I continue to try and teach him the cultural tics that he missed by not being raised here. As this conversation continued, I gave it one last ditch effort.

"Hon, *I know*; I miss it all too, but that's just not how it works here. Everything is carefully meted out. ADMIN knows how much food we all eat, how much waste we produce, how much energy we use. Any change is noted and must be approved. You watch; when the baby comes they will adjust our ration automatically and give us just enough more food, electricity, and rubbish space to allow for an extra little person, but no more. They are very strict and egalitarian in their values. We can dream about your mother's cooking, but forget venison. You can't hunt . . . you know that. Just try and appreciate the bit of variety we do have here. Did you forget we have chewy provisios along with the crunchy ones, and also, the ones with apricot or blueberry flavoring?" I gave him a gentle nudge with my elbow and he feigned a smile.

He's right about the difference in foodstuff, but our provisio is definitely more efficient. In any case, I hadn't thought of the past in terms of food.

"So—okay, Vidd—let's unpack this idea, then; what do *you* think future humans might say about us?"

He pondered my question and gave it respectable consideration for several moments, then shook his head.

"Well, by then it would be nice to see a reversal of the ultra-templated self that has emerged from this tek-driven world. Hopefully, everyone will return to their senses and start relating to each other in ways that make more sense! *Hopefully*, future people will be back to appreciating the land and the water and the beauty of this magnificent planet."

Wow. The man's sure got it done. He didn't think twice about an answer.

"You sure are filled with hope, Mr. Florencia."

My smile was measured, but genuine. I wish that kind of hope would stir in me. Thoughts of Marissa, Libby, and Grand'Mere living here, among us in City Centre began to float through my mind. I found myself wandering toward the pensive. Sometimes when he talks like that my heart tumbles toward the pensive. Instead of hope I just feel an empty yearning. For what, exactly, I'm never sure, but it always seems to involve the folks back in the mountains of old Pennsy.

The only way I can wrap my brain around his hope for a better future is to think about work again, and what we might be able to accomplish there. In spite of how unrealistic it sounds, I find myself getting caught up in the passion for a better world, too. Yesterday was one such time. He gets so enthralled when talking about the mountains, green hills, and fresh food. I know he misses it all, everyday, and I can't help but wonder if we could be agents of change here, paving the way for a new City Centre—one that might even call our families back from the mountains. Is that crazy?

"Oh Viddie, I just didn't see it prior to all those months in FRANCO, even with both you and Russa filling my mind with ideas about the artificiality of this place; I just didn't get it. But now I do. Being back, after I shared that life with you all—I get it!"

He went to the kitchen and brought me a second cup of tea. When he got settled in the lounge chair in the corner of our bedroom, I put my swollen feet up on the bed and we took right up where we left off.

"That's packed with vitamins for you and the baby. Have a sip and think about the next step in design this way: Do you have an idea about what kind of virtual experience you want folks to have if they purchase an early American package? I mean, you're asking them to take a virtual trip back in time. What's your aim; I mean, what's in it for them?"

Breathing in the fragrance of the piping hot roobious and enjoying the deliciousness of its steamy brew, I realized that Viddie's question was perhaps the most important one to be asked. There can be no marketing of the package if we don't understand the consumer take-away.

"Well, yeah, I've been thinking about that, too. But you know, Vidd, I'm beginning to see that perhaps these Xtreme Vaca Packages that we produce might have much more importance than simply giving folks the ability to relax or detach from work for a few minutes a day. We can make them do double-duty by creating so much beauty that it draws forth curiosity."

"Now, I thought that's what we've been talking about all these weeks, no?"

"Well, yes . . . in a way, but the ideas have been coming together in my head more steadily, and now they are just more fully formed. I mean, we know that no one here pays a shred of attention to the beauty out there. The utter detachment from nature is contributing to the collective misery. So I asked myself, how did I begin to really see all the beauty? I mean, *really* see it. I wouldn't have seen it had not my eyes been opened by the beauty of your mountains."

"God's mountains, baby. I know, I know. They are majestic, aren't they? It really is a shame isn't it?"

"It *is*! And the more I think about it, the clearer it becomes. Man alive—the LAB staff and almost everyone else I've ever known here are empty, colorless people, just *colorless* and vacant."

"Well, that's a sorry proclamation. But think about it: you say 'people you have known.' Have you really even known them, *mi amor*? I mean, how can you know who they really are if they don't even know themselves?"

Ooooh. That stung, and I'm sure he didn't mean it to hurt me. But, man—just hearing that makes me cringe, probably because it's true! It's only been since I returned from the mountains that I can say I've begun to know my own mind, but I do hate to admit it. It's sad. The whole culture strikes me as so sad sometimes. How did we get here? How did this devolve so quickly? I looked over at him and he was still waiting for answer that I certainly did not have, but I did offer a comment.

"Even with a bit of flamboyant flair thrown in, everybody has the same vacant, empty eyes. Viddie, it makes me want to cry, and I don't think it's just the hormones that are wreaking havoc in my system. I feel it deeply. It's *sad*."

He took my hand and smiled knowingly. "Been waiting for you to come into your own with this, Em. It's one thing to live it and another to know it deep in your knower. It's clear you're beginning to really understand the difference now, but I'm sorry that it makes you sad. It's a sad thing, for sure, but we can't just pretend that it's not a problem. When I think about my upbringing it's hard to imagine anyone ignoring the earth and all its treasure the way everybody does here. But once your heart is awake, you begin to see everything anew."

"Oh Vidd, you're right! I mean, there are colors and flowers—even weeds around here—remember those lavender lollypop weeds that I pointed out this afternoon? *They're gorgeous*. I feel like I am just seeing them for the first time, yet clearly they've been here all along. I want to help others wake up to this beauty. I so much want to do this!"

Viddie came over to my side of the bed, laid down really close, and began to whisper love things in my ear. *Oh how I need his love*. How did I ever do without it? After a few moments he proceeded to remind me of the major role Marissa and Liam had in establishing FRANCO, and his voice cracked a little just like it usually does when he talks about our story.

"I'm glad your parents found their way up to the mountains. I'm so glad they joined hands with my parents to establish an alternative culture, and I am so glad that you found your way to us. . . . It's just a shame that this world of ours got so messed up and that we have to be separated from our family and friends and the people who love us most. I think it happened because no one cared to look down the road to consider some of the rippling effects of a world that exalts machines and diminishes human contact. It just didn't have to happen that way. And maybe we can do our little part to change the outcome of it all. Think how easy it is to begin using some new piece of tek that makes everything so much easier—your P/Z, for instance. Did you or any of the others ever think that that using it every day might completely internalize your communication systems, making the external devices obsolete?"

"Well, yeah, actually, we did. It seemed a much more efficient way to do business and to function, in general."

"Really? Okay, so . . . did you realize it would also affect your innate ability to remember things?"

Now it was my turn to shrug, a bit callously, I admit. It felt like we were beginning to go far afield. Maybe it was my own fault. In any case, Viddie continued with the train of thought and reflecting back on it, I'm glad he did. It was a bit comical too. We got a bit muddled with a misunderstanding about a particular phrase. What a sight he was—hands gesticulating, voice projecting. He stood up and got all animated when he spoke.

"Yeah, baby, I mean—how easy it was to get caught up with all the fantastic possibilities of the technologies back— what, 75 years ago? And really, are they any different than us? Your very own parents were at the helm of all that innovation and they escaped by the skin of their teeth!"

"Skin of their teeth? What the heck does that mean? Yeah, I know they got sucked into the propaganda, but there was never any skin on their *teeth*! We started using the skin along the cuticle of our fingers, but not *teeth*. What are you talking about?"

"Oh my good God, Emi—ha, you are truly a crack up! You never heard LJ or Earl or anyone at FRANCO use that expression? *It's just an expression.* Uhhhhh. You got me off track. I was trying to make a point."

"Go ahead," I said straight-faced and quickly. "I'm listening."

By this time he was so worked up that he stood and seemed to use the room as a stage. With hands continuing to help him find expression and his face more animated than before, he continued his response.

"Em—with all the stories I've heard I am sure of a couple of things. One, our generation is no different than they were. We are all susceptible of being dazzled by tek and drawn into its sway without thinking one dot or iota about the way it'll change us. And, the other thing I know is that when the tekworld began to dominate it became integrated into the very value system of everyone alive. People here have forgotten how to relate. Heck, it seems they have even forgotten how to smile. Everything is business, business, business. And yes—you have changed, but they've all pretty much stayed the same. Hence the frustration."

I stood up and started to make my way into the kitchen to heat up my tea.

"Oh my, you are certainly beginning to sound like Russa now. All that talk about the technological imperative. *Ha!* Viddie, seriously, you have a very cool outside perspective and I appreciate your ability to analyze it all, but while you were speaking *I* just had a brainstorm!"

"Another one?" He followed me to the next room and urged me on.

"It's in the same vein as we've been talking, hon. Think about this: We use the XtremeVacation packages to introduce them to historic America and re-create a virtual environment where people can actually relate to one another. We can help our subscribers understand the beauty of the earth without a formal tutorial or without giving ourselves away. We could market them as adventure packages, but totally draw vacationers into virtual worlds that are slower, sweeter, and filled with the simple things—all the things we love. I mean . . . we could draw on the glorious environment of FRANCO, sort of like a re-enactment of community life. Wouldn't that be *so cool?*"

His sweet smile evaporated immediately and his eyes looked like they were about to pop out of his head. "You are an idea-a-minute, do you know that? *Ha ha ha*—oh, you are brilliant and beautiful and so creative. The Lord has been so good to me. It's hard to express just how thankful I am to Him."

Casting my eyes away for a moment, I felt my face get flushed. It's hard to know what to say when he talks like that, especially since it's couched in such love. It's popped up a few times these last months, but when he mentions the Lord—man alive—I just don't know what to say. I mean, I love this man to Mars and back, but his *Lord*? Can't really get behind that part of him, but . . . well . . . there *is* this tiny piece of me deep inside that seems to light up when I hear him profess his love like that. I mean, *as if* there actually might be someone out there to thank for this life of love.

"Yes, darling I know. You are thankful, as am I, but I . . . I would really like to know if you think we can pull it off. The idea—I'm talking about the idea; will it *work*?"

He pulled back slightly at my sheepish response and cocked his head with that friendly, but tentative smile.

"*Hmmm*. Not sure. Do you think your boss would go for it? It's definitely a *cool* idea, but . . . what about . . . well, honestly, I've got a bit of reservation tugging at me on the inside. Not sure if there would be any rippling effect. Do you think trying to change the whole world is a bit too radical, my love? And what if . . . well, do you think it would lead your design team onto finding FRANCO? You know we couldn't let that happen. Oh baby, I'm not sure."

Day 30—The Fatigue

Two little drops of hot tea dripped on my shirt. Not enough to burn me or make me change my blouse, but I got up to wipe it off so it wouldn't leave a red stain. When I looked in the mirror to check out the damage, I saw a remnant of toothpaste at the corner of my mouth. *Ugh. What's the matter with me?* No one told me how dragged out tired I would be at nearly 9 months pregnant. Grand'Mere left when I was seventeen and I wasn't even interested in the opposite sex yet. Too much going on with my post-grad opportunities at the LAB. 'Course, Marissa and Liam were long gone from my life and the fact of the matter is, I simply had no social life. Nada. Zip. Nothin'.

Just saying "social life" (even the phrase) sounds kind of odd coming from my lips, but *pregnancy*—well, pregnancy is nothing any of us ever talked about before. The only woman with whom I have interacted in the last decade was the female medic who helped me through a debilitating season of influenza that hit me when I had just turned twenty. Yeah, ol' Doc Martin—another hoary-headed soul. She was all business, but she knew her stuff. I mean, I remember her surprise when she treated me for the flu. She said, "Well well well, Dr. Hoffman-Bowes, you are the youngest person I've ever treated with influenza, and fact is—I haven't even seen that strain for twenty years. What have you been up to, young lady? You been playing in the dirt?" I remember it like it was yesterday. She looked at me inquisitively and all I could do was shrug. Didn't pay much attention because all I wanted was to get back to the design floor.

Ugh, I feel so exhausted. Viddie made me vegetables again last night in hopes that the extra nutrition would bring me strength. It was really tasty, but now we won't have anything fresh for at least ten days. *Man alive*—that guy is as stubborn as I am!

Day 31—The Run

Tender petals of creamy yellow-white and purple feel as smooth as anything I've ever felt against my cheek. These little blooms have popped all over the place this week. It's like the earth is alive again. *Ha!* A little like me. Everywhere I turn it seems new feelings and experiences are popping up across the landscape of my heart. Surely, these violet flowers must have bloomed every summer, but I do not remember ever seeing them before.

Hard to believe. So hard to believe.

So here I sit, once again in my familiar little spot—a stump in the sand surrounded by wispy kelp, some tangled, some single, stray, strands—watching as my Love runs along the wet shoreline, listening to the gentle rhythmic crash of the waves against the earth.

Deep breath.
Deep breath.
Ah, it feels so good, so right to be here.
Drinking in the air
Like a cup
Of peach tea
Brisk
Bold
Brrr . . .
I laugh at the wind as she tries to chase me away.
I'm staying right here, oh laughing Breeze—don't you dare!
Been away too long
But now
Now
Now . . . I 'm here.
I love you even when you are biting.
I want you even when you give me a chill.
I need you
Everyday.

Ha! Sometimes I just can't resist writing what is bubbling up inside me. Even if no one ever reads it, it is so freeing!!!!

Wow. A vision of my younger self just soared through my brain—a flash of the occasional days I'd drive by the ocean and venture a sideways glance toward the water. Getting out of the car, touching the sand, really *enjoying* the beach was just . . . well, it was unthinkable. Oh my how life has changed. But now, *now, spiaggia* is ours! Using the Italian name for it helps combat all the bleak, dark associations I've always had with the ocean and my emotions are in full flower. It's a whole new experience. And no one is there . . . *ever.* It's all ours!

Mmmmm. The salty air, the whipped up wind or gentle breeze coming off the water—how it delights my heart. And I have Viddie to thank for it. Had he not showed me that the water wouldn't harm him, I simply would not have believed it. It continues to shock me that everyone else is snookered. How I wish I could shout to the world: Jump in, jump in! The water's fine. The earth is fine! There's nothing to fear . . . but fear itself. (Oy, who said that?) *Arrrgh.* I know so little without my OLSM.

I do love the joy I feel bubbling up inside me. It's foreign, mostly, but there is a vague recollection I find myself having once in a while—a memory of a much earlier time. Was I in a stroller? Was it with my parents or Grand'Mere? It is vague, indeed, but it pops up now and again, especially when I'm down here at *spiaggia.*

It would be nice if my body cooperated with my emotions. Lately, I feel increasingly cumbersome and this little girl has begun doing a daily afternoon dance inside of me, so it usually takes a while to get comfortable. Today, however, she's quiet. Her little bottom is sticking up on the left side of my abdomen; I can hardly wait to meet her. It's a fair-skied, sunny, 72 degrees today. The weather report says that it will swing back to the mid 40s tomorrow, but the warm weather is really on its way.

Day 33—The Drama

I love it when the weather report is wrong. Ha! Mid-40's—boo! It's taken all morning to warm up, but it's a lovely 70-something again down here today, and am I ever glad about that!

After more drama at the LAB this morning Vidd brought up the value of writing stuff down, and reminded me of how in the early weeks of our marriage I hadn't touched my art book. Fact is, he was the reason I started up again. Anyway, we ended up having another of our increasingly common heart-to-hearts on the way down here today and he pointed out the fact that sometimes he can see what's good for me before I can simply because I'm not accustomed to thinking about "tending to the soul," something he is very good at.

I remember those early days and him saying that writing might be a good idea just for the sake of processing all that has happened. After a bit of reluctance I retrieved it from my backpack and the minute I did I realized how much I have truly come to enjoy the whole process of writing. To this day it strikes me as so ironic. What a funny, *funny* thing—*me*, loving something as old-fashioned and quaint as writing.

Speaking of Mr. Florencia. "Oh, there you are. You're back sooner than usual."

He bent down to kiss my forehead.

"Kiss kiss. Yes. Yuk—*eeew*. I see you are extremely sweaty. Are you done running already?"

He leaned down and placed both hands on his knees. His heavy breathing was out-of-character. When he spoke he did so with short staccato type words in between deep breaths, and he winked at me as he looked up from that bent-over position.

"Wooooooo—*that* was intense." He wiped the sweat off his forehead and shot me a huge grin. I made room for him on the stoop.

"Sit down hon. What on earth did you do to yourself? Are you okay?" I stood up from my part of the stump and placed my hand lightly on his bare back. When he looked up at me his face seemed angelic—like a little boy.

"It's a hot one today, *mi amor,* and I thought it'd be a good day to sprint instead of jog it. It's no problem, just catchin' my breath."

"Viddie, you're scaring me! I never saw your face this red. You barely drank your water. Come on, take a break." I called after him as he got up to finish his run.

"No. No. You go ahead, sit down. I'm gonna move into jog now. Just another two miles or so. I'll be back soon. I'm fine."

Turning backward as he jogged, he waved gently as his voice trailed away. I waved back, shaking my head, and smiled as he blew me kisses every few yards.

Where was I? Oh yeah, aside from the vehicle that writing provides to help me express what I'm feeling, it also sort of provides a rhythm to my days that helps me process all the changes.

In truth, sometimes it feels a bit silly because I really am talking to myself on paper, but whether I am writing to remember conversations from the day before or I'm writing out my thoughts as I have them, it just . . . well, it just feels good. It's a safe place. It's especially helpful lately since I've been feeling so ill at ease at the LAB—I need a place to go, and writing has become that for me. Not sure what it is, but when I run my hand over the rough leather and loose binding of this journal, I think of Marissa who so thoughtfully had Harold-in-the-camper make a new one for me. I run my fingers over the intricately etched mountain scene on the front and can almost smell the musky scent of smoke rising from the center of Stone Camp.

Yeah, the rhythm of writing sort of gives a nice flow to my day. It reminds me of the laid- back life we shared up there, and it brings a welcome peace, but then–*ughhhh*—every time I go there in my head, I think of Russa. Fact is, a day does not go by that I don't think of her. Memories of rich conversations and long walks fill my mind with such pleasantness and some sadness, too. It's a winsome wonderment—I still can't believe that a friend as close as a sister is gone from this world.

And—the more I write the more I think about what it means to be Mrs. Belvedere Florencia. It's not just a change in name and living situation. For starters, the thought of being married barely scratched the surface of my consciousness before meeting him. Marriage is so increasingly uncommon these days anyway, but actually *being married* sure has given me a new perspective about how the world works. It's in the midst of our relationship that I've noticed so many things about myself that were absolutely foreign to me before now. Probably the most significant thing is that there's a new sense of self emerging within me—I can feel it. It is a self that is far sturdier than I've ever known. Marriage seemed to reveal it, but I'm noticing it even more as I write and reflect. Yeah, it's like—well, when I write it helps me wonder, and lately I can't help but wonder if it's this growing discipline of writing that is actually helping me reflect. Like a circle, of sorts. I mean, thinking deeply about who I am is not something I really ever did before I began to write—so it's gotta be connected. *Hmmm.* I'll have to think about that some more later.

Oh, here he comes.

"Hey baby. How's it coming?" Catching his breath, Viddie bent over with his hands on his knees, motioned toward my journal, and gave me a quick wink.

I breathed deeply and looked up.

"You're in better shape this round. Just shiny; no sweat."

He leaned over and laid a kiss on me, and then joined me on the stoop.

"Told you I was gonna jog. You didn't question my veracity, did you?"

Ha ha ha. "Veracity, eh? When did you start talking like a member of the LAB?"

"Uh . . . maybe since I became one?"

I kissed him back with a quick peck. "You're definitely are a part of it all now."

"Anything you're a part of, I'm a part of, *capisco*?"

His dark curls, wet from the run, kinked up much more than they do when his hair is dry, and the sharp line of his jaw made me want to jump on top of him at that very moment. With a due measure of restraint, I laid my book in the sand. "That is true, my handsome man. You are part of the team, but *you belong to me!*"

"*Uhhhhh*, yeah. Of course I do. And that needs to be said?"

I snuggled next to him and fit myself in the crook of his arm, not caring about the sweaty skin.

"Well, no, maybe not. It's just a little reminder that may not be totally necessary, but . . . but . . . I see the way Powers checks you out every time we're there. *Ha!*—that woman better watch her Ps and Qs!"

His light laughter rippled like a quiet roar and he wrapped his sticky arms around my shoulders. "I love it when you say something that you picked up from FRANCO! Do you know that?"

My heart just expands like an old accordion when I feel his appreciation and affection like that. I know the smile on my face must have reflected the depth of emotion I was experiencing at that moment because I noticed his eyes got glassy and, well—that's an indication that the boy is feeling homesick. I knew I struck a chord.

"Yes, my darling man, I do know that, and I was thinking how much fun it might be right about now to play our memory game for a couple minutes. C'mon—before you leave me again for the final leg of your jog—why don't you sit for a moment and play a round with me? Okay—can you picture LJ's tattered, black eye patch and his whitish-gray mustache twitching as he strums a hundred-year-old folk melody while Liberty plays hop-scotch with a limestone rock she retrieved from her rock collection?"

His eyes lit with that familiar joy of a boy-become-man. What fun when he lets me see who he really is!!!! The more I am privy to his open, authentic, self, the more I realize I have been blind—even half awake—my whole life till now. Oh, what a school I am in these days! He broke into my memory with one of his own and nearly crushed my heart as he pulled me into some of the beauty I experienced this time last year.

"Oh yeah, I can picture it, alright. It's a good one. But how 'bout this one, Miss Memory. Can you . . . *hmmm.* Let's see. Can you picture the green-smelling grass and rich, dark, dirt that has just been unearthed by one rakishly rugged farm boy who is readying the ground for Marissa's green bean patch?"

I could almost *smell* the spring air! The immediate sense of being there, right back on the side of the mountain where we met—encompassed me and utterly took me over at the very moment he released his words. My mind's eye sparkled as I pictured the frayed overalls he wore; I soaked it in, re-living the pale, but welcoming sunshine that surrounded us that brisk spring day. The warmth that enveloped me at that precise moment was something to bask in. Clearly Viddie won the round and knew it. I smiled; he winked, and gave me a quick wave as he trotted off to the water's edge to finish his run.

Our memory game is always fun, but sometimes it is so winsome that I feel like my heart could break and then spread into a million pieces that somehow fly out into the universe, touching every star and moon and planet, only to return to my chest, enlarged and full of gold. Ahhhh.

Being with Viddie is a way to function in this complex existence that has allowed me to release much of the cumbersome baggage of my parental legacy. It's allowed me to experience who I am in ways that I never imagined. I don't see myself as an orphan anymore, and it's not because I know that Marissa and Liam are alive. It's actually, well . . . I don't know exactly; it's just that I feel that I have a home today in ways that I did not ever have one.

I do wonder how they are—Marissa, Liam, and oh-so-sweet Grand'Mere—but living here, with him, has taken precedence over all my past. I am done; done with the angst, the mystery, the sorrow. Even that nagging, raucous machine that used to grate at my soul no longer has dominance in my life. I see now that much of what I experienced then was coming from the inside of me—just a cavernous vacuum of a person who thought the only reality was outward. My days must be more than calculation, marketing, and work. *Ugh—that's so hard to admit,* but there's really no use in denying it any longer.

And—ugggh; I do *also* wonder if I will ever stop analyzing all this. So much of what I'm learning lately is really a sort of un-learning of the things that were normal when I grew up. For one, I've been thoroughly rethinking the social order here in City Centre. Why did I feel so alone growing up? Was it really because I lost my family at such a young age, or are there other factors that instill such a deep and residing sense of individuality? I mean, I never was truly isolated or . . . or . . . socially inept, but the need for others seemed so intrinsically unnecessary. I'm not sure, but one thing I know, ADMIN has worked diligently over the last four decades to create a new world—one *they believe* is safe and secure.

Consequently, the concept of community has been cut like a flower without nourishment. As we've normalized the use of advanced technologies, we've lauded values like efficiency, safety, and privacy without thinking a bit about the losses we've incurred. At this point I'm wondering if it has been something more radical than simply an unforeseen consequence. What if the government has been working all along at keeping us—all of us—separate from one another? Ugh. I don't think I could bear it if I really thought they had purposely misled us all. So much to think about—my head hurts!

What's been especially helpful, aside from the writing, is that Viddie is very good at listening. Both in the practical and the philosophical, he's a darn good sounding board. For instance, in the beginning of our marriage I was at a complete loss about what to tell the department about my sabbatical and how to keep FRANCO a secret, but Viddie said I should just show up and tell them I got married and was ready to come back to work. Don't know why I didn't think of that. Duh! He's always telling me that the right solution is usually the simplest one. He was correct! They didn't come back at me with a lot of questions—not even a memo from Allessandro. With the exception of Jude, (and I still have no idea what's up with *him*) they all just accepted me back at face value. On top of that, it just so happened we needed a new research assistant so I was able to bring Vidd onto the team without any questions. What a hoot, having my man there.

Oh! Here he comes.

Better finish up.

Day 34—The Angst

The scalding burn of this world and its grueling necessities continue to vex my soul, but now that I know we humans have this thing called soul, I often wonder if we wouldn't be better off without it! I mean, what's with this tendency to build fiefdoms and futile systems of false importance and . . . and . . . create havoc in places that once were full of harmony? *Arrrggghh.* Up and down and up and down. I feel like I'm on an old-fashioned merry-go-round sometimes! My own fledgling little soul has been twisting and turning for days. Ever since that nasty little pushback from Jude—and then the Powers-Margene drama— ugh! For the past few weeks the two of them are always *tete-a-tete*, whispering about one thing or another; clearly I can't trust either of them. Fact is, I feel like I am losing control at the LAB. It's just not the place it once was. I mean, where is the camaraderie and cooperation and *fire* for the cool projects we're working on? What happened to my staff? These people are passionless. *I can't stand it!*

The ghosts of post-Devastation haunt every crevice of the halls of the LAB. Our work there provides an alternate reality for the weary workers of this contemporary abyss called society, but *sometimes* it seems like it's not the most important thing I could be doing. Truth be told, it's more than sometimes. *Alas.* I see no other option.

In spite of the growing discontent that seems to be creeping up my spine with greater regularity these days, I really don't have any desire to give up my place at the LAB. *That's* the rub. It's like, I want it . . . and I don't! *Uggggh.* What I am noticing, though, is a drift in direction. This desire to create vacation packages that are not just enjoyable relief for customers, but products that will produce positive change in their lives, is coming on strong. It has crept up from a mere idea to become something of a yearning. More and more I want to work on the natural vacations. I want to bring legit history into them. I want—I want them to be fun, but in some way, educational, too. Is it arrogant to think that I can change the world and make it better? When I shared these thoughts with Viddie, he was his typical encouraging self, but he really made me feel good when he outlined all the areas in my life that he thought were excellent. Along with helping me see all the angles involved in my new ideas, he told me I was a visionary, and (his words) a dynamo. Ha! *What a doll.* And then last night, when we fully discussed all that I've been thinking about, well—he made me sit on his lap and wouldn't let me up until he listed all my good qualities. Ha ha.

"Vivacious, Warm, Intelligent, Thinker, Visionary, beautiful . . ."

My face was surely flush with a little embarrassment as he continued to regale me, but the last thing he said sort of stuck out. He told me I was *Leader Extraordinaire.* It opened an entirely new can of worms, as they say. I came right back at him with a boatload of stuff that's been rattling my security there.

"I don't know. I want to be confident and believe what you're saying, but they've all been so strange. Starting with Jude and Ms. Powers. They've both managed to build up quite a bit of their own cache with ADMIN, and speaking of the higher-ups, you know that Allessandro has carefully avoided me as much as possible during this entire time, don't you? His current response rate to me is frustratingly slow, and his words are sputtered out in one-word answers. Even our daily briefings have deteriorated into stupid holographic memos delivered by his bot."

I snuggled closer and just allowed myself to settle into Viddie's encouraging thoughts. There was too much too untangle. When I finally did speak again, I'm sure I sounded whiny, but he's the only one I have to talk to about it.

"Did I tell you I saw his hologram activated the other day working very closely with Powers and Margene? Yeah—well, when he noticed my gaze, he quickly turned away, said something privately to both of them, and then they all looked toward me and away again, as if on cue. Hon, it's getting stranger and stranger, especially with Allessandro. I think he's unwilling to accept that I am married and expecting a baby . . . and have concerns other than what happens at TLG. I dunno. I just really don't know what's up with him. He's just so different."

"C'mon, Emi. *Baby.* Think about what you're saying. Just wait . . . *wait* before you imagine a whole story, now. Think, for a minute. I mean, the behavior you're describing about your boss is identical to what you said about the man long before I met him. Allessandro *is* weird. I remember it clearly. So, really—*c'mon.* He may be a poor communicator; maybe he's even ticked that your devotion is not completely toward the LAB anymore, but he's gonna have to deal with some new arrangements; that's all there is to it. You're still the main player in the field and everyone knows it. Speaking of which, when is the last time you even negotiated your contract? You could re-work the responsibilities. I'm sure we could take some time off."

Ah, we're back to that. Hmmm. His words are loud and clear in my head and he fills my ears with a logic that is increasingly difficult to ignore, but there's the other side of this whole situation, too. Main player or not, the field is not the same as a sports game. In fact, it's not a game at all. Something strange *is* happening at the LAB. Not only is it not the place I once thought it was, but there are some rather clear signs that my own place there is in some sort of jeopardy. I piped up with my concerns.

"Okay—so, you do make sense, but really, well, things are just not the same as they were before I left. Maybe it's me. I dunno, but I'm beginning to feel like a stranger in my own department. Less and less of what we do at the LAB makes much sense. You know, hon, I remember our first meeting at the LAB. We gathered in the brand new Travelite Global area and our first meeting was nothing less than inspirational. We were charged with re-developing the social element of society to sustain the mission of the new government—that is, to keep the world safe and protect the population from extinction. We were inspired Viddie, truly inspired, and tasked with the goal of providing enjoyment, hope, and recreation."

He feigned a smile and squeezed my hand. *Hmmmm.* I wonder if he gets it. It's hard to explain where I'm at with all this, but articulating my feelings was helping to clarify my thoughts. I couldn't help rambling on.

"Hon, you know it's important to me that you understand the significance of my work, so I hope you don't mind that I'm taking time to remember those beginnings. Our task was really quite straight forward and . . . well, I thought it was noble. Propaganda wasn't anywhere on the table. I really didn't even detect a scent of it."

The words were barely out of my mouth before he cut in. "Now wait right there . . . just a moment before you go on. Could it be that you didn't even know about propaganda at that point? I seem to recall regular leftovers of your early conversations with Russa. Didn't you talk about the importance of marketing and selling ideas—and if I recall you two really tussled about the ethics of your job, didn't you? "

"Oh Viddie—we did, but—*I don't know*—you may be right. Your memory is better than mine, but, yes, there were some hearty *discussions*. All I know is that prior to this we were never asked to lie or leave out a portion of the truth or . . . or . . . mask anything. The civic importance of our work was drilled into us daily. It's true, we were asked to weave the thread of the Principles of the Golden Triangle throughout all our vacation packages, but that was for the sake of morale—the morale of *the saved.*"

"Huh? *The saved?* What do you mean by that? It sounds like you're calling the current population, the saved?"

"Yeah, yes, we do. That's right; that's exactly right. We're safe . . . safe from the poisonous earth—*saved.* It's part of our national identity. It refers to the ones who were left. Us. All of us. Vidd, you've gotta remember, people were still reeling from the loss of homes, families, traditions, and everything that had been normal in this country up until the Devastation, and the country desperately needed a reinforcement of identity and purpose. I . . . I . . . I thought my job was all very noble. I mean, who wouldn't find purpose in Pride, Progress and Perfection?"

He raised his eyebrows and leaned a few inches away from me. I could tell by his reply that he was tentative.

"The 3 P's—how can I forget? Forgive me if I don't share your passion for those values, baby, but I do understand how important it is to believe in *something*. We all have to place our faith *somewhere*."

Did I detect a hint of sarcasm in his tone? I wasn't sure, but one thing I am sure about: Belvedere Florencia has always been the safest place for me to share my thoughts—even my intermittent double-mindedness. *Even* in the midst of my plethora of uncertain emotions and changing opinions, Viddie is patient, never belittling, shutting me down, or making me feel awkward. I felt free to go on.

"And, you know, honey, I do believe our foundational principles are important, but I'm just no longer sure they are the only reasonable choice. Is that heresy? Oh I'm just not sure anymore, but quite honestly I do believe what we do at the LAB continues to be important work, helping the working class find ways to de-stress through fun, interesting Xtreme Vacation packages."

Viddie shook his head. A look of slight defeat framed his face. I continued with my train of thought.

"But there's something up with everyone at the LAB—I'm quite sure of it now. It's definitely more than just the bothersome surface-level interactions and annoying personality of the new female employees. It's as if there is an agenda that I know nothing about, and it feels like any day now another shoe is gonna drop. Don't you feel it too? I mean, when you're there, don't you sense a rumbling sort of undercurrent?"

"Maybe so. A little bit, I guess, but you are the one with the history here. I'm new to all this triangle stuff, the principles, etc. All I know is that it's important to have integrity—to do what you say you're gonna do and to look out for each other—cause we all share this space and time. I think that might be what you're feeling. The lack of it, I mean."

Stomach acid started to creep up my esophagus; I could feel the heartburn rising in my throat. Ugh. *I can't wait for this little one to be born!* Viddie sensed my discomfort and added his own take on my mental meanderings.

"Emi, human beings are not meant to be alone. We can't go it alone. But that's not the way your peers have been raised. The Saved—if that's what you called them—need more than provisio bars and work to live fulfilling, joyful lives. Now that you've tasted a more satisfying life, rich with people and nature and love—well, don't you see? It's harder to handle the lack of it all around you. What can I say? I've been taught to work and love and care for the people I live with. I really don't understand this isolated way of life; I can't even imagine who I'd be if I hadn't been raised with such a deep sense of belonging and connection to others."

I rested both hands on the top of my abdomen. It feels so strange to have a ledge there. It's like I have my own personal shelf space available for a coffee cup, a water bottle—anything I want to place there, I've got a ready-made table on top of me! Ha. *Crazy.* I really can't imagine what it will be like to be responsible for a whole other person, but I am quite looking forward to getting my body back.

"Now that's a thought. I wonder who I'd be if I had not been raised here. What if Marissa and Liam had taken me at six and raised me up there with you, outside the walls of this faulty system? Maybe I wouldn't feel so conflicted. Maybe I wouldn't be dealing with this inexplicable push and tug that's going on inside me. Heck–maybe I wouldn't even know anyone in ADMIN let alone have to deal with Allessandro's secretive ways. Honestly, Viddie, he is SO weird. You are so right. That's the perfect word for him: weird."

"*Mi amor*—I've only been at the LAB for eight months. They're all weird, if you ask me. I mean, what guy wears only white to work?"

I couldn't help rolling my eyes at him; he still understands so little about the protocols here.

Day 35—The Language

Viddie and I are so different in so many ways, but more alike than I ever imagined. For instance, he is challenged by the pace we keep here, always looking for more sleep and I, enthralled with the new found freedom of enjoying the outside air, am always wanting to go-go-go. Four hours sleep and I am fine for another twenty.

On the other hand, our differences are fun sometimes, especially when we engage in language games. English and Italian are drastically different, and although his English is impeccable he often drifts into Italian. That's what his nuclear family spoke around their table. I know he misses it, so in spite of having so little real knowledge of Italian, I try. The one word I know by heart is *spiaggia*, but there's also several others creeping up in my consciousness. How can get away from *bacino, bambina, mi piace,* or *mi amor? Ha ha ha.*

No doubt, he thought his invitation to an early beach day would draw me out of my quiet ponderings and as usual, he was right.

Day 36—The Gift

Late afternoon light dapples through the leaves and lands in a well-defined rectangular shaft under the poplar just inside our car-cover gate. Funny how it refracts, giving the impression that the whole entire sun is intent on bursting onto this one little spot on the ground. Oh, and how the shadows trick our minds when we view the world out here in natural sunlight. What a deliciously delightful day!

As I sit out here I realize it's something I never do. I mean, when's the last time I took a moment to just stop and observe what's going on? Uh . . . *Never.* Typically, I just jump into the back seat of the '70, click the starter, and go. But my body is cumbersome these last few weeks and I am not jumping anywhere. My gait has slowed considerably and I find I need to take a little breather here and there. I guess that's partly why I've been noticing so many new things on my street and in the surrounding areas. Like the songbirds that come to serenade by the window slat in our bedroom, or the gray doves that peck around our trash cylinder in the mornings. Where were these eyes last year, just 18 months ago, when I regularly stepped into my car and drove off to the LAB to accomplish the oh-so-important work of virtual vacations, so busy, but so unaware of the world around me? Where were these eyes back then when LJ's vacant flat seemed invisible to me or the honeysuckle growing up my back wall was in bloom? It's as if these eyes have been replaced by a new set and they are brighter, sharper, clearer than I ever remember in the past.

"Emi?"

"Oh!?!? You startled me."

Viddie appeared seemingly out of nowhere. I guess I was a little lost in thought. *Ha!* I popped my head up from my writing to acknowledge him, as he grabbed the step-stool from the car cover and pulled it over to join me where I sat on the stairs. Now a perfect afternoon has become more perfect. Is that possible? I cocked my head and looked at him in awe.

"Sorry, love. Whatcha lookin' at?"

"What makes you think I'm looking at anything?" I countered with a wink. "I'm just catching up on my journal. What are *you* doing?"

Leaning over to rub my stomach, Viddie shot me a sly smile and brought his stool even closer. He leaned over to rest his head against my upper arm. "Uh . . . Just checkin' on you. I mean, it's really any day now, isn't it?"

"Whew. I guess so. I mean, I *hope* so. Look at my feet. They're like . . . twice the size of normal!" I laughed right out loud but he got really serious.

"When do you see the medic again? I don't think that looks healthy."

"Don't say such a thing, Belvedere Florencia. They are perfectly fine . . . just fat—ha ha ha. A little fat—okay, JUMBO—feet."

He chuckled too, but his knitted brow let me know he was concerned.

"Okay, okay. I'll mention it tomorrow. I'm seeing Medic daily now that we're in the two-week window."

"I doubt you'll have to mention it. He's gonna take one look at your feet and . . . well . . . they are *big* . . . really big."

The frown I was feeling from that last statement must have showed up on my face, because he reacted thoughtfully. Yeah, my feet are out of shape right now, but it felt kind of weird to hear him point it out.

"I mean, I love your feet. I'd love them even if they were three times the size, but something just doesn't seem right. In the past couple of days I've noticed your breathing is heavier than normal too and I don't want to take a chance on a problem."

"It's not that I'm trying to ignore some potential problem, Vidd. I'm just not interested in being sad or miserable, no matter how out of shape my feet get. The baby will be born soon and Medic says I'll bounce back to normal size and . . . well, I'm just happy, in spite of the discomfort. And, I'll have you know, I don't have any intention of being any less than happy. There are enough miserable people in this world; we don't need one more. In fact, the bigger I get the more time I have to think, and more and more I am realizing that my mission to help folks relax and enjoy a virtual vacation needs to expand—I mean really expand. More than recreation, more than rest, more that education, even.

I plan to inject happiness into the world and I will do it diligently with better, more beautiful, interactive vacation paks."

His eyes widened and for a second I thought he was going to jump into my vision wholeheartedly. "Oh my love, you are so full of passion now, and I love it! I love you, but slow down just a little bit, yes? We're gonna have a baby *very soon* and she's gonna need every bit of that passion and energy."

"What are you saying, hon? Don't you think I should expand the TLG mission? Think of it: It'll help the continent. People will wake up! They need to be educated. They need to come alive!!! It sounds like you're putting the brakes on. *Why?*"

I felt so let down. The minute he tried to moderate my excitement, I felt completely defeated. *Ugh.* It seems as though I am either extremely positive or extremely negative lately. Up and down, up and down—*these hormones!!!*

I'm looking forward to being a mother, but the baby's not going to need all my energy. I don't think he understands that I've got a responsibility to use what I have inside me to help the public.

He got up and picked a thin green shoot from the ground, and then joined me on the steps to our flat. We sat with our shoulders touching, leaning in to each other for several minutes before the conversation continued. The sun shone brightly and I could feel little beads of sweat begin to form on my forehead.

As he turned toward me he asked a probing question, one that completely switched gears but easily revealed how observant he had been when we first got to know one another in FRANCO. What he said cut me to the quick, and it was in the very asking that the answer was made clear to me.

"Baby, I want you to really think about this: has there really *ever* been any joy in those work relationships? Think for a moment before you answer. Was there even a bit of joy among you or has there always been malaise—the same malaise that seems to surround everyone in this place?"

The question hung in the air, suspended as if by some invisible hand. I gave him a quick glance and noticed he was chewing the side of his lower lip, shaking his head slowly. Without even a hint of response from me, he continued and although his language was positive the tone was decidedly opposite. "Emi-girl, you've got such a generous, big heart, but baby–you can't save the world. I don't believe waiting a little while to start these new projects is gonna hurt the effort one dot or iota. C'mon now. We've discussed this before. So I'll ask you again: Has there ever truly been joy?"

I shook my head slowly. *Joy? I dunno.* But the prospect of some new projects is calling my name and that might give me joy. He was right, though. Finding the right timing for a new project is essential.

He gazed at me with an expectant look, still waiting for a response. But how could I really think about joy? I mean, joy is a huge word—it's a big commitment.

The seamless communication we enjoy in City Centre makes it far too easy for all of us to simply ignore one another. I've got more of a stake in this whole thing than anyone else I know. I feel partially responsible for making the OLSM so easy through the P/Z. It's hard not to think about the mistakes I've made in the past and how they may have affected the lack of joy in this world we've made. I mean, I think of the way the OLSM project was birthed. Great idea, right? Clearly, the LAB would not have made OLSM the trademark norm for all communication in this post-Devastation world had I not thought to pair it up with the P/Z100. Had I discovered the residual effect of my decision while it was in development, I would *never* have gone forward with mass marketing.

Now, everyone in the new world perceives emotions to be a sign of weakness, and so they cover them up or deny them instead of giving life to them. How do you think you would feel if you knew that you were the orchestrator of such a depressing symphony? I let out a deep sigh and decided to answer his question directly.

"I really don't know about joy, Vidd. My mind's racing with the possibilities of using my talent for good—for the good of our world! And as far as your bleak estimation of my world, I thought you knew that ADMIN was high-minded. Mistaken in some things, perhaps, but always for the ultimate good of the country."

He cocked his head and shot me a quizzical look. His tone continued to be doubtful. "It's not that I don't trust your story, Emi, but when I see what all this closed communication has

118 / The Poet's Treasure

produced, it's hard to believe that ADMIN doesn't have its own warped agenda."

"Vidd, I guess I haven't really made it clear. This is a good government, at least generally. They've made mistakes, but it was a frightful time trying to regroup after the horrors of The Devastation. OLSM was ADMIN's solution to the chaos that absolutely reigned here. We were all mandated to stay in our individual domiciles and there was a lot of pushback. People (Grand'Mere was one of 'em) found it hard to comply, and there wasn't enough government personnel to oversee the safety of the population so even more havoc came into play. They needed a means of communication that would not draw the public out onto the streets or necessitate any sort of physical gathering out in the elements, and I think they did a pretty darn good job! Clearly, my family couldn't deal with their methods, but without the major help of ADMIN, well, I just don't know how anyone would've survived!"

The wind kicked up with unexpected fervor and gave me a little chill. It was probably time to head inside, but we were far from done with our conversation. I continued to explain the rationale for our tek as we walked up the stairs to our flat. Our narrow staircase made it impossible for Viddie to walk beside me, so I kept turning my neck to try and finish the explanation.

"Just keep your eyes ahead of you, *mi amor*. We can finish talking about this once I put the tea on."

"You need to hear the truth about the part that the OLSM played in City Centre's renewal, hon, how we believed that using it could save us, and I'm not gonna stop trying to tell you until I know that you understand."

He shot me a reassuring smile and scooted me through the door, calling after me as I padded my way to the lounge.

"Okay, okay—I'll listen. Save me a spot. I'll be right in with a hot cuppa."

When we settled down to our tea, I attempted to quell his fuzzy thinking on the matter and unmask some of the guilt I felt.

"Part of the way we are able to edit our emotions comes from manipulation of the stress hormones—totally necessary protocols for the OLSM to work properly. And you know, I had a heavy hand in all of it, don't you?"

"But you're not to blame. You can't take it on. You never would have imagined any of this. What's foreign to me is how it works. I can't imagine how everybody can avoid their feelings. It sounds more like denial of emotions to me."

"*Hmmm*. Yeah, I guess without experiencing it, you would be confused. Well, it's as if a shade comes down on the emotional center of the brain and people become content to live without the ups and downs of a normal human emotional scale. Instead of love, food, and any other pleasure points, they . . . we just learn to center life around work."

Viddie was quiet and listened. I could almost see the inner wheels of his brain turning.

"I'm glad you let yourself feel, *mi amor*. You need to really feel how much you are loved, and I hope you can feel that."

I squirmed my way into the crook of his arm and rested there. It was good to feel the love. It was good to . . . feel.

Day 37–The Effort

The idea is growing on me.

If I can just crack open their minds a bit with a luxurious, nature-centered virtual vacation package I really think they might come alive again, regain their passion, and help them find a greater purpose in living than just . . . just . . . I don't know . . . just existing!

Viddie hasn't seen the entire scope of my work so I'm sure he can't imagine all that I can accomplish. He hasn't experienced anything more than snippets and images—never the whole package. If in fact I have been used to cloak a deceptive vision then I can use my skills to create a better one. Whatever it is, I've just got to do something because all day long I see the flagrant emptiness in all of their lives and I am more and more aghast. *Lately it seems like it's all I see!* Everywhere I turn the misery hits me smack in the face. From the weekly drops of provisio to our office shoots, the rabid controls on use of water and power, and the fear of breathing in more than 30 minutes of outside air a day—*ugghhh*—I know they don't even realize the real life they are missing! This morning I searched each set of purple-lined eyes and they are all vacant, grossly vacant. No wonder I had such a hard time believing in the human soul! There is so little evidence of it here.

Breathe. Ah . . . I've got to stop getting so worked up. I'm trying, but everywhere I turn there is another indication of this malaise.

And this Powers woman—*ugh*. She's the worst of the lot. To be sure, I don't know if my reasons for disliking her are *completely* fair, but every time I see her, I notice something else that bothers me. First, what's with the turquoise blue blush she brushes on those gaunt cheeks of hers? *She tries to come off like she's just so hip.* No one but the hologrammed celebs wear that shade, and she doesn't even wear it well! And then the way she half closes her nearly translucent eyelids and lets them flutter for a few seconds while she's already begun to talk. *Ugh.* She makes it look as though she's thinking some ponderously deep thought and then makes everyone wait for an answer—just a few seconds more than is appropriate. *Ugh.* When she finally opens her eyes and gives that long, side-winding look it's, well . . . is just ridiculous! *And her speech—it's so tedious!* When she opens her mouth to say something it's so painfully slow, almost like she's sashaying through a forest of words with no path or direction, looking up at the trees, searching for ripe fruit. *Ugh.* On top of all of this nonsense, I am quite un-amused about the way she cocks her head just slightly to the right when speaking to Viddie. *That* makes my blood boil! The other day when she came around with the daily affirmations again, I noticed it immediately. As soon as she left the front office, Vid bee-lined over to my drafting glass and plunked down the "Acquiescence" frame for me to see.

"She gave me 'acquiescence' again. Just what is this supposed to mean, boss lady? That woman has totally lost me!"

"Well I should hope so," I said, without looking up. I'm sure there was probably a tinge of sarcasm lurking in my tone.

"*And,* my darling wife . . ." he said, snuggling up to my shoulder and ignoring my tone, "just what is *that* supposed to mean?"

Surprised by his overtly bold display of affection, I gave him a gentle push in hopes that he would remember company protocol. It's been awkward enough bringing my husband in to assist us; if Allessandro got wind that there was anything but utter professionalism between us while we're on the drafting floor, I'd have more than a bit of heat coming my way. I can just hear that dreary voice chiding all of us to "keep it virtual."

Day 38—The Sleep

The thunderous downpour gave way to a gentle patter that felt as comfortable as one of Grand'Mere's fancy duck down blankets on a chilly mountain night. Spring showers are still cold this time of year. I can hardly wait till June when things really warm up.

It was the end of the day and I was just finishing up my notes from yesterday with a cup of hot ginger tea. As the two of us lounged on the sofas opposite one another I glanced up from my journal and caught him looking wistfully toward the door. The subtle sadness on his face is not really common, but I do see it here and there when we're home, occasionally on cook nights, and at times when we're at the LAB together. It bothers me. I want him to be happy. Clearly Viddie loves me, but that he pines for FRANCO is befuddling. By now, he should be accustomed to his new life here. I've given a good deal of thought to this problem and can't quite figure out how to help him. Yes, it's beautiful in the mountains. Yes, they are lovely people. Yes, he was raised there, but . . . we're not going back. I wish he could just let that part of his life go. It would make it easier for me to stop thinking about them, too. Last evening when I saw it, I tried to draw him out of his wistful reverie, and in spite of being slightly annoyed at his demeanor, my tone was decidedly upbeat, hoping to spark a conversation.

"Hey you—whatcha thinking about?"

He glanced my way, smiled and gave me a playful wink. "Oh, just a bunch of stuff. I finished the baby's cradle this morning, everything except the paint. I'm working a little bit on our table, too. That's gonna take a bit longer because I'm definitely not using the Drunge wood. Since you told me that they're the government's indentured workforce I have no desire to contribute to slavery or add to their sweat. I saw a few of them in the standard yellow vests along the skyway and I don't want to contribute even one dollar to that operation, speaking of which— do they ever get released? How many years do they have to work outside before they can go home to their families?"

"Aw, hon. They're not slaves. Don't say that. You make it sound so bad."

"*Hmmmm.* Okay. I won't say it then, but I'm afraid it's still true. They aren't free to come and go as they please. Bottom line. Unfree."

"*Vidd*—they don't have families or *any* tek skills. ADMIN'S not enslaving them, hon—they're taking care of them. The Drunge have been the government's outside workers for as long as they've been alive. All of 'em are either orphans of The Devastation or they've somehow been in non-compliance with the Principles so they have no way of surviving. They're never getting out—no. But at least we know that they're not slowly poisoning themselves with the lumbering and planting and such, right?"

I attempted a smile and chuckle but the sound got caught in my throat. Viddie didn't laugh at all.

"Isn't is ironic, Em? We know that they are not in a toxic environment, but ADMIN doesn't. The government would just as soon contaminate the poor fellows! These are guys with no families and they are 'punished' by being forced to do the work everyone else is afraid will kill them. Yet—look at 'em. They're old and strong and rugged. It's probably the very thing that everyone else is so afraid of that is keeping them alive so long. The sun, fresh air, hard work . . . don't you find that ironic?"

Now that's a thought that hadn't occurred to me. He's right though, the outside workforce that plants and picks our weekly real food rations and other perishable goods are kept like indentured servants. They're not really imprisoned, but they don't have anywhere else to go so ADMIN takes care of them and puts them to work in the fields and skyways doing everything that others find too risky. I just never thought about them before.

"I do. Yeah. It's nice that you have gone out there to find your own materials for the cradle and such, but frankly, I would be careful. If ADMIN catches you they're gonna be suspicious. They'll wonder why you're not afraid of the environment, Vidd. I'll say it again: I hope you're being careful."

The thought that ADMIN doesn't know that the Drunge force is *not being* contaminated strikes me as utterly odd. I need to think about this further.

"Are you sure you want me to use the dark stain you picked out for the baby's bed, Emi? I kind of like it raw."

"Well, that's one way to totally ignore what I just said. Are you being careful?"

"Careful as I can . . . so, the paint? Should I stain it darker or leave it light?"

Whatever. His *laissez faire* attitude is maddening sometimes! I shrugged and gave in. Fine. We'll talk about the color of the cradle.

"I ordered the dark stain and you have it right there in the car-croft. Don't you think it would look nice stained dove gray? This way it would match the rest of the flat. What are we going to do with it if we don't use it?"

He scrunched up his nose and thought about it for a minute.

"Yeah—it won't go to waste. I'll be building stuff from time to time; I wouldn't worry about that. I'm happy to just leave it raw. It does really look nice the way it is, and . . . well, it would be one less bit of chemical around the baby when she sleeps."

"Oh my. I hadn't thought of that either. Do you really think the paint will retain its smell? I don't want the baby inhaling any fumes either, but I can't imagine why the smell wouldn't fade once it dries. Viddie, how about the sturdiness? Are you sure the pegs will hold? The stock cradle in the shopping ledger is seamless. One piece of graphite. All we need is the soft cushion and then we don't have to even deal with stain."

The disappointment that colored his face was indisputable. I saw it even as the words popped out of my mouth and I knew it was one of those times that would've been better if I had kept my opinion to myself. But I certainly did not realize that my suggestion was going to be taken as a mandate against his wood-working skills! For goodness sake, it was just an option, and— *yes*—I know that he survived in the woods his whole entire life, building, hunting, and working the land, but . . . it just seems harder. Why go the long way around with everything?

I hate arguments. Glad we don't have them very often.

Day 39—The Idea

Wow! What a difference two extra hours of sleep makes!!! I feel wonderful!!!! That lethargy from the other day has all but vanished. I wonder if he's right—that I just need to get more than the standard four hours. *Hmmm.* Medic said the same thing: *You might push your sleep to five—even six—hours, Mrs. Florencia. A baby can be draining on a body's resources.*

I dunno, I guess it makes sense. When Viddie scooped me up from the lounge and placed me on the bed two hours earlier than normal I thought I'd bounce right back up and go refresh my tea, but amazingly I fell fast asleep. As I was fading I felt his hand on my head and heard him mumble something about health and blessings.

I fell into a deep sleep and don't even remember getting up once to pee and then I started dreaming. I haven't dreamed that vividly since FRANCO. Russa was alive in my dream and she called to me from the flat next door. The voice was muffled but I knew it was her and it startled me, but I followed it without a second thought. I inched my way through the opening, which has gotten smaller every time I've tried to get through it these last weeks, and there she was, right next to the cooler—the open cooler—on the kitchen floor. It was the same cooler that is actually there next door—just like everything else in the dream. But Russa was different, different than I remembered her. It's hard to explain, but I will give it a shot.

Clearly it was her, but it was a better her. That quiet smile of hers spread like butter across her broad, glowing face, and she took my hand and looked at the amethyst ring and said, "*See this? This happens when someone believes. It doesn't have to be you, just someone who will hold onto it. Dreams never die as long as there's even one person holding true.*"

I remember looking at her quizzically and attempting to speak, but no words would come out of my mouth. Oh how I wanted to tell her about coming back to the flat and my marriage to Viddie and . . . and . . . the baby, and I tried, but couldn't quite articulate. Her eyes sparkled with a gentleness that also had flecks of fire in them. The gentleness was blue, sea glass blue.

Her gaze seemed to penetrate my very skin with peace. The oddest part of the dream was that she spoke with her eyes—not her mouth—and although there were no words I understood her clearly. She said, *"Be happy, my friend. Don't be afraid."* When I reached out for her hand she disappeared almost as if she evaporated, and I woke up suddenly. It was oh-so-vivid! Now all I want to do is revisit LJs flat again and try to regain the warm, peaceful feeling I had seeing her. Even though it was just a dream, the feeling was real, so real.

My stomach is grumbling. I'd better get a provisio and continue this later.

Day 40—The Letter

My darling Emi,

Before you come barreling into the lounge to ask me why I have dared to write in your journal, please take a deep breath, sit down, and read what I have to say. There are a couple of things I need you to know, but whenever we talk about this subject I never seem to be able to find the words. This was the only way I could think of to get your undivided attention. So read on: *please*.

I am aware that this journal is sacred and the last thing I'd ever want to do is invade your space. Yes, and I know that I did not even ask if I could write in this book, but this is the only way I know how to broach a subject that is most important. I promise I have not riffled through your pages or read one single word that you have written. I just want to be heard. I want you to be able to re-read what I have said here and give reasoned thought to it.

Hon—right now you are like a herd of untamed horses running all over the mountain side, so full of vigor and strength, but running off in every direction. I will reiterate what I've told you in the past: I'm wild about your passion, just like those horses, and I smile every time I think about how different you are today from the distant, elegant beauty that showed up in FRANCO close to this time last year. Your personality has blossomed like the apple trees in June. You have grown so much *mi amor*; you bless my life continually and in countless ways. I love you.

Here's what else I need you to remember: I grew up in a family and an environment that was bursting with love. The passion I see in you is pleasing probably because it was such a normal feature in my family. I'm thankful that you have had a taste of this same lifestyle and hope that one day (okay, maybe far in the future) we can return to it. But FRANCO is a unique little enclave of people living intentionally in a community setting, drawn together by the belief that the God who created all things takes pleasure in being included in the lives of His creation. Believing, as well, that He created us to experience the joy of living and truly knowing each other instead of just existing in the world's system of rules, regulations, and corrupt authority. Some people might call us anarchists, but I don't think that's exactly right. We don't want to overthrow anything. Instead, we'd rather just live peacefully, and work hard to make a beautiful life together. I don't believe this setup is a social anomaly; I think it's the way humans are meant to live. *Together.*

You may be thinking right about now that you know everything I've told you and that this letter is unnecessary, but I want to be extra sure that you understand the context of what I'm about to say.

You've been wondering about the roads in former times, and the people who travelled on them. Well, I think about them too, and I'm sure there were couples just like us 100 years ago who dreamed of better days and loved each other with the same kind of passion that we share. We aren't better than them just because we have a more organized system. They were vexed by the challenges of their own time, just as we are here, but they got home from long, eight and ten-hour days and were happy to have a simple meal with their families. And if we think back even farther, the folks who paved the way for a country based on freedom and values of democracy, citizenship and equality were happy to farm, cook, and share a meal with their families— maybe chicken and dumplings, green salad with radishes, and corn, freshly picked from the field, or the stuffed artichokes, spaghetti and meatballs, and garlic bread that my ancestors loved. They spent lots of time preparing meals. It was hard work without the modern conveniences, but guess what—they did it together and then enjoyed the fruit of their labor.

In both time periods these people placed high value on simply being with one another. Heck, in the 1800s, by the time they finished cooking and cleaning up, taking care of the horses, and giving their children baths, they were exhausted and fell fast asleep until the next morning when they started all over again. The women had long dresses and . . . not very colorful clothes, I imagine. Today we've got it easy, so easy. No need to sleep more than four hours, complete nutrition in a bar, no cooking or clean-up—all the conveniences, but what about our community? Where is it? It's all so efficient, but *what for*? Where are the people? Here in the flat it's . . . it's just us. You know I'm thankful for us and I always want to keep it that way, but here's the bottom line: If you keep bucking the protocols at the LAB and insist on trying to change the culture there, I am afraid you will end up hurting us more than helping us.

There, I've said it. And I've said it because it's true. With all the listening I've done lately, all the planning, designing *and* consulting on the upcoming VacaPacs, I thought it only right to be explicit in sharing my concerns. Yes, we must do our part to preserve the important traditions in our families and in the wider world, but frankly, the longer I observe what goes on at the LAB the more I am concerned about your zeal to be an agent of change. It's scary to me. Don't you think I'd like to see the world change as much (or more) than you? *You know I would!* But what I see happening at the Lab between you and your colleagues—especially Allessandro—may well be a forecast of what is to come.

Please, listen to me. Your desire to change things in this world is noble. It's commendable! But you are just one person; we are one couple, and we cannot save the world.

Mi amor, please listen to my heart here. I am not timid, but we need more than boldness to create change. You are headstrong and I have no desire to fight with you. What I am expressing here needs to be said, but saying these things to you is difficult because I don't want to tamp your passion and I don't want to snuff out hope for a new world. Please believe me when I say to you that I don't want you to give up on the world, but I cannot sit idly by and watch you throw your entire self into a project that is likely to fail and will probably hurt you in the meantime. People will not change through simulated community life. They have to know that something is missing first . . . they have to be hungry for it . . . for something more than what they've got. If they look for it, they will find it.

So that's that. It's not a rebuke, but a charge. Please, let's go more slowly. Please, think carefully about what you try to accomplish at the LAB. Please, let's keep our priorities strong and clear, so that our love will never suffer the fate that this last half-century has brought about.

I love you.

Don't ever doubt it.

Day 41—The Response

Belvedere Florencia! If I did not love you as much as I do, right now you'd have this book crashing over your head. How could you look in my journal? I can't even speak to you! How could you *write* in it? *Really.* This is the one place that is truly mine! My thoughts, my frustrations, my dreams—it's not right that you have written in my book. If you ever have even the slightest inclination to do that again, please don't. Grab a piece of paper and leave it on my pillow.

Now to your points.

Sheesh. I hardly even know how to respond! I have no words.

You're the believer, I am not, and you want me to stop trying to change this miserably lame culture in which we live? I don't get it, not at all. Your God has shown you a better way to live and you don't want to share it? I don't know your God but I want to change the world to be in harmony with his purposes and his ideas and . . . and . . . you are trying to talk me out of it? What's wrong with this picture?

Day 42–The Journal

It's been hours since we had a real conversation. Feels like weeks, but it's really only been since yesterday. I am having a really hard time getting past this letter thing. I need a fresh start. I can hardly even think of any words to write here.

Ugh—the words are stuck. The baby's stuck. Work is stuck. We're stuck. Things aren't terrific. To make matters worse I can barely move. According to the Medic this baby was due yesterday. Where is she? C'mon, girl! I want my body back!

Yeah, there's no doubt Viddie and I are not in sync. The deep freeze of discord has settled on us and is stealing the joy that seemed to lap at my feet these last weeks. I don't know how to get past it, but I know I must! I am just so angry with him. This journal is the place I run to. Even though I love him desperately, I can't help but feel more than a little violated. This is *my* sacred space. Now I feel as though I must hide it somewhere for safe-keeping. *What an ugly and unexpected feeling!*

"Oh, OH OH—Viddie? What . . . what's this? Water? Viddie, there's WATER! My water . . . Uhhhh, uhhh Vidddd . . . Viddddddiieeee!!!"

Day 44—The Exuberance

She's here! She's here! Russita Bellini Magnificat Florencia is here! Whew-ee—that's a lot of syllables—*ha*! Our little one made her appearance three days ago. Five pounds, two ounces . . . a miniature human being with a perfect little nose, sweet pink cheeks, and her father's long lush eyelashes. It all happened so quickly that we never made it to the clinic. She was born at home with Viddie's help all after only 30 minutes of labor. It was all so quick.

Oh dear . . . she's stirring again.

Day 45—The Name

"Look at those eyes—ah, *Bellini*. She has your eyes, Emi-girl. They are little beauties."

Viddie has this habit of standing over the baby and me as I nurse her—*Bellini*—that's what he calls her. I told him if he keeps calling her that we may forget that her proper name is Russita. (Once we saw her face it was clear that her name was not any of the other options we discussed).

He always nods and smiles saying "*right, right.*" I need to be careful to call her by her *proper* name," but then the minute he sees her with her eyes opened he says it again "*Bellini Bellini, my bella Bellini*!" I guess it's the best of both worlds; an Italian nickname to follow a beautiful namesake. Russa would approve.

Never have I experienced the emotions that stir in me over this child. They are unlike any I've ever known, and it's really hard not to go a little overboard. Heck, I'm even tempted to use the word, miraculous. Somehow the connection we have feels as though it was the very reason I was born—to bring this little one into the world. This innocent, milky white, curly-headed doll-baby is everything to me . . . to us. The feeling is so completely lovely and magnificent that I wonder why more people aren't having babies. I mean, I know the unspoken pressure not to add to the population numbers is always there in the back of all of our minds, but given the sheer joy in bringing a new person into the world, I'm surprised more people aren't having babies. In fact, come to think of it, I have to stretch my imagination to remember the few people I've known over the years who have had babies. Let's see . . . it was Roger's wife, the sanitation agent at the LAB who had a little boy about 8 or 10 years ago and . . . *hmmmm*. There was another. What was her name? That's right! It was Rolly's daughter. I never met her or the baby, but he mentioned it—gosh—was it, yeah—it was shortly after I started work at the LAB. She had a boy too.

I love my little girl.

Day 52–The Change

Can hardly believe it's been nearly ten days since Miss Russita Bellini Florencia has made her appearance. Such joy. Such joy! No time. *No sleep.* I need to write some things down. Arrrgggh. *No time.*

Day 54—The Notice

We heard from the Medic today.

The message was waiting in my daily cache as soon as I connected to OSLM. It seems the normal inoculations and other medical protocols that are scheduled during delivery must be taken care of within the first month of life, so we've got to get her in there for that. Plus, they want to do the necessary infant protective shots on the same day. *Ugh.*

It's been a rough first couple of weeks around here. She's been sleeping a lot and I've had that crazy condition with my blood pressure—*whew.* Don't know what I would have done if Viddie hadn't been here. I could barely lift my head for almost five days. Now that I'm on my feet again we'll probably take her in sometime in the next day or two, but I don't like the pressure they're putting on us to have her shots. Frankly, the notice from Medic was a little disturbing. If there's one thing I have taken with me from FRANCO it's what Marissa told me about the way the LAB treated her while she was pregnant with me. They tested early neural connections with me in vitro without Marissa and Liam's consent, and although the result has only helped society to better communicate, it's not left me with an overwhelming degree of trust for the medical researchers here.

There's no way I'm going to take a chance with Russita. I don't care how many memos they ping me with, it's not gonna happen. We'll have to let them know when we get there.

Day 58—The Return

After we discovered the inside route to LJ's flat, Viddie wanted to scope it out more carefully, so we've been back a few times. I never find it very comfortable to go there. Even now, when my waistline has returned to normal and I can get through the opening without squeezing, I keep feeling like we're doing something wrong . . . like Security Officials are gonna storm in and fine us or . . . or . . . something worse. Not sure what that would be, but I don't want to find out.

Actually, it's *really* uncomfortable. Earlier, when we were in there, we decided to take the open cooler from the kitchen and use it ourselves. Viddie insisted that LJ would want us to have anything useful that we might find and we both know that he is never coming back. I guess after twenty years with no new occupants in the flat, the city is probably not even aware that it is empty. *Anyway.* It'll be nice to have some cold drinks when we go down to the beach. As soon as I saw it there on the kitchen floor, that dream of Russa popped back into my head. I wonder what she might say, if she were here.

When we returned to our place, I mentioned that it might be best to keep the cooler in the attic because our kitchen area is far too small to hold anything more than it already does. We pulled down the stairs and ventured up together. Russi was up and wide-eyed, happily snug in my infant carrier. It's so easy to take her anywhere in it, but when we got up there in that hot, dark attic she immediately began to fuss. I tried to pacify her but she was still squirming and making all sorts of baby grunts.

"I've got to bring her down, Vidd. This isn't working. Move, please." I schooched around him, moving carefully to make my way down the six small stairs backwards without upsetting her further. It wasn't particularly easy with a baby on my chest.

In the midst of all this, Viddie put his hands on a small stack of dusty books that were behind the stairs. His reaction was one that was just shy of flabbergasted. He could hardly believe that I hadn't told him about the books, but I had never even seen them before! I could almost swear that the last time I was up there I looked behind the stairs, but I guess I missed them. They were awful dusty.

"Look at this, Em—five little golden books! We actually have this one back home. Mom read it to sis and me all the time when we were peanuts. And *look*—its The Velveteen Rabbit, Peter Pan. Scully Saves the Day, and Little Blue Truck. Oh man—there's even a Baby's first Bible Stories and Peter Rabbit. *It's a treasure trove, woman.* I can't believe you didn't find these earlier."

Russi's tiny complaints rose to a new level. She began to flail and raised that little voice of hers to decibels neither of us had yet to hear come out of her. I nearly lost my balance. "ShhhShhhShhh. *Shhhhhhhhhhhh.* It's okay, baby. C'mon Russi, mommy's here. *Shhhhh.*"

Viddie turned his attention from the books to the baby. "Is she okay? What's wrong?"

My own voice shot up in volume because she was so loud. "I don't know. Maybe she's just hot. It's stifling up here."

By the time I got her settled and happy, I was bushed. Thankfully, we haven't had to deal with too many screaming events like that one. Russi was fed, dry, and napping when Vidd finally came down and joined me in the lounge. His arms were full of old books and a number of other small items. He plopped everything he had been holding onto the carpet in the middle of the room.

"Hey, that's a mess! Vidd, what are you doing? Do you see how dirty those things are?"

"Look. Look at this, Babe. These must all be books Grand'Mere read to you when you were little. Wow!"

"Oh my goodness—I do remember Tinkerbell. She was a little fairy, I think. Yes, Grand'Mere used to read that one to me, for sure!"

Day 60—The Tek

Low supply of diamond dust. *Yikes!* I haven't heard the sonar alarm go off like that in ages. It's so rare that we have a public warning and guidance to switch out of OLSM protocols. I wonder what that means for this week's upload to our customers. *Hmmm.* We've got so much stored up here at the flat, I wonder if I should just bring it in to the LAB to get us through the low inventory. Viddie's outside tinkering with something—I think it's the rubbish chute. Gonna go find him and get his advice. Oh! Here he is.

"What in God's Name was *that*? Just about scared the shirt off me Em, and what does it mean?"

He was slightly breathless. Looks like he took the stairs three at a time. *Ha!* I love it when I know something that he doesn't.

"First of all, I can't believe you're invoking *God* over the sonar. LOL! *Vidd!!!* I have never heard you do that. It's just the public warning system that overrides OLSM. It's an early alert system that warns of impending disaster and/or resets the OLSM authentication protocols—whatever is necessary. It was put in place when I was a teenager—you know—to give the public a heads-up when there is an emergency situation at hand, or on those rare occasions when low supply of diamond dust alters our social protocols. That's all we've ever used it for. It happens once, maybe twice a year. No problem, babe. We're already managing quite well without it, aren't we?"

"Whew—that's right, we are. But really, that blast is louder than anything I've experienced in nature. It sure gets a person's attention."

"Yup, and that is the point. When diamond dust is low we are required to communicate face-to-face as much as possible. Sometimes it lasts for a few hours; once in a great while it's gone on for a few days. *Hmmmm.* Not sure *why* it's low, but I guess that means I'll have to go into the office today. Gotta make sure production is on schedule."

"How 'bout me? Do you need me there today? I'd love to stay home and kick around downstairs. I've got a new project coming together and it involves a lot of whittling. Can't bring that to the LAB now, can I?"

"You're fine. Do you want to keep Russi here with you or shall I take her? She just went down for her long nap."

"Oh, I'll keep her here, no prob—as long as you're not too long. She'll probably sleep the whole time you're gone, anyway, right? In fact, *ha-ha*—I just may have to make some noise to wake our little sleepy head up. By the way, I know all about the way you all use diamond dust on your forefinger to make a neural connection to OLSM, but why is it diamond dust—what is it about the dust that makes it so integral to the process?"

What a day! I do love it when I'm in the driver's seat. There is so much that he knows for which I am clueless. What fun to be his teacher once in a while!

"Uh . . . yeah . . . if we ever had anything sacred, diamond dust would be it. The stuff works to protect and shield the brain. It's like an invisible interior helmet."

"That's wild, Em, really wild. I don't understand the brain like you do, but *it is* fascinating."

"Isn't it? The more we observe its functioning in various situations the more we are privy to its vastness, but stretching beyond its current function is risky—which is why we don't take chances like using it without the diamond dust."

"Go on. How *does* it work?"

"*Hmmm.* You really are interested. Okay. Well. Just as the organic myelin works like a shield to surround the nerves fibers, there is a need to wrap the synapses in the language section of the brain with a protective covering so that nerve impulses have a sturdy bridge from one to the next. We could still use the OLSM without the Diamond Dust, but over time the brains' language transmitters would fray, prohibiting internal communication and worse—diminishing the ability to even speak. It would work equally as well to communicate if we had crystals or chunks of diamonds, but they're hard to synthetically replicate, hence, too expensive. The dust works just fine. It's the conduit for the skin-to-neural pathways that we all need to keep clear headed and it does double duty because it protects the myelin that keeps the-transmitters healthy. Silver and gold work just as well to connect, but ADMIN switched to diamond dust when they saw that it better maintains brain segmentation and overall cognitive health. It's all in the nerve pulses, baby. LOL!"

"Ha—it sounds a little bit like all the gold dust stories I heard around the campfire growing up. The oral histories of the passionate mining for gold in the Old West—oh, what that gold promised! If I heard one I heard a hundred, mostly from Harold-in-the-Camper. From the California gold rush to the search for—*El Dorado*—when the world was younger people placed great faith in what gold could do."

"What does *El Dorado* have to do with diamond dust, babe? Were they doing brain segmentation back then? Ha ha ha."

"No, no. 'Course not. Don't be silly. I just mean all the myths about the sacred gold thrown into a lake . . . bringing a better life, creating prosperity. It all sounds quite a bit like your mission of the three Ps. You know, OLSM connecting everybody, making the world safer, more efficient, yada yada."

"*Hmmm.* You sure have your opinions about this, don't you? I've got to get the office, but let me just remind you that OLSM is no myth. I mean, it does work doesn't it? The world is safer and things do run more efficiently today than at any other time in history, Vidd. *El Dorado* was just about a hope of miracles or magic of some sort, wasn't it? This is no dream."

"You're still not getting me, Em. I'm talking about the myth of *efficiency*—the myth that a more efficient life is a better life. Think about it, has the ability to talk to each other within the walls of your brains and live inside the walls of your homes really done much to foster better lives? It's a shadow existence, babe. C'mon. You know that. You've seen it."

Oh my goodness—there's the baby. She's up. That's strange. So much for getting out of here early this morning.

Day 61—The Message

Yesterday's short check-in at the LAB turned out to be *hours* longer than I intended. By the time I got home Viddie had already gone through the entire supply of breast milk that we had stored in our freezer-cubby and my shirt was wet through with two gigantic circles of milk that was leaking out. Never again will I leave her home, at least not while I'm still nursing.

I kicked off my heels and carried my shoes up the stairs so I could get there faster, but when I arrived, there was Russi, quiet as a mouse in her daddy's arms as he rocked her back to sleep. I tried to whisper, but was a little winded from the stairs, and blurted out my story without thinking about the volume.

"*Shhh.*" Viddie turned toward me with another shush, and blew me a kiss immediately after, but the message was clear. Russi wasn't quite asleep and I best shut up. I headed to the bedroom to change and get comfortable before I told him the new level of drama kicking up at work. All she needed was a few more minutes. When I got out to the lounge, Russi was fast asleep in her cradle so we took the opportunity to have a chat.

"I'm sorry, honey. It got crazy there. Wait till I tell you what's going on at the LAB now!"

I plopped down on the lounge across from his chair, put my feet up on the small table, and let out a deep breath.

"So? What happened? Tell me."

"Okay. Well, when I arrived there was a message blinking on the P.I. board. The headline was: *The Paradigm of Positivity: Hoffman-Bowes Florencia.* Being that the Public Internal is an external board everyone in the company can see and everyone else in the world has access to when they are cued into it through their OLSM, I was really taken aback when ADMIN connected my name to that phrase. We rarely use it, except for emergencies or announcements that directly affect government relations, yet we were mentioned!?!?! What the heck do you think they meant?"

"Whoa. That *is* news, then. Did they say anything specific about me? Man alive—I really have no idea what it meant. Maybe they're just finally getting comfortable with your new status and . . . I dunno, they felt it was time to announce it to the public?"

"Don't know. By the way, speaking of the public information system, we could get you on it in a flash, but that would mean further background checking and questions about family of origin, etc. If you're still set on staying off the comm system, I respect that. But it's up to you."

"Nah. I'm fine. I like things just as they are. Anyway, you tell me everything I need to know."

"Okay, so you've got to hear what they said today. Allessandro not only referred to me as "the Paradigm of Positivity" but he formally congratulated "the Florencia's" on our new arrival. So, fine, right? Yeah, but up till now, they haven't spent much time letting information out to the public, but now, all of a sudden, they're using the P-I to spread news of our baby? I don't get it. It doesn't make sense."

"So, these kinds of announcements—news in the lives of the big wig executives—they aren't public knowledge?"

"No, not really. ADMIN picks and chooses what info they will release and what they keep close. For instance, they never announced that I was on sabbatical, at least to my knowledge. And the fact that he framed my role in the most formal of terms—executive Vice President of Marketing at Travelite Global—should have made me smile, but there was something in the tone of the press release that made me cringe. It was Allessandro speaking, and when he spoke, his voice boomed in familiar fashion, but when he pronounced our name, the grinding sound of his teeth made the muscles on his cheeks move strangely, and he just sounded so insincere. You should have seen it, Vidd. I'll pull it up on my glass for you. *Clearly, it was insincere!"*

Just what am I supposed to make of all this, I don't know. Nine months of almost absolute silence and now that the baby's born he's gonna be civil? I don't get it. I simply cannot make out what is happening here. There are too many changes in protocol, procedure and the public dissemination of information.

Something's up.

Day 63—The Pomp

We went to work together yesterday and brought the baby, of course. Since she was with us, it made sense to contact Medic. I wanted to make sure we let her know that Russi wouldn't be having her initializing shots for at least a year, but I still wanted her weighed and measured.

It happened just then—before we even had a chance to take her down there. Just as my message to the Medic went through, another came in—the shifty blond visage of Ms. Powers appeared on my private screen. There she was, the MVP herself, in all her flat-faced glory and giddiness. Her face took up nearly the entire frame, but her shoulders were visible as she held her fingers under her perky little chin. As soon as we connected she raised her hands in feigned excitement and air-clapped with tiny, fluttering speed. The skinny chevrons on her temples were as glaringly orange as ever, but I noticed today that they each curled back a bit toward her ear lobes. Some sort of fancy new look, I guess. She spoke at a shrill, inauthentic pace, slowly spitting out the words as if she had practiced them fifteen times prior to speaking. "Kudos, kudos, kudos to you both. Oh, happy happy day—a new little baby for the LAB to love. When will you bring her in, Miss Leeya? We haven't seen a new baby in years—we all want to ogle over her."

There was not a molecule inside me that wanted to respond kindly to this woman, but protocols are protocols, and had I ignored her, record of it would be archived and the compu-judicial would have marked me with a first warning, so I denied my instincts and answered politely. "She's here today, Ms. Powers. We're here, in the executive suites. We had to bring her in for her checkup with the Medic, but we're leaving now. Perhaps next time."

"Now? You're here now? Oh my . . . hold on. Margene and I have got to come up and see her. Stay right there!"

With that, our connection was cut off and I looked at Viddie, who was now holding Russi because she started to fuss.

His questioning face matched his words: "What was that all about?"

I know I was abrupt and shouldn't have been but that woman makes me crazy! I turned to Viddie to see if he caught the gist of it.

"Were you watching her on the wall? Did you see that face?"

"Well, yeah; I could see her image coming through on your wall there, but I couldn't hear what she said. What's going on?"

"Let's just get going. I'll tell you about it in the car."

He looked around, shrugged, and agreed, but simply was not moving fast enough. I urged him along.

"Can we get going? *Now?* Hurry honey—they're coming up now. *Please.* Let's get out of here."

He immediately grabbed the baby's carrier and the fob was out of his pocket before we even turned around. But then, just as we moved to make our way out of the complex, the twin terrors of TLG stood facing us under the executive arch. There they were, Powers and her tag-a-long, Margene. Standing in tandem, the same height and frame, they almost looked like twins; except for Margene's feathery, poppish ear bobs and neatly combed dark locks, I could've sworn they were sisters.

Margene's hair was pulled back from her face revealing a strange fashion tic—no chevron. None at all. Hmmm. Now that's something I had never noticed before. Now that she was up so close it was clear that the distinctive inch-long marine-blue insignia that are a part of every citizen code category were . . . well, they were simply not there. *So odd.* Plus, in spite of the similarity in their features, Margene's casual style was in stark contrast to the faux sophistication of her cousin—whose straw-colored hair, by the way, was also pulled back in an elegant up-do.

Their atypical appearance made it difficult not to stare. *What?* There is diamond dust layered on the hair combs, too? Who wears their hair like that these days?!?! The look was over the top even for Monica Veslie Powers. I was literally shocked to see several gemmed decals dotting her pure white dress. She was all gussied up like a character out of an old-fashioned movie scene. Gushing the minute she saw the baby in Viddie's arms, Powers got so close to her face that I thought she might touch her!

"Ms. Powers, *please!*" I stepped between them and partially covered the baby's face, but my actions did not prove successful in getting either of them to back off.

I half-smiled, nervously, I suppose, and tried to graciously leave the premises. Clearing my throat, I felt no need to make apology. "She's brand new and just hasn't had her immunizations yet. If you please ladies, we need to get her home."

Viddie watched the drama unfold with wide eyes and no words, but Powers was all agog with news. She nodded her head in seeming agreement, but then began to prattle.

"Oh, Leeya, I can't believe you're still sticking to such formalities. Why, we are ADMIN family now, don't you think you could begin to call me *Mon?*"

My inner antennae went up. What could this woman be talking about? *Family?*

"*Oh Ms. Powers*, I think it best if we just keep it professional, why don't we? First names are really more appropriate for close family relations. Now, if you'll excuse us."

The woman wouldn't let up. She stepped firmly in front of the executive arch and spread her petite arms open wide.

"Well, yes, yes, *of course* . . . but perhaps {giggle giggle} oh my, you don't know? Hasn't anyone told you? It was announced in this morning's First Call. You must have had your OLSM disengaged."

The last few weeks I have occasionally missed the pre-dawn communiqué. Typically there's not much happening on the 4:30 a.m. call. At this moment my lack of sleep is making the thin veneer of patience I have for this woman wear even thinner. However, I was able to maintain enough inner calm to get to the bottom of her silly game.

"Yes. As I am nursing the baby through the night I find that I need a bit more sleep than normal. I was not on this morning's communiqué. Pray tell us, then. Yes?"

"*Oh dear,*" she placed her hand in front of her lips in feigned surprise. "You *really* don't know, then, do you?"

"*Miss Powers!*"

Clasping her hands in front of her milky white chest, she looked at me squarely. "Let me be the one to tell you the very grand news, then, Leeya: It involves a new order around here."

I raised my eyebrows and shot her an inquisitive look. A new *order*? What on earth . . .

"Yes, it involves your darling boss and . . . it involves yours truly. Ready? Brace yourself, my dear. Alli and I are planning to be married in August. *He he he!!* We are to be wed; Soon soon soon! *Soon* we'll be official!"

More feathery little hand-claps barely making a noise accompanied her glee, but she didn't stop there.

*"And, w*e want you and Belvedere to stand up for us. Of course, in return for your endorsement we will provide entrée to the grand feast, and to thank you we will give you two tickets to sit with us at the table of the New Council of Elders."

I blinked and then blinked again. In the past I have been known to have vivid dreams. This had to be one of them, but it was not.

Council of Elders?

Standing up for them?

Family?

Have I been catapulted to a parallel universe?

Day 65—The Page

As if there's not enough to get worked up this week, here's what I found lying on the counter between the sink and the cooler this morning. One thin page of white paper, jaggedly torn from *my* journal, written with my pen—AGAIN, my husband helped himself to my art book.

I wanna scream!!!

This is what it said:

I am overwhelmed with troubles and my life draws near to death,
I am counted among those who go down to the pit;
I am like one without strength.
I am set apart with the dead,
Like the slain who lie in the grave,
Whom you remember no more,
Who are cut off from your care.
You have put me in the lowest pit,
In the darkest depths.
Your wrath lies heavily on me;
You have overwhelmed me with all your waves.
You have taken from me my closest friends
And have made me repulsive to them.
I am confined and cannot escape;
My eyes are dim with grief. [1]

Dear Viddie's God, have mercy! This man is scaring the life out of me!!!! Is he truly in the depths of despair? *This is so totally disturbing.* I hope I'm not driving him mad with all my ambivalence and anger about work. *Man alive*—why is his pain so deep, his eyes dim with grief?!?!? Ugggh. If he's really that miserable, something's wrong with me because I had no idea!

Confusion crept up my spine and messed with my heart. I really don't know how to respond to this . . . message. If he truly is as devastated as he says, what hope do we have of being together for more than a short season here at the flat? And the baby? Is he going to leave me with the baby? Take his life? I cannot bear the thought!!!

When I confronted him about it this morning, I couldn't even bring up the fact that he TORE a page from my book, because the fear combined with the winsome beauty and concurrent sadness of his words cut through me; I had to respond with my heart. BUT . . . *but* . . . what ensued really blew my mind. Even though I still didn't know a clear way to proceed, I stomped into our bedroom waving the paper over my head and spoke loudly enough to wake him.

"What on earth are you talking about, Belvedere Florencia? What is going on with you?"

I thrust the paper onto the bed covers as he wiped crackles of sleep from his eyes. He slowly picked up the paper and then put it down again.

"Oh that," he croaked. "That's not me; that's David."

"*David*? What are you talking about? We don't even know a David."

He shifted into a sitting position and leaned back against the headboard. I shook my head in utter confusion and folded my arms across my chest. As I stood there, I felt the angularity of my chin become more pronounced. I'm sure my eyes matched with a menacing gaze.

"Well it looks like your handwriting and I know that you wrote it. I don't even know where to start with this—the use of my book again, or your sad-sack poetry, which, by the way is another thing! When did you start writing poetry and in what universe is it alright to not tell me?"

Sheesh.

With that I turned back toward the kitchen to go get a cup of tea and he bumbled out of bed, trailing me, reaching for my back as we walked.

I stopped short at the kitchen arch and he bumped into me. Quickly turning around, I stared him down. He began to chuckle and certainly did not look as if he was ready to lay down and die.

"Good morning, *mi amor*. Come over here. Did you sleep well?"

I gave him a gentle push and felt my heart soften. "Viddie, stop fooling around. You're scaring me. *Who* is David and why did he rip a piece of paper from my journal?"

"David—he's the Psalmist, Emi girl. You remember? The statue of the Hebrew shepherd boy up at Holly Hill? Same guy.

He became King of Israel in ancient history and wrote all the Psalms in the Bible."

"Viddie, stop! What's going on with you? Why are you in the depths of despair?"

"Not me, my dear . . . it's David, I promise you. He was lamenting for the people of Israel. He was lamenting over the loss of his son. I'm not . . . I am not devastated; I was just practicing my memory skills . . . writing down some of the psalms I memorized as a child. Don't want to lose them."

"What? You were just practicing . . . your memory skills? *Hmmm!* You are a riddle, a riddle for sure! If you're not suicidal, I can stop being scared, but tell me why I shouldn't tear your hair out for messing with my journal again?!?!?"

He was beginning to look a little sheepish.

"Oh wow—I think that trip through the woods did something to you. Did a bear hack your brain? You wanna tear my hair out, eh? Well, I can give you one extraordinarily good reason not to."

His voice was fully awake and he pulled me near as he drew me into a soft hold. "Because you love me, Emi girl. You don't wanna pull out papa's hair because you will miss it. You *love* my hair."

There's that wickedly sweet smile again. *Uhhhhhhhhhhh*—he's so hard to resist! I felt my own half smile appear, but pulled away from his embrace so I could continue to chastise him.

"Didn't we just go through this? And, if you're practicing psalms, or whatever they are, can't you find something more upbeat that you've committed to memory? And while we're talking about it, I'd rather you ask me for a piece of paper from my book. Vidd, please don't tear anymore out. Besides—the stuff you wrote was dark!"

"Baby, David was the shepherd boy who became King of Israel and his strength came at least partially from acknowledging his doubt and confusion. David cried out in pain; he didn't stuff it inside. That's the first step to feeling better, *mi amor*. If we never face our pain we close ourselves off from ever feeling better. But, to answer your question, sure, *yes*—I've committed large swaths of poetry, psalms, and other scripture to my memory and most of it is not dark. How 'bout this one? Listen: 'I will keep him in perfect peace whose mind is stayed on Thee, because he trusts in Thee.'"

"Actually, I don't recall where in the scriptures that portion is from *exactly,* but it's a good one, eh? Oh—oh, and here's another from the son of our Psalmist friend, another king named Solomon. It's a proverb. Proverbs 8, to be exact. Listen to this, my love:

> Does not wisdom call out?
> Does not understanding raise her voice?
> At the highest point along the way,
> where the paths meet, she takes her stand;
> beside the gate leading into the city,
> at the entrance, she cries aloud . . ."[2]

That man.

Uhhhh. I guess I could chock it up to simply being one more wrinkle in the vexing thing I am calling my life these days.

I need a little beach right about now.

Day 66—The Walk

"Are you ready for a little stroll with our *bella bambina, mi amor?*"

Viddie came cruising around the corner, already prepared for our daily outing. Having gathered everything we needed for our day at the beach, he brought the '70 out of the carport and started to load it. The cooler was filled with ice, some provisios, and several sparkling bubs. It was enough to keep us hydrated for much of the afternoon.

I had the baby situated nicely in my linen infant-carrier. She was all swaddled and ready . . . and adorable. Those little pink cheeks were beginning to fill out. Already, she looked a couple of pounds more than when she was born. The cradle contraption was in the hatch, and I couldn't have been happier for the moderately mild day. The sun wasn't as strong as I like it, but at least there was no rain.

"You betcha! I am ready, *mi amor!* Let's do it. I have her little blanket here in case the clouds roll in. Plus, it's not the warmest day we've had so far this month. I thought June would be much warmer."

"Hey! That's my line." He raised his left eyebrow the way he does when he makes a goofy face and mocked my choice of moniker. "You are a copy cat!"

"Ha ha ha—yes it is; I am a copy cat because you are *mi amor* too." I jabbed him in the rib with my elbow and we both had a good chuckle.

When we arrived at *spiaggia* and he opened the car door, the wind off the ocean kicked up sending a cold blast through the back seat. A chill shook through my chest and arms. I tucked the blanket around Russi.

"*Whew!* I'm glad you brought the extra blanket along for the baby. It sure doesn't feel like June."

He handed me my nice woolly sweater, put down the cooler and shut the door, but I wanted to get out there even if it was a bit cold. I opened the window slat and looked toward the ocean with wanton eyes. Oh, how I wanted out of the car and onto the beach. The nippy breeze sparkled with a salty freshness that nearly called my name out loud. He wanted to wait. *Boo.*

"No sad sack look from you, Emi girl. Let's let it warm up just a bit. It's still only 8:30. I'll warm up with my jog, but you'll be just sitting there. Why don't we just finish talking here in the car while you nurse her? It'll warm up considerably by the time she finishes."

I shrugged and feigned a compliant smile while continuing to peer out the slat toward the waves.

"Would you look at her, *mi amor?* Look at that—did you see that? She's smiling in her sleep. Awwww . . . *bambina.* It's her first real smile. *I think it is; is* it? Ohhhhh, Bellini. You are daddy's little *bambina*, aren't you? Oh baby girl. Kiss kiss. *Baciami.*"

What a kick I get out of watching him gawk at her. She's like a daily little gift . . . a surprise every day. Each day we find something new about her . . . something she's doing that she hasn't done before. I caught myself smiling right along as he continued to ogle and goo.

"So, tell me, Mr. Italian Papa, do you have any plans of ever calling this child by her proper name?"

"*Ha ha ha.* Maybe. Maybe, soon; I will try. I just can't help it. She's cute as a button and I look at her and all these nicknames begin to roll off my tongue. She's such a little bundle. *Ha ha ha.*"

"Have you noticed that every other thing we say involves the word 'little?' Ha ha ha . . . everything's little these days: a little stroll, a little blanket, a little kiss. Everything is miniature. She's miniature! Yeah—you go ahead, push her first, but seriously—let's not forget that her name *is* Russita and remember, we both agreed on it. Are you sure you weren't just going along."

"You know me well enough by now to know that I wouldn't have agreed if I didn't love it. I love the name . . . it's just she makes me all a-mush and I can hardly help myself. Look at her. She loves *spiaggia* too. She's sleeping like an angel!"

"Yes, she is. Okay . . . so are you ready to go? Let's get out there; it's nearly nine o'clock. Doesn't it feel warm enough now?"

I opened my side of the car and the fresh air filled my lungs with the faint smell of mussel shells and other mollusks. Oh, I love the saltiness of it all!

"Okay, okay. I get to push first, though, right?"

The rolling baby cart he built was made with the wheels he removed from our laundry bin. It takes ever-so-long to order these things from ConsumerHQ—I'm glad he is so talented with woodwork. The contraption is pretty cool. We lift the entire cradle up out of the frame he built for it and then place it in this thing and *voila*! It's sort of a stroller and a cradle, depending on what the need is at any given moment. I've never even seen any strollers available through HQs Big book. With so few babies being born these days, there's not much of a call for them, but my resourceful husband figured a way. *He's so cool.*

"*Mmmm*, smell that air? I already feel a little light headed with all the fresh air and honeysuckle swirling around us, don't you?"

"Not light-headed, no; just happy. I love you so my Emi-girl. I'm so thankful you married the likes of me!"

"There you go again, with all your thankfulness and gush. You are so sentimental, do you know that, fine sir?"

He chuckled and nodded. "Yes, I admit it. I am mush. Total mush. I get around you and the baby and there's no stopping the sentiment. It just gushes outta me. What can I say?"

We breathed in deeply and turned toward the water, staring out to the horizon, savoring the moment before we set out on our walk. He pushed back my bangs and kept the other hand on the baby cart. After a quick hug, we continued down the old concrete path that followed along the shoreline.

"There once were wide boards covering this path, Vidd. Did you know that?"

"I did not. Where'd you find that factoid, milady?"

"I've been doing some research on the time periods we've been discussing, and a hundred years ago this area had what they called a *boardwalk*. Folks walked, ran, jogged it and pushed their babies just like us. It was crowded. The image I pulled up in the 20th century image archive had a bunch of information that showed how popular this beach was."

"*Mmmm.* Yeah, I suppose most people enjoyed the fresh air back then. It would only be natural. What a shame that it ended and we are here alone—just us three."

My mind was a-swirl with so many things. So much of my day is taken up with diapenz, nursing, bathing, and sleep that I just love it when we get a chance to talk about grown-up things.

Day 69—The Talk

The day was considerably warmer than yesterday. We went down to *spiaggia* again and walked the entire length of the platform—about three miles or so. I was bushed when we got back to the flat!

Yesterday, when we started talking about all the changes in the world we got majorly sidetracked because of that Powers woman. Today was better. The history of the Shore came up again and we had a really good discussion earlier.

There's never a time when Viddie seems uninterested in the way I was educated. I brought up the lack of dialogue we are experiencing at the Lab and he brought up Rome.

"*Hmmmm.* Something similar happened in 6th century Rome. Did you ever study that in your archives?"

How this man knows all he does about world history is beyond me. I am the one with the world at my fingertips, housing all knowledge in the outboard memory of my OSLM that anyone could ever want, but *he's the one* with so many details about cultures and civilizations for which I have never even given a thought. How the heck does he know what happened in Italy in 568 AD? *Sheesh.*

"Would you like to enlighten me? I'm afraid I must have skipped over a few bits of my world history archives when I was first taking it all in."

"Really? I would think that with access to everything there is to know about the history of the world that your head would be jam-packed with it."

His semi-sarcastic tone was coupled with a firm wink and that oh-so-familiar scrunched up expression filling his face. I knew he was just giving me a hard time—busting-my-chops, he calls it, and the crooked smile that I have so come to love appeared before I could get upset. Rather than defend myself, I thought it best to simply explain.

"What I know . . . I mean what is really mine are the things Grand'Mere taught me—the stories she told me, the poem's she had me memorize, the fairy tales that her mother told her—all of these became mine. The rest—my entire education, dear—

would best be called *information access.* We were given access
to different digital archives at different stages in development
and taught to choose those items that interested us. Using the
search term could lead us to one subject or another, but it was all
where we decided to spend time. I always found myself in the
science and tek archives. It was a completely different method
of learning than how you were taught, dear. Need I remind you
of this?"

"Well, actually, yes. It's completely foreign to me, you
know that. I need your help understanding this crazy culture; it's
nothing personal so please don't take it that way, right?"

His soft tone soothed the growing angst that began to rise
up inside me, but our discussion was just one more instance of
the growing disparity I am noticing between his brain and mine.

"Fine. So . . . okay, go on. Tell me about Rome. How does
it pertain to us here in the late 21st Century?"

Viddie peeked into Russi's stroller and pulled down the light
blanket from her chin. She continued to sleep soundly and we
continued to walk. The crashing of the waves just forty yards
away kept me mildly distracted, but I was happy to have the
lesson on Rome, so I listened well . . . out of one ear.

"Okay, then. Just nod if what I tell you is stuff you already
know, okay?"

"Yes, sir." I saluted him, smiled, and readied myself for
another one of his tasty stories.

"Okay. Well, in its heyday Rome was the city of the world
boasting as many as a million and a half people. You know that
expression 'all roads lead to Rome?' Yeah, well—that was
partially because anything of any import ultimately happened
within its walls. That was the fourth century, but after much
vandalism, invasion by the Goths, and the city going up in
flames, by the late 6th century the population bottomed out to
around thirty thousand."

"Sounds a bit like the Devastation in this century, back in
the '30s."

"Exactly. That's what I'm talking about. Here we were, ten
billion people on the planet and now—what—a mere thirty
million? It seems highly unlikely that our world could rise
again, but that's why we need to do what we can and stay true to
the things we know are true!"

"So, how'd they do it? How did Rome go forward?"

"Well, it took some time for sure but here's an interesting little factoid: Gregory the Great—a guy from an old Roman family—was much of the impetus for change. 'Round about—I think it was 590 AD—he had a vision to restore Rome to its greatness. He began working from the inside out, a little bit like your vision to inspire others through the VacaPacs."

I smiled at that, and looked up at him as we found ourselves getting back to the platform of Old Bath. We decided to continue our conversation in the '70 where we could sprawl out in comfort while I nursed the baby. His tone was so confident and pleasing to my ears. I felt encouraged by the direction of our conversation.

"Oh Vidd—you have such a way of inspiring me. Do you really think we can have an impact in this century using virtual reality? After that lengthy message you left for me in my journal, I didn't think there was much hope really making it all happen. I mean, what you're saying here seems to be strong evidence for the kind of cultural change that we need. Think of it: everyone accepts and uses the VR tools already. If you think we can tap into their hearts and minds by creating really persuasive vacation packages, I will not let up. I will hang on and push them with everything in me."

He rubbed his chin, seeming to thoughtfully consider what I had just said, but then the expression on his face changed considerably. Viddie's not usually an enigma, but I couldn't quite read him at that moment.

"Yeah. I sure do remember; I mean, how could I forget? We never talked about that letter, Emi. The baby came and the issue just sort of got lost in the zaniness of life."

His tone suddenly became serious. Did I detect a change of heart? Hmmm. I wonder if he's ready to relent a bit and let us branch out in culture-shaping. Hmmmm. I knew I had to tread lightly and figure out what he was feeling at the moment. Sometimes I don't read him right. Either I'm completely clueless or he's just a bit less than direct. Not sure who's really to blame.

"Yes, I know, dear. Not only do I remember, but it took everything in me not to bring it up. Do you know that?"

"I do remember how angry you were with me, and I do remember that writing in your book is a major no-no, but again—we never discussed the issue itself, Em. Do you want to do that now? I mean, I still have concerns, but you were interested in what I was telling you about the rise of Rome and I was kind of on a roll."

I smiled and nodded. There are times when he is relentless. This was one of those times.

"Well, far be it from me to side-track your flow, 'specially since the baby's cooperating so nicely with a long nap. Go ahead."

He cleared his throat and then went in a completely different direction with his thought.

"Speaking of co-operation, she woke up within fifteen minutes after you left for the office the other day. Thank God you left those three little bags of frozen milk. I zapped 'em and she drank through all of it. You'd better do some more pumping soon."

I smiled more widely now, and as I moved from my cozy spot on the lounge and schooched closer to him, I teased, but told the truth. "You're a champ, Mr. Florencia. Russita Bellini is a lucky little girl to have you for a father."

His generous smile appeared once again and he continued with his explanation of the rise and fall of Rome, intermittently rubbing my back and playing with my hair. Our conversation was devolving, but slowly.

"Sooooooo, it took several centuries for Rome to come back but the world did flourish again. It was Gregory who worked to help Rome expand beyond its borders, but he didn't do it single-handedly. There were others who made a difference, in the renewal of Rome and the repopulation of this beautiful planet."

"So, if I'm reading you right, you're saying that we could really make an impact in *this* century by exposing folks to a way of life other than the deadened artificiality everybody just seems to accept today, and . . . that we could really have an impact. People will see. They will want more? You are telling me this story . . . to encourage more brainstorming and perseverance concerning our XTreme Vacapacs? . . . So you agree?"

"Uh, not . . . not really, Emi. What I am telling you is about a religious leader who was the catalyst for positive change. I wasn't so much thinking about your work. I'm sorry . . . I still don't think that would be enough to really turn this culture around. But, but . . . I could be wrong."

"Fine. Tell me how Gregory did it. How'd he do it, Vidd?"

Before we got too much further our conversation was interrupted by our beautiful little Bellini-girl. Crying and clamoring for more of mommy, we put our thoughts on hold, yet again.

Day 71—The Security

If you work at the LAB, no matter if it's with TLG, as an ADMIN official, or one of the several other corporations housed in the main government building, you have access to everything because the communication process is so open. That's why the vetting process is so complex, too. Once in, you don't have to deal with the three-tiered authentication process that everyone outside of the complex does, which is why, when I saw the encrypted glass-sheet with the purple security lines running through the header just hanging out there in the locker room, I was hard-pressed not to let my eyes take it in.

It was just 10 or so seconds before I heard Margene flushing the toilet so I wasn't able to read much, *but what I did see was alarming*. Some sort of eradication plan is in the works, having to do with organic material of an uncertain nature. I just read the first part of the send paragraph in the memo that mentioned something about ocean liner vacations. The upsetting aspect mostly involves the fact that I have not been privy to any of it.

When Margene emerged from the hygiene cubical she picked up the glass-sheet and smiled delicately, unaware of her carelessness with the confidential memo.

Things are getting spooky.

I don't like it. Not a bit.

Day 75—The More

Fatherhood has done marvelous things to my husband. Although I have no recollection of him ever being anything but helpful and kind, these days he's reached new levels of chivalry and charm. It's as if he has taken on a new coat of arms, one that has "fatherhood" inscribed in a half moon across his back. I swear, it's an invisible robe!

Now that it's clear that my toxemia is completely gone and I'm going to be okay, we seem to have passed through a threshold that has led us to an open wood, of sorts, in our hearts. We haven't argued for weeks, and now that my blood pressure has stabilized and my feet have gone back to their normal size, I feel more myself. My energy is back and I am eager to revitalize and get on with my life's purpose, only I'm not quite sure anymore what that means.

Questions about ADMIN's ethics continue to nip at the heels of my consciousness, but for the most part I keep my concerns to myself. Occasionally I open my heart more fully to my husband, especially on days that we have time for a good conversation.

When I processed my findings from the other day, I decided that I really must speak to Viddie about it. He may not understand City Centre culture completely, but he's got wisdom and I know I can trust him. The hardest part was verbalizing the initial question, but I finally got around to it last night after Russi went down for what turned out to be a very short nap.

So, fatherhood has changed him, but the ways that motherhood has already changed me are hard to even calculate. It's been such a short time, but my perspective has changed so much since Russi was born. It's hard to even write about. I ended up sharing my thoughts with Vidd, and that helped me understand some of the changes that I've noticed in my life.

Vidd drew me onto his lap once I put the baby down, but after we cuddled a few minutes, I decided to open up.

"Could it be that I invested my entire self in the work we do at the LAB and used it as a substitute for really living? Oh, Vidd—it's as if the promise of another life, albeit virtual, was the only thing I could give to others to inspire hope for something more than the flat, daily existence that encapsulates us all. Now I'm seeing that so much of what I did was merely to deaden the longing for something more—that little sprout that makes it way up out of the dirt of our human hearts to try to find life outside of the small, enclosed space of self—it searches for light. It needs to be watered. It shrivels without nurture. And it's what you've given me. You—you've watered and shined and pruned and . . . and loved me . . ."

A fat knot in my throat kept me from going on to fully express everything that was going on inside me, but in spite of all the emotion welling up it was clear that the entire sum of my adult life up to now has been a pitiable waste.

My husband's strong arms gathered around my shoulders and as he held me no words were necessary to let me know that he understood. He was there. I was safe. It was enough.

Russita's miniature cries reached my ears from the basinet in the next room and I broke away. Wiping the water that was quietly spilling over my eyelids, I looked at him intensely.

"There's more. I'll be right back."

Day 76—The Realization

"How 'bout I build us a table?" His words tumbled out in such a matter-of-fact way, but the question seemed to come right out of nowhere, and when I asked him why, his answer made me smile.

"*Why?*"

"What do you mean, *why*? We don't have a table; hadn't you noticed?"

"Hon. We don't have a table because we don't need a table and where on earth would we put one, anyway? Besides, what do you call that thing in front of the lounge? Uh . . . I believe that's a table, yes?"

"It's a twelve inch square, Emi! I'd call it a foot rest before I'd call it a table. It's far too tiny and short to use as a table. I dunno. Maybe I just feel like building something. And, it'd be nice to have a little table for the flat. Think about it: we could put it up against the wall heading toward the kitchen. It'd be small, really small—but a good place for us to sit down together and eat our weekly meal."

My stomach rumbled a bit at the thought of food. These days we are going through provisio bars like there's no tomorrow! I swear, he must have three to each one of mine.

"I imagine a table would be nice if we spent more than one night a week sitting down to a meal, but it's going to take up space that we really can't spare. Seems to me the hand-trays we use in the lounge work just fine for our weekly rations."

"*Emi.* That's just it; we don't sit down together to eat. We're always munching those crazy bars in the middle of doing something else and . . . I mean, it could be so much more."

He held up a crumbled wrapper from the cranberry flavonoid bar I had for lunch and shook his head. "Don't you ever get sick of this stuff?"

"Actually, no." I returned his look with my own expression of apology. "I didn't mean to leave the wrapper on the floor either. Sorry. I completely forgot it was there."

He got up, tossed it in the trash, went to get one for himself and called to me from the pantry.

"Which one do you want, babe?"

Hmmm. I've got a cacao-flavonoid here on the lampstand but if I yell for the Milky Yo, I'm sure baby girl is gonna wake up. Creeping ever-so-gently out of the rocker I tip-toed to the cupboard and used my chin to indicate my choice. Whispering my intentions, I was happy to see that there were still a couple of my faves. "That one. It's the best," I whispered. "Bring it to our room; I'm gonna put her down."

Russi continues to be such a good little sleeper. She cozied into her cradle immediately and seemed to be sleeping soundly. I joined Vidd back in our bedroom and slipped back into the rocker as he handed me my yummy Milky Yo.

"Thanks, hon. So, even if we could fit a table against that wall, do you think we'd sit down together to consume our provisios at the same time? Let's get real. I don't mean to be harsh about it, but you know these things go down in like . . . like two minutes."

"That's just it! If we had a table, wouldn't we be more inclined to make time to cook? I think we should. I can get started on it this weekend."

"Aw, hon, I'm sorry to remind you, but the world has changed in the last forty years, and there's no room or way to eat meals as you remember them. I mean, the few live foods we receive each week in the chilled doorbox come mostly from the hothouse HQ, with the exception, of course of the tiny crop the Drunge workers produce, and there's not enough clean space in each district to grow more. We don't even have the option of getting more real food, so really dear, I don't think we need a table."

An over-dramatized wink came my way along with another one of his big ideas. He's been hedging that we should start up a little garden of our own and he brought it up again when we were discussing his table-building project.

"*Ahhhhh.* Glad you brought it up, my Emi-girl. That's another thing I've been wanting to get started on—a potted garden."

His confidence just amazes me, but he just doesn't realize the challenges involved. He says we could begin with tomatoes and zucchini squash because supposedly they grow very easily in pots and then, little by little add other live foods. *Oh Belvedere,*

Belvedere. You and your romantic notions. That man is always thinking of ways to stretch beyond our current constraints. Eventually, he'll learn, I suppose, but our little talk about the table revealed something to me about myself, too.

Until now, I never realized how conditioned I am to think in a certain way—the LAB way. And, as free as I think I am, well, my ideas are fairly well conditioned to expect only one possible *correct* outcome. When we were hashing out this last little bit about the garden, I realized that I rarely think about what could be, only what *is* already. That is quite a realization because I must say, I do consider myself the most creative person on my staff. In fact, I don't know anyone (aside from Viddie) who has so many creative ideas, and here I am limiting him so. *Arrrggghh.*

During a long pause he continued to stare me down, rocked his head back and forth a bit and cloaked his eagerness with a quizzical look. *Adorable and so hard to resist.* I gave in, as usual, and let him have his say.

"Okay, so tell me, how can we grow vegetables inside our little sun-starved flat when the entire rest of the world cannot? You're telling me that we know something better than ADMIN about the land around here?"

My question emitted outright laughter coupled with a look that exhibited utter surprise. His eyes went all-googly—so much that I had to laugh out loud too—but when I thought about it later, his idea sort of blew me away.

"Really, Emi? The whole rest of the world? You know better than that. Besides which, we know SO MUCH more than Admin—you know that by now, my lovely lady. Please tell me you know that."

His puppy-dog eyes seemed to scour my soul with a love that drenched my heart like raw honey in its comb. I remember that big hive we encountered on the back side of Grand Lake last summer—it was raw, real, smooth, sweet nectar from the bees' hard work. I felt a bit raw inside as I returned his inviting, penetrating look. He went on to explain how easy it would be to use some dirt from outside to plant seeds from the few vegetables we get each week. Slowly, my heart started to soften to the idea. I can't believe my thinking is still so conditioned to believe in the toxic earth lie. What's the matter with me? I listened in rapt attentiveness; my man was on a roll and it seemed there was no stopping him.

"We use one or two tomatoes or peppers—whatever they send us in our ration box—and dry out the seeds and *voila*—we have our own supply in 6-8 weeks. If we get good at it we'll have more than we need and I can teach you a method of preservation that my mother uses that's called canning. You use glass jars and boiling water—it's easy, and everything stays fresh. We can make cool recipes during the winter months. *Oh man*, potatoes, tomatoes, garlic, onions, green beans—whew—my mouth is watering just thinking about a bubbling pot of *giambotti*."

"Jam Boatee? What on earth . . ."

My hack-worthy pronunciation gave him a good chuckle and then he proceeded to tell me all about the thick vegetable stew his mother always made every week in the winter. I never had the pleasure of trying it because she had so many summer recipes, but the excitement in his voice nearly made my mouth water. Pure joy peeled across his face and his twinkling eyes made it hard to kibosh the scheme he was concocting about building a table. I cannot resist this man.

"Fine then. Maybe just a little one. But don't go crazy, Mr. Florencia. Remember, this place is only 700 square feet!"

Day 77—The Words

Pent-up Passion
Pouring out;
Oozing from my skin
Waiting for an outlet;
Rushing waters
within.
Where were you friend,
—if I can call you that—
when the days were longer
and my eyes were young?
I did not see you standing there
In the corner
Past my stare.
I did not know you,
—not at all
But now you're everywhere
—everywhere I turn.
You are my friend
—I do call you that—
You are part of everything I yearn.
Come and stay
Make a place
Oh Passion
You are home.
Flow through me,
Come and dance,
Don't let me walk.
Please don't let me walk
alone.

Day 79—The Daily

"Do you really think I'm like my mother?"

Viddie had just finished changing her diapenz and gently rocked the baby in his arms. He turned and looked at me with a mixture of incredulity and wonder.

"What? What are you talking about, baby?"

His query was no more than a whisper as he intermittently shushed Russi, who at that moment began to make tiny, familiar, noises like she was hungry. At least that's my default perception. I figure she must always be hungry with that teeny tummy of hers; can't hold much at one time. I gently took her out of his arms and sat down to nurse this precious little one while he grabbed one of the folding chairs we keep in the hide-away spot for the broom and the mop. He unfolded it quietly and placed it as close to me as he could so that we could continue our conversation at a level that would allow Russi to fall asleep as she nursed. In fact, he sat so close to me that our knees were touching. I felt my body heat rise slightly, relishing our time together last night. I'm sure at least the inference of a smile crept across my face. He looked at me like he knew what I was thinking.

Our conversation began in whispered tones.

"You called my mother *a peach* the other day and told me that I take after her. Did you mean it?"

He cocked his head, looked at me squarely, and grinned with an impishness that is just so Viddie. His response came with his own version of a whisper, which is always only mildly softer than his full, bassy voice.

"In some ways you are like her, yes, but in other ways—no, of course. You are your own person. But to tell you the truth I can't believe you remember that I even said that. It was just said in passing, *mi amor*. Don't take my words so seriously; really!"

"Really?" I could hear my own volume rise, just a tad.

Eager to know exactly how he thought Marissa and I were alike, I urged him on.

"Okay, so how? Tell me *how*. I mean . . . I can't even imagine that it's true—my mother and I are as different from each other as the ocean is from the street, but . . . okay, let me have it. I want to hear your thoughts. How do you perceive us as similar?"

"You are so funny, Emi. *So funny.*" He leaned his forehead against my shoulder and let his lips rest on my arm, then looked up.

"Emi—my exquisite and exciting, *elegant,* wife—YOU are a trip; *such* a character. Do you even realize how complex you are? I just can't get over how totally complicated—beautifully complicated—you are, and how much . . . *well,* truly how grateful I am that you married me."

Russi pulled away from my breast with a loud suction noise and wide eyes as if she understood every one of her father's words. She craned her tender neck around, stared for a moment, and then quietly went back to my breast.

"Shhhh. *Vidd!* You're getting loud. Do you hear yourself? She was finally going to sleep, and now you've startled her, besides which, what are you talking about, Mr. Mush? I asked you about my mother!"

My hand rested on my knee while we spoke. I've always liked the feeling of my cottonblend spants against my skin, but I have become so accustomed to wearing this chocolate-colored pair when I'm not at work, that they've become a little grungy. They really do need a good washing. Viddie lifted my hand and kissed my palm.

"Oh, c'mon. You know you love the mush. You eat it up. It's better than your cocoa-bits provisio. *Ha ha ha.* Admit it!"

It was hard to keep myself from laughing out loud. He's such a stitch. It's true: I may pretend, but I am a glutton for his affection. He's got me right, that's for sure. I shot him a smile as I felt my face flush and he . . . *goodness*; he did not let up.

"I love *every* inch of you; every jot and tittle, every curve and curlicue. I'm just saying—sometimes I look at you when you're all riled up and wild-eyed and you . . . you remind me of her. And you may not realize this because I don't think you have ever tasted a peach, but they are sweet and tart and luscious and indescribably good!"

He scrunched his nose and poked his tongue out toward one side of his mouth, making me laugh out loud. Russi opened her eyes immediately, didn't stir, and kept sucking.

"Shhhh. You're making me laugh. She was almost asleep again!"

Day 80—The Rage

Work was wretched today. I feel like I don't ever want to step foot in there again. Powers was strutting about in her overdone stir-o-steen. I mean, it's one thing to match the company's signature bright blue lipstick with a simple blue stripe along the temple, but she goes waaaay overboard. Who does she think she is anyway—adding muted orange to the chevron!?!!? *I* don't even add orange. *Man alive*—that woman is audacious and *sooooo unrestrained!* Arrggghh!

Surely she should know better than to flout her status! On top of all her nerve, word came back that the latest version of Xtreme 1208 needs revision. The colors are off—*colors that I approved.* Allessandro finally contacted me about it today, but it was just to say *get it right.* Ugh. *That man!*

There's such a growing feeling of disconnection and so little peace. Worse yet, the feelings of mistrust that have been bubbling up inside my brain are coming to a head. Until now, I never understood that old saying "ignorance is bliss," but now I feel it—In spades*! (Ugh—there are those spades again!)*

What I did not know didn't hurt me, but now that I know how much the people of this great country have borne the brunt of ADMIN'S mistakes—or their agenda, I still am not completely sure—all I know is that I'm quickly losing all respect for them. I'm getting to the point that I don't even care anymore about our contract with them; I mean, where has it gotten me? To top it off, when I think of all the trouble my parents had with this mixed up government, how they were used by them, how ADMIN's deception sent them fleeing—*oh dear Viddie's GOD*—it all seems like a crazy, incredible dream. Actually, it's funny, but now that I think about it, most of all that transpired *was* a sort of dream. Everything except FRANCO, that is.

And that's just the tip of the iceberg.

It's so hard not to get negative sometimes. My own storied past as a would-be lunatic—and *all* of the ensuing drama—including Jude's bipolar behavior, my entire teams' cloaked accusations, even the virtual hook-up with Allessandro have foisted me into a growing melancholy. Clearly, this stuff will take me right down in the pit of depression, if I let it.

Been there once before; don't wanna go there ever again.

Idiots and ideologues—that's what they are, and I'm not afraid to say it out loud. I just wish I knew for sure what they were doing, and what our part is in the whole plan. If they really believe they can create and maintain a safe society by keeping us all shut in, I wonder why they haven't tried to . . .

"Hey there Emi-girl, whatcha doing?"

I about jumped out of my skin when Viddie wheeled into the car cover.

"Heyyyyyyyyyy—you startled me!"

"*Ha ha ha—you* are having a rip-roarin' convo with someone in here. What's going on?"

The joker. His question surely belied his experience. Clearly my husband knew I was talking to myself, because he's caught me doing it before. Sometimes I can't help it. Anyway, I decided to let him poke fun and laughed along with him.

"Why, yes, in fact, I am," I said, bantering in a bit of a self-mocking tone. "I am having a fine little rant about ADMIN and the *stultifying* lifestyle they seem to encourage at every turn."

Viddie planted a solid kiss on my lips and held my face in his hand for a second. Then he started tinkering with the wood-staining tools that were on the bench and looked up at me as he organized things there. His interest was welcome and a comfort to my soul.

"Same old, same old? Or did some new development upset you?"

"No, nothing really new. Basically it's more of the same. But Viddie, it's so disturbing. It started with the corrections Allessandro made to our design this morning, but my angst goes deeper. I hate the fact that it's starting to feel as though the smiles that are plastered on everyone's faces are really daggers being thrown at my chest instead of my back."

"What on earth happened, *mi amor?*" He put down the tools he had begun to clean and came closer.

"It's so much more than just a minor problem with the edits. The negative vibe I get is repelling. I wonder if anyone is actually happy there, because frankly, I don't see a shred of happiness there. And it goes beyond the LAB—far beyond it.

Vidd—*do you see it*? Whenever we *do* see someone living in City Centre, they are always docile and meek *and polite*—but happy? I don't see happiness on any of the faces, do you? I don't hear *happy* in any of the voices. I don't see *happy* smiles, just fake ones. They are coddled and clueless, all of 'em. I am at a loss to think any of them will ever be happy—and the weirdest thing is—they don't even seem to want it!"

"Whew. You are on a roll, woman! Keep it goin'! Rah, rah, sis boom bah!"

When we get going together it sometimes turns into a bit of a circus. He did some sort of tangled cheer with his arms and hands all over the place and as aggravated as I was at that precise moment, it was hard not to fall into a good round of laughter watching him. He looked like a lunatic—a goofy, googly, loveable, lunatic. I roared. Couldn't help it. Then, after a momentary pause, he locked me in his strong embrace and began kissing my face all over until I broke away, intent on finishing my rant.

"Not so fast, mister; I am smack in the middle of an important diatribe, remember? And although you have done much to pull me down off the ledge, I have no intention of not finishing what I wanted to say."

He took two steps back and folded his arms across his chest. "So, I'd better let you have at it, huh? Go ahead, Emi girl. Rant away."

"Okay. *Good.* Yes. But wait. Are you sure you're not sick of my complaints about work? I mean, I appreciate your good heart, but this must be boring for you."

His voice took on a more serious tone. "No, no. This is important. This has been your life for . . . for all your life, till now. What's important to you is important to me."

"Good. Okay. So, here's the deal: It's much deeper than just the lack of contentment there. I am seriously beginning to think that there is more to all this than just an error in thinking or miscalculation about the state of the earth."

"Go on."

"Yeah, well—at first I thought it was just the myth of a noxious earth that the LAB has propagated for all these decades, and perhaps that was the reason for so much underlying discontent. I thought that it was possible the government really didn't know, and maybe, just maybe ADMIN trusts the LAB's department of research so completely that they . . . they just bought it. And now the entire population of this world has just come to expect unhappiness as normal. I dunno. Or . . . or maybe their own fear kept them from investigating or believing that the earth could renew and replenish itself. Now, Vidd, if that's what it actually is, it's an awful enough miscommunication, but now it seems the evidence is mounting that all of their tactics and protocols are part of an intricate web of deceit, built on half-lies, innuendo, and the good intentions of those who work at the government HQ. And . . . *and*, if it *is* more convoluted than a simple misunderstanding or well-intentioned agenda gone wrong, well then I am outraged, absolutely outraged. Do you understand?"

He broke in without apology.

"Hold on there just a minute! One little minute. Call it what it is, Emi girl, *please.* The LAB has propagated a lie. Pure and simple. It's not *if.* It's outright deception, and it would be surprising if you didn't feel outrage."

"Fine. Let's go with your idea that it's a lie. But *why?*" I continued in rant mode while giving a quick look at the monitor to check on Russi.

"Please tell me, Vidd. Why on earth would they create a complete fiction to keep people stuck inside our homes? If they knew that we would all be safe to breathe as many hours of fresh air as we wanted . . . that . . . that we could enjoy the sun and sea and vegetation to our hearts' content . . . if, if, if they knew they didn't have to ration fresh fruits and vegetables for a meager once-a-week real-meal, why would they hold us all back? *Why-oh-why* would they insist we stay enclosed within our walls? Why would they make it impossible to communicate outside the walls of our brain hemispheres, pulling us away from each other's presence?"

Viddie pressed his lips together, shaking his head back and forth in short, staccato movements that made it abundantly clear his opinion was already well-formed. "Think about it. You all have this seamless communication system, but what good is it? None of you talk about anything. It's like . . . gosh, Emi . . . it's like forbidden territory to speak of what's going on—that's problem number one. Just think: if we were part of a public discussion about the earth and we could tell what we know and have experienced, others would try to step out and freedom would be the result. But, no. Nobody talks. Nobody says what they're feeling, and on top of that, you're taught *not to feel*. But *why* they have created a fiction is a much bigger question than that short answer tells. If you want to know why, I say it's because everyone has let *ADMIN* get away with it. No one dares take a step out into the water or risk finding a bit of greenery for themselves; it's like you've all lost your explorer gene!"

I answered weakly, clearly trying to convince myself of the veracity of what I already half-knew in my gut was true.

"We . . . we like to explore *virtual* lands."

"Aw, c'mon, honey. You all just blindly believe. I swear I think that's part of why you are so aggravated. It's hard to admit. But—they tricked you. They tricked you all."

My head started to swirl. So much was starting to come together. If Viddie was right, there is no telling where ADMIN will take us. Now it was his turn to rant.

"Zero dialogue exists, so no one can really make an intelligent judgment, let alone persuasive case, but *Emi*—you're asking me why, and ultimately I've gotta put the ball back in your court: Isn't it clear? Don't you see it yet? Someone *wants* to control things, and in that attempt there is no room for discussion, inquiry or . . . curiosity, at all! *Someone*—I am not sure who, but *someone* thinks their vision of a 'better earth' deserves to be preeminent."

By now my head was reeling. I so desired to combat his words and fling them back into his face. Every one of them felt like pelting rain against a closed window, *my window*, and that's what made me even angrier. *Could it be that my mind has been just as closed as everyone else's?*

As hard as it was to hear him so nimbly put his finger on the problem, I was becoming increasingly convinced that this alien, this mountain man husband-of-mine, is absolutely correct in his estimation of the situation here. I've been arguing with him about the wonderful respect and trust we all have here, and now I'm not so sure. There's growing evidence to the contrary, but I am determined to keep from implicating them before I have all the facts. Unfortunately, instead of feeling more composed and assured, his argument made me really start to feel scared. My heart was beating faster than normal and fear just came bubbling out of my mouth like dirty water from a sewer. I felt my nostrils start to flare and my voice went up a couple of decibels.

"I'm really beside myself about this, Vidd. What are we gonna do?"

He took both my hands in his and looked me squarely in the eye. His attempt at comfort was undoubtedly authentic, but the reality of the words he'd spoken, stung. Actually, I was leveled. A bit of tension rose in his voice as he spoke, and even though he was trying to downplay his assessment of ADMIN'S intentions, the words pierced me like an arrow and seemed stuck there, right in the middle of my chest.

"Emi, listen. We can do what we can do—it is not hopeless! Rome flourished again. Let's just do what we must and go forward with your plan. And who knows, perhaps ADMIN'S new agenda will work to advance the plan. Moderation in the VacPac expansion strategy may do exactly what you have envisioned. We can continue to work the new Xtreme packages and start with . . ."

"Vidd, wait. Listen. We haven't gotten one step closer to understanding what's really going on at the LAB, and the fact that you think it's all about control does makes some sense. If there's manipulation and real deceit going on we could be setting ourselves up for a fall. And who's to say this has not been ongoing? I mean, why else would we all be pressed to live our lives so nearly completely within the walls of our homes? Maybe the LAB's agenda is only about making money—keeping a consumer population doling out the bucks? I dunno. Plus . . . *plus*, Vidd—listen. Stay with me. I know I am talking in circles, but I think things are starting to get clear. As you were speaking I kept seeing that initial encryption glass before me. Clearly, the memo wasn't for my eyes or ears, but that Margene—you know, she is a little ditz. I know what I saw. What looked like gibberish to her was an obvious message to Allessandro about this new thing—this eradication plan—some sort of effort to eliminate unnecessary elements of our world. What elements? What? Toxic waste? What are they talking about? Oh man, it's just . . . it's hard to believe Powers entrusted her with it. Anyway, I think you're right. We need to get more information. I'm going to look for an opening with Zeejay."

Day 82—The Information

Soon it will be July and then the fall. Winter is right around the corner. There's no time to wait for an opening. We need answers *now*, so I cornered Zeejay yesterday before I left the LAB. After conveniently removing my P/Z, I put it in my side pocket, took him into my confidence, and point-blanked him.

"What do you know about what is going on here with our new mission? It must involve a decision that was made last year, while I was gone."

Zeejay stared at me blankly. His lips were tight and he began to move his face in short, horizontal motions, clearly dismissing my question. I grabbed his forearm and stared him down.

"Listen, whether you consider me a worthy boss or not, I am still in charge here and I asked you a question. I expect an answer."

He broke the hold I had on him and crossed his arms. I softened my tone and took a step closer.

"Zeejay, I brought you on. I helped you understand design. I have been more than your superior. I have been a friend to you."

"Really? A friend? Leeya, c'mon. We're not friends here, you know that. What Allessandro says, goes. They send down the agenda and we accomplish it."

"Zeej, do you realize by now that I am not part of the agenda-setting? Maybe we haven't been actually friends, but we've worked together for over a decade and developed beautiful Vacation Packages together. We have had investment in each other's lives. Can't you tell me what you know about the current strategy here?"

He seemed to soften to my own softer voice, and relented, if for a moment.

"Fine. I guess I owe you that. I find it hard to believe, but if you truly have not been brought into the agenda, I'll tell you what I know, but you aren't going to like it."

My interest was piqued. "Yes, please. Please, do."

"Okay. So none of us have all the details, but it has to do with something that Allessandro's been touting as the new vision. 'Course, that's not the official name of it, but there have been whispers of the vision for months. It involves keeping the general population happy, healthy, efficiently productive, and well fed."

Wow. No mention of keeping them properly inspired or motivated. Plus, it's much expanded. We never involved ourselves in health and proper nutrition before. *Strange.* In spite of his hostility, something inside made me feel like I could trust him. I was dumbfounded, but motioned for him to continue.

"Yeah. And the plan to accomplish this goal involves our department and the new packages we're creating—the interactive packages that we'll be rolling out in the fall."

"You mean the ones we've got in the pipeline—the NatureTrailsXTreme and AlpineVillage Packages?"

"Uh. No, we've got others in the queue that have priority. You haven't seen MaidenX-One or OceanlinerX-One?"

Day 83—The Ambivalence

"I don't like what's happening to me, Viddie. We have everything in the world to be happy about, but the stupid flack that I'm getting at work keeps bringing me down! It's not that I feel hopeless—more like helpless. This new agenda is keeping me in an almost constant state of confusion. One day it seems to me that this interactive vacation strategy could be the very thing we need to crack open the minds of a people whose minds have been closed by fear. And, then other days it feels as though there is something about the agenda that is just not right. Since my position at Travelite Global is still intact, I believe it affords me the clout and ability to make positive change for the more than perhaps 99% of the rest of the people on this planet, yet there still seems to be so little that I can do. Our generation has so much, but it's as if we have been anesthetized."

He listened attentively, with tight lips and a solid sort-of quiet that made me feel a little nervous. After a few moments, he spoke up.

"Hon, that may be true, but don't you see it? Your position may be intact, but more and more it seems it is intact in name only. I still don't think they'd have the nerve to fire you, but it does sound serious. I'm sorry to point that out, baby, but you told me yourself that when the memos arrive on engraved glass it represents the most serious of messages. They just laid all this on you without any care about your input or perspective. The MaidenX stuff—or whatever they're calling it—is something that's been in the works for some time, and clearly there is reason to be concerned. Yet, yet . . . we shouldn't fret. This cycle keeps happening and it's highly likely that our world is in the midst of new growth right now. As we walk into our future it will be people like us—people who know there is more to life than work—who help others step out into uncharted territory of real relationships, community and genuine love. Folks who truly know the difference between what's real and what's artificial have the responsibility to help the world go forward. And, baby—that can happen no matter if there are super duper nature VacaPacs or not."

His gaze was tender and full of passion. I could feel the passion oozing from him as he spoke. I sat there, dumb, unsure about what to think as he continued.

"I mean, I don't have the answer. I don't know *how* we'll do it, but it *can* be done. Besides, you know, it's just . . . well, you know how I feel about it. Experiencing the truth second hand never really works. I mean, reading about (or seeing) community and the beauty of nature can stir up interest, but we've got to experience things for ourselves to really know a thing. While an appeal to our emotions has got to be part of the motivation, without the bravery to step out, folks will just stay stuck, believing the propaganda that's being pushed."

After some time thinking about the communication breakdown at the LAB I have come to the conclusion that it's time to take a bit of the blame. I mean, I used to be queued into every second of what was happening there, sleeping with my P/Z intact, offline only if I ran out of diamond dust, and how rarely did that happen? Lately, I connect only when it's absolutely necessary. Mostly I'm queued into OLSM when I get to the LAB and I'm at my glass-board. Maybe Viddie's right. I need to rethink my aversion to Powers and realize that as I'm taking a step back I am leaving a gap. Maybe things aren't devolving as quickly and grossly as they seem. Maybe I'm just being oversensitive because *I'm* taking a backseat.

Day 84—The Game

"I'm sooooooo exhausted."

"Go back to sleep, *mi amor.* I'll rock her if she wakes up."

Viddie tried to coax me back to my pillow but I knew if I didn't get up then, there would be no time to queue into that aggravating First Call. Now that the dynamic duo were getting married, I had to be sure not to put myself in a position of ever having to hear that I wasn't on the communiqué again. Especially from *her.* Plus, Viddie was up and it would be a good time to have him help me process whatever drama might be stirring today.

"It's okay. Besides, I can't get comfortable enough to sleep. My mind is so fixated on what's happening at work. I can't seem to relax."

"How 'bout we figure it out together?"

"What do you mean?"

"Why don't we help ease your mind by going back to that memory game we created when we first got married? It's been a while since we traded off one liners of our best memories of life at FRANCO. How 'bout that?"

That oh-so-familiar teasing smile that I have so come to love flashed across his face before I could say no. His skin was ruddy from a week of sunny days, and he hadn't been to the office with me since Monday so his jaw was covered by two-day old bristle. I could stare at him for hours. Rather than push him off, I thought it best to simply stall.

"Oh hon," I replied groggily. "You always win that game. Besides I have to think about what's going on at the LAB . . . and figure out what to do next. I need some thinking time; I still don't have a clue as to how to proceed."

"You'll figure it out just fine. Right now, it's better to relax your mind a bit and give it a break from Allessandro and his women. Look. I'll start. I'll say something about someone or something that we loved up in the mountains and you play off that and try to one up me. Like this: I see Grand'Mere stirring thick, piping hot, potato soup in her big black kettle using the wooden spoon to make sure it doesn't stick."

"*Mmmmm* . . . her potato soup with the leeks and onions and creamy broth? Oh wow. That totally makes my mouth water."

Viddie leaned over and cradled my face with one hand. Smiling, he cocked his head and gave me a half smile. "Now it's your turn."

I let out a long breath and closed my eyes.

"Ah . . . there's so much. Okay. Here goes: I see us standing in the meadow between Rubble Ridge and Grand Lake, locked in an embrace under a swirl of white clouds; the sky, streaked with lavender stripes and soft gray hues—the color of mourning doves—surrounding us. You, with breath hot on my neck, whispering words that dazzle my ears and drench my heart in the rich delight of your warm affection."

"Emilya *Florencia*! You are so poetic!! When'd you get to be such a little wordsmith?"

There I was, only half awake, digging out the miniscule bits of dried sleep that lingered in my left eye, trying to yawn and cover my mouth simultaneously, when he literally jumped on top of me and began covering my face with tiny kisses. He was so playfully intense that I could barely breathe. We erupted into a fitful laughter and I tickled him until he cried *uncle*.

"Okay, okay, girly; you definitely won. How can I say anything that competes with Cloudland?"

"Ha ha ha! Wait, wait! I've got another. How 'bout this: I smell fresh blueberries bursting inside of fluffy muffins as the heavenly aroma wafts just outside the hearth area of Fiorella's earth shelter."

"*Oh, no*—cloudland is it. Babe, you got me. I'm done. You win this time. I can't imagine anything better, not even my mother's best blueberry scones."

I snuggled in under this shoulder and just rested there for several moments, content; completely content to stay right there all day. He looked down at me and winked, and softly caressed my hair.

We sat quietly for a couple of minutes and simply enjoyed the stillness. First Call was up next, and I was ready for the day.

Day 89—The Progress

"There's really nothing here besides what we've already found, hon."

Yesterday began like any other day, but then Viddie wanted take another look at LJ's old flat so I wrapped Russi in the swaddler—she loves that thing—put her happy baby self close to me, and placed a little pacifier in the folds of the cloth. We didn't find anything new, but it satisfied his curiosity—*ha ha ha*, until next time!

We sat on LJ's kitchen floor for a long time talking, just airing out all the events of the last few months, and tried to be very objective in reevaluating our purpose in City Centre. Along with the numerous and unexpected needs associated with having a baby in our lives, Viddie and I busied ourselves by thinking through the various scenarios and possibilities for the future.

It wasn't long before my creative juices started up and we hopped on the topic of work and we plunged into the new Vaca ideas we've been working on. Who knows if we'll actually be able to follow through with these VacPacs, but talking about them helps to ease the uncertainty I feel about . . . well, just about everything.

We sat quietly thinking and speaking on and off about it all afternoon. The more I thought about it, the more I realized that I really wanted my new Xtreme Vacapacs to be produced! Work has always been a means of such satisfaction for me, and now that these ideas about new packages were percolating, well, I feel more motivated again. I mean, how else would we be able to alert the public of an alternative way of life, or interject some of the important pre-Devastation values into society? Yeah, the more I think about it, it's true; work has actually taken on new importance. Heck—this is the world our daughter will be raised in. We've got to stand strong and stay with our mission!

Plus, the stats were in. For the past six months every marketing report noted the same thing: the public has been clamoring for new virtual vaca-spots and our opportunities to introduce them to different ways of being alive seem endless. But—ugh—I feel so conflicted at times. One day, going forward; the next, giving up. *Ugh.* I'm hoping these motivated feelings will stick and I will feel less of a push and pull inside me.

As much as there are opposing agendas here at the LAB, I actually don't think I can give up. We've been weighing these conflicting agendas quite a bit lately, some days we can hardly speak of anything else. *Something* good has to win out, so in spite of the anger and uncertainty I continue to feel, the deep significance of my work keeps bubbling up. Virtual vacations truly might allow us a way to help folks experience nature again!

After our noon hour provisio we went back to our flat and laid Russi down for her full midday nap. We shared several cups of our favorite roobious tea with a touch of honey and it made our creative chat quite a cozy time together, continuing to talk about what it would mean to keep working at the LAB, and put up with their new mission.

It's good to have a partner in all of this. How blest am I to have someone who cares about the things I care about and wants to work with me to effect change.

Day 93—The Wish

Twisting, changing, charging down a path
with a machete.
If I could get my hands on a knife that big,
that's what I'd do.
Cut away the weedy growth that obscures the way
and change it into one that's
Clear
Straight
and
Certain.
I'd leave the wildflowers, though . . . leave their
fragrance dancing in the air
Sweet
Clean
and
Comforting
Air.
The clouds could come along for the ride,
I don't care.
So could the rain.
Getting wet doesn't bother me
Anymore.
As long as I don't get lost, I'll be fine.
The woods are dense and like my thoughts
Cluttered with unnecessary debris.
I'd like to carve them up
Yeah,
Carve them up
with a machete.

Day 94—The Patterns

"Look at this!" I am absolutely mesmerized by the smoothness of the snail shell and can hardly believe the spiral design of this little mollusk's house.

"Do you see it Vidd? Look at the way it swirls in, getting smaller and smaller. Did you ever notice that it's quite similar to the spiraling layers of stars in the universe? It's as if there's a pattern and everything around us is connected. Here, look. The opalescence on the water is exactly like the inside of this oyster shell!"

I lifted the shell up to his eyes so he could get a closer look. He gave it dutiful attention and then smiled at my wonderment.

"Exactly? Is it exactly like the inside of the oyster?"

"Viddie you are teasing me again!" I splashed a little of the water at him as we waded through the tiny breakers. "No, seriously. Do you see the way they are similar?"

The baby nestled on my bosom and slept soundly, wrapped tightly in the body scarf that I carefully tied around my back and chest. Her tiny head was fully covered by the cloth so I was free to use both my hands; one was busy entwined in Viddie's, the other held four or five of the daintiest of the shells we found throughout the afternoon. We stopped for a moment when I noticed another exquisite gift of nature—a slipper shell.

"Oh no—I can't fit any more in my hand. Can you carry this one for me? Look—it's pink on the inside and several shades of white on the exterior."

"Of course. I've got this whole other hand that's empty and ready to be your shell basket." He laughed and the baby stirred.

"You know, if I believed in fairies, this could be a little shoe for her. Ha ha ha! *Fairies!* It does just look like a miniature shoe though, doesn't it? *So cute!*" A small wave crashed at our ankles and Viddie turned his attention to the baby.

"Look at this little foot, *mi amor.*" As he spoke, he tenderly rubbed Russita's heel. Funny, how it didn't wake her or even cause a stir. He continued to reminisce.

"Remember before she was born when we walked this same stretch of sand and you'd feel a poke in your abdomen? We'd see this little ball of skin roll around on your belly and think it was her heel—or maybe it was her elbow. *Ha!* We were never sure, right? Now look at her . . . my baby—*our* baby girl—cuddled across your chest, so peaceful and sweet. This little foot—wow—what a miracle."

Viddie continued to tenderly caress the baby's foot and when I looked at him, his eyes were glassy. He brought up the fears my parents shared with us about the research the LAB was conducting when she was pregnant with me, and what they told us about my inability to ever conceive a baby of my own.

"I'm so glad your parents were wrong about that, Em. I can't imagine a life without this little girl. Can you?"

"Absolutely not. She is part of us—so beautiful. And, Vidd—who knows what really went down when the LAB supposedly messed with me in my mother's womb? All I can say is that I am thankful Marissa and Liam were wrong. *So thankful.*"

We gazed at her with a wonder and a love that neither of us had ever previously known. This moment was like so many in the past few weeks when we would just stop and stare at her in utter amazement.

"*Mmmm.* She certainly *is* sweet—like her daddy."

He gave me a playful poke in the ribs and then took the shell from my hand.

"I never quite thought about the patterns the way you have, Em. I mean, I think what you are seeing is a really cool part of the design of the universe. Ya see? The universe makes sense; it's purposeful and orderly—all these things come from an intelligent Maker—the One True God, God Almighty. Tell me you don't know that in your heart of hearts? I know you do. If you search there, and ask Him to reveal Himself, He will. I'd know it, even if my parents hadn't raised me up in the belief of a deity. Nobody had to tell me. I could just look at the stars when I was a kid and . . . well, something inside me just rang with the knowledge that He is there."

These little God-chats were starting to pepper our conversations here and there, so I was not as flustered as I once had been, but it still didn't make a whole lot of sense to me. The momentary shot of anxiety that rippled through me was quashed by his tender, reasoned tone.

"I just believe in Him, Emi. It's where I choose to place my faith. Everybody has a measure of faith. I put mine in the Lord."

"Yes, I know well what *you* believe, my dear. What I don't know is how you can be so sure. How on earth do we know what we can believe if we can't see it?"

"*Hmmmm*. Not an easy question. I do have a sort of threefold test, but I've got to make sure you really want to talk about this."

His tone moved from lighthearted to serious. As he cocked his head, a long, soft curl fell across his raised brows. I snuggled closer to him and pointed to one more shell.

We walked a few steps away from the water and sat down together on the warm sand. Despite the grip of quiet terror that still lingered at my core, I nodded and let him go on, smiling weakly.

"I do want to hear your take on these shells. And a test? Sure. Go ahead."

He cleared his throat. "It's not actually a test, but more a way of knowing. First, I listen to what I have heard from others that I respect, then I listen to my own experience. Next, I listen to my heart and ask myself if what I am believing truly resonates inside me. Finally, I look for it in the Bible and when they all meet, I know it is worth believing."

"You're kidding, the *Bible*? Viddie we haven't ever talked about the Bible."

"Oh yes we have, Emi-girl. Remember the Psalmist, David—the king I quoted a while back?"

I placed the little cache of shells next to me in a neat pile and shushed the baby a bit when she began to awaken.

"What . . . the guy you were talking about when you ripped a page out of my book?"

"*Mmm*—yeah—that's the one. Those words are part of the Bible. A part of the Old Testament—in the Psalms—they are ancient songs."

"H*mmm*. Interesting. I guess . . . what? I didn't even know they made Bibles anymore. Where is there a Bible in FRANCO? Did your parents bring one there in their big box?"

"Well, yeah—we do have a few Bibles up there, but most of them are stowed away to make sure they stay intact and preserved from the elements. So, I never really read much Bible, but I learned through mnemonics. My parents—your parents, too—almost everybody up there have sections they've committed to memory. My parts included most of the Psalms, some of the Proverbs, Song of Songs, and there are . . . well, a few random New Testament verses that pretty much everyone knows."

I listened in rapt attention, quite shocked that I saw nothing of this while I lived in the community. Discovering this little fact about my husband quite boggled my mind. I mean, I know Christianity was linked to the Bible, but where the heck did FRANCO get one? Even twenty years ago paper books were scarce.

"So, what Christianity verses do you know? Can you really just rattle them off?"

The gentle late June breeze blew lightly through Viddie's dark curls, which were now growing a bit longer again. Almost time to pin them back in a mini-ponytail. We decided we didn't care if our co-workers looked at his lack of haircut a little strangely because—heck—they are all strange as strange comes. He glanced at the ocean and furrowed his brow as if he was thinking hard. The strong fragrance of beachside honeysuckle danced past our nostrils and I closed my eyes to drink it in while I waited for his response.

"Some. Yeah, definitely. You're talking about New Testament passages—Christianity didn't even develop formally until a few centuries after Jesus walked the earth. Yeah, I know a bunch of 'em. They're all right here." He gave his chest a single, hard pat just under his left shoulder and winked at me with that crazy, adorable smile.

What a guy, *this man*. How did I get so lucky?

"Uh, my darling husband, I do think those verses are up in your head where your brain is lodged? Ha ha ha—you are something else, mister. You definitely seem like an alien life form! *Ha ha ha.*"

"Laugh all you want girly, but it's not often that you ask me to give you a Bible verse; I've got to give a little thought to this one. I may not get this opportunity again."

His soft chuckle helped moderate the tone that had suddenly become ultra-serious. I could tell this meant much to him.

"By the way, handsome, your little test asks four questions, not three."

Day 95—The More

Prior to green grasses swaying in the gentle breeze I was
content
> *—not fully, but satisfied.*
Satisfied in my oblivion.
No swaying vegetation or fragrant days to anticipate,
> *but quiet acquiescence to a life*
>> *—unlived.*
Misery, not quite horror, plagued me from time to time,
> *but only because a vacuum seized my mind*
>> *—nipping at the heels of my existence.*
Not so, today.
Refreshing wind off the ocean blows back my hair and
although it is
> *too brisk sometimes, it is not biting*
>> *—lets me know I am alive.*
Foggy car windows obscure my vision,
> *but as I peer through the cracks I see the color green*
>> *—maybe for the first time.*
An azure sky calls my name, bids me to follow.
> *I move and stretch, sway and dance.*
>> *—fly, dream.*
Softly rippling waves deliver more blue,
> *mingled with gray*
>> *—I sing.*
Ah cantare.
There's more!
Finally.

Day 97—The Bug

I feel like there's a bug in my brain. Not spyware. I'm protected from internal hacking; been protected from the start. Most of us take care of that risk, but me—I've made doubly sure. Grand'Mere always taught me to be cautious of the TEK, so when she first brought me to the LAB to intern for her, I made sure to upgrade to the most secure version of the OSLM. It's nearly unhackable . . . at least the DeepArchives. I've got government grade, so I'm not worried, but it just feels like I've got some sort of flying insect roving around in my head, wreaking havoc in the normally well-ordered rhythm of my synapses. *UGH.*

I woke up feeling so off—and there's no reason. Viddie and I are fine. Baby girl is fine, but I'm just feeling so defeated today, and we haven't even begun our work. I'm beginning to think Viddie's right about my brooding. Maybe it is more than hormones.

It's so unlike me, but the last thing I want to do is work on the vaca packages, and I don't even feel like getting up and going for a walk or doing anything!

This malaise has been growing, settling on my soul here and there like the fine, cool mist of morning before dawn. It's not steady, but it does seem to be coming at me with increasing regularity, and sometimes it's not only disquieting, but it sends an actual shiver down my spine. When I've spoken with Viddie about it, he shakes his head and never seems to have an answer—like he's never experienced it or something. I don't know how to shake it. Must be the extra weight and cumbersome body that I am dragging around since the baby was born. I'm up a solid ten.

"Hey there, *mi amor.* You slept late. How are you doing this beautiful morning?"

Placing a steeping cup of greenVita by my bedside, Viddie's warm smile gave me a bit of a lift. I wormed my way up against the bed head, took a deep breath and blew him a kiss.

"Not so fast, milady. I wanna real one!"

He swooped down for a quick peck on the lips and remained close to my face, staring deeply into my eyes, and then did the same for Russi who was lying happily alongside me. I had to turn away and chuckle.

"What a character you are, Mr. Florencia—a character, indeed." I shook my head, smiling. "How long have you been up?"

"Oh, since about two. You were ripping up the covers, tossing back and forth and I just got to thinking about how really great life is living with you and then just couldn't get back to sleep. I think it was about four when Bellini started to stir. I heard her and got up to rock her. She went back to sleep and was quiet until now, when I brought her to you."

I yawned and stretched extra long, drawing Russi to my breast. "Nice. Good job, Dad."

He nodded and grinned.

"Thanks, hon. It's a pleasure. Yeah, I feel great today— like I want to go for a run. Should I wait for you and the bambina or do you mind if I just get out there around the block?"

"Oh, why don't you wait? It's better if you run on the beach where no one can see you, you know that."

Day 99—The History

"And where, may I ask, have you been? Making progress on our table, yes?"

Viddie strolled into the lounge looking like he had been spit out of a 3-D printer. Hair strewn in seven different curly directions, with a single corkscrew coming down right between his brows—he had stain on his fingers and stubble on his face. It was clear he was accomplishing much in the carport. His smile spoke of deep satisfaction.

"Uh, how'd ya guess?"

Without waiting for an answer he motioned for me to follow him.

"C'mon. Bring Russi down and check out my progress. I carved some baroque-style filigree into the legs; I think you'll like it."

Baroque? *Unbelievable.* How this man knows all he does about world history, art history, aesthetics—everything—is beyond me. He's been living on the dark side of a rock his whole life and I am the one with the world at my fingertips! More and more I see that housing all knowledge in the outboard memory of my OSLM is vastly different than really knowing. In any case, he's the one with so many details about cultures and civilizations at his disposal. He knows so many things that I haven't even heard of! Sheesh.

After we checked out the table (it really is lovely), he washed up and we headed down to *spiaggia.* Yay—the beach always has the power to break me out of the doldrums. Vidd was full of energy and put off his jog so we could continue a conversation we have been having about the state of our government. He came and sat down next to me on our favorite stump at Old Bath and we dove right in to where we left off.

We ran the gamut of contemporary culture, discussed the precursor to the fall of the USA, the bombing of the World Trade Center at the very start of the millennium, and the breakdown of culture and civility before the Devastation. He had quite a convincing take on it. Then we meandered into reasons why history so often repeats itself. Generation after generation nations war against each other, people rage against their neighbors and commit violent crimes; it just doesn't make sense. Why does it have to be this way? I wondered this aloud and he was quick to offer his perspective.

"I'm sorry to say it's true, but it's just part of the human condition. We mess up. We try again. We are victorious. We mess up again. The cycle is something that we can count on, Em. It just keeps happening. Prime reason, if you ask me, of why it's important to study history! Otherwise, people just keep repeating the same mistakes. And as we walk into our future it will be people like us—people who know there is more than devastation, darkness and fear—who have the responsibility to help the world go forward. For us, the question remains: what is our particular role for this particular moment in time?"

I leaned back to ponder his question. A cluster of petrified barnacles that were stuck to a semi-buried bolder scratched against my thigh. The sun was delightfully warm and the breeze coming off the water was just enough to keep us comfortable. He hunched over, grabbed his toes to stretch out, and we delved even deeper into our culture chat as the baby slept soundly on my chest.

"Do you think *everyone* has a particular role, Vidd? I mean, what if we don't fulfill our role? What about people who are clueless about all this?"

That led us rather quickly off the political underpinnings of our crazy, mixed-up world and straight into philosophy. Ha! Russa would have loved it! Right in the middle of being deeply enmeshed in the history of ideas, her namesake woke up in an unusual fit of tears—probably with a mess in her diapenz. It wasn't long after that we packed up and headed home. It was a really peaceful day. Lovely, in fact. I enjoyed talking about life with him, even if we don't agree on everything.

Ah—*and there she is again.*

I'll have to finish writing the rest out lat . . .

Day 101—The Future

"*Shhh, shhh, shhh,* baby girl. Go to sleep. *La, la, la . . .* Vidd, could you hold her, hon? Here. I've got to go down to the LAB and check the galleys on NatureTrail. Looks like they're trying to get a hold of me. My OLSM is flickering and it's driving me to distraction! It's days like these I wish we still had screens."

"I would love to hold her; come here baby girl . . . come to Daddy."

He cradled her in his left arm and continued poking around in the small cups of dirt on our tiny counter. The little kitchen garden he planted hasn't produced more than a couple of leggy shoots and while they are all nice and green, none are large or strong enough to be re-potted. Where we'd move them, I have no idea.

"Do you want me to come with you?"

Russi gurgled and attempted a swat at her Daddy's mouth. I put her in her white jumper with the pink rosebud collar when she woke up drenched in pee at 3 a.m.— the adorable one that matches the color of her sweet lips perfectly—but it still had a little spittle on it from the morning's feeding. I should've changed her.

"I'm fine. Thanks. Shouldn't be too long . . . but change her, would you? She's got gunk on her clothes."

"*Ha-ha*—it's hard to see the gunk when those little beauties are shining up at me." He was totally in Daddy-mode—starry eyed and oblivious to everything but her little face. However, I did manage to get a response out of him when I poked his side and stuck out my tongue. He continued to gawk.

"*Ha ha ha* . . . oh, baby. Will do. I will definitely change this little peanut. So . . . how long do you think you'll be?"

"Not long. I just have to make sure all is running smoothly and check out the messaging system—make sure I haven't missed anything significant."

"Sounds good. When she goes down for her nap I'm gonna do a little more work on the driftwood chest. Maybe I'll have it done by the time you get back."

Ever-eager for a building project, Viddie definitely doesn't mind being alone, and that's fine by me, really, because I'm so accustomed to being by myself. What an optimist he is, though. *Ha!*

"Really, by the time I get back? That's doubtful. I shouldn't be more than an hour, but . . . well, *great*—maybe you *will* have it done. Have fun, honey!"

I kissed our *bambina* on the forehead and watched her lips curl up slightly upward. *She's really starting to smile.*

Little did I know that when I decided to come into the LAB I'd be walking into a battleground, and my quick check-in would turn into four hours of non-stop engagement! By the time I arrived back at the flat my shirt was saturated with breast milk. *Ugh.* What a trying morning this was. When I got there, my staff was clustered around Jude's glass board, ogling something. Zeejay motioned for me to come a little closer. It was a memo engraved in the glass. *Official.* Oh, wow.

"What's going on, guys?" My question produced a number of diverse looks, spanning from incredulity to disdain to relief. Ion looked somewhat sullen, Zeejay seemed baffled by my lack of information, and Jude quietly shook his head. Where Powers and Margene were, I hadn't a clue.

They made room around the station for me and as I zeroed in on the message, the reason for the glass engraving became clear.

"Okay guys. Let me just see what this is all about." I peered more closely at the work order and continued to inspect the glass. "I'd like each of you to report what you know about the scope of this project. It seems we've got a few changes to the mission statement and a bit of organizational adjustment for the company at large. I'm sure there's nothing cataclysmic here. Hmmm, let's just see."

I pulled my hair back into a high pony tail and realized I really should have washed it two days ago. Ion mumbled something about job security and Jude stood up straight and raised those hairy eyebrows of his, taking care not to make eye contact. Zeejay was the only one who spoke up.

"Looks to me like we're doing more than expanding our mission, Leeya. This morning's First Call indicated that there will be fundamental changes. Seems the LAB is finally allowing us to create specs for the next generation of vaca packages. From where I stand that's gonna mean a totally new line of software, new tools, and *totally* new design products. We'll need to know what sort of timetable we're dealing with."

Hmmm. My mind started going in a hundred different directions. This must be the Oceanliner thing. I looked up at them and spoke aloud instead of using my P/Z.

"Must be the XtremeInitiative that we've heard about."

Zeejay continued where he left off. "Yeah. I think you're right about that. And it's gonna be a major deal, 'specially since it'll be the first interactive package we've created that's not strictly VR."

Wow. I wonder if it'll be just the thing to spark the public and open them up to life outside their walls. My heart started beating faster.

Jude, still simmering with some sort of vague resentment, offered his two-cents. He spoke to my query while continuing to avoid my gaze. "That's right. TLG is expanding beyond the virtual to the actual. They're gonna use high compression tek . . . the kind that was used over a hundred years ago in early space travel. It'll allow people to vacation on a real barge that's been electronically wrapped—sort of—covering them with aeronautic quality compression. Sounds like it'll be possible to spend up to ten hours on the open sea without having to breathe the air."

Shrugging my shoulders, I shook my head and let the team know that I hadn't spoken with Allessandro about the timetable yet, but I assured them we'd get a process together and nail down the specs just as soon as possible.

My eyes zeroed-in on the inscription and as I looked at it more carefully I heard myself whisper aloud. "Next generation?"

Ion looked the way I felt inside—dazed. He didn't say much, but Zeejay chimed in right after Jude. Decidedly more upbeat, he seemed genuinely interested in getting to work.

"Kinda cool, isn't it?"

I couldn't help but agree. "No doubt, it's cool, but it's a lot of change in a short span of time. It must have been in the works for months."

How in the world Jude and Zeejay were privy to such information was beyond me. I couldn't quite figure out if their thoughts were based on some sort of inside info or just the prognostication of an experienced design crew. My continued attempt to pull some info out of them drew out some questions. I'm actually glad I came in because these changes seem to be on the fast-track, and it really would have been horrible if I didn't hear about them until the Public-Internal memo. I spoke directly to each of them as I scanned the room.

"Gentlemen: We have much work to do. We'll have to gather all our creative faculties and work together to come up with designs that draw the public into a new way of thinking about vacation. They will not be prepared. There's been no hint about new protocols—no discussion that the toxicity of the ocean has subsided or that it's safe to be in the water. Part of our job will be to provide solid, straightforward information housed in impeccable design. *Hmmmm.* I wonder where they're going to find people willing to take the risk?"

"What do you mean, Leeya? No one's been out on the ocean or had any kind of vacation other than a virtual one for almost fifty years! I can't imagine that there won't be many people willing to brave the waters, to really experience the rollicking waves of the sea; I imagine people will be eager. You know–there are always early adopters." Zeejay finished his commentary with a definitive turn back toward his own work-glass. His direct, unfaltering attitude was intact. *Ha*—some things never change.

My next stop was to head up to the executive suite. Like it or not, Allessandro was gonna have to bring me up to speed. I needed details, and in a hurry. These new packages could be a very good thing, or the worst thing that ever happened at the LAB. I was determined to find out. Ironically, as I turned to leave, Jude addressed my exact concern, but once again, deftly avoided my eyes. His voice was a little sheepish.

"Allessandro sent out a public notice about restructuring the organization, revisiting our mission, and expanding the vision of Travelite Global. He announced the appointment of a new head of advertising and made it clear that the changes came as a result of discussions at the highest levels of ADMIN. You weren't here when it happened, but we . . . uh, we figured you knew."

WHAT?!?!? The simmering frustration within me melded with fear and outrage. This was even worse than I suspected.

Whatever has been going on here has been outside of my influence—completely! The challenge at the moment was to stay cool for my staff. I took a breath and composed my inner terrain.

"And the new head? Would you care to fill me in, Jude?"

Zeejay looked up and the two of them exchanged a glance, both sets of eyes displaying a hesitance to speak. My second request was not as polite as the first.

"Gentlemen!"

Zeejay turned quietly back to his work, but Jude finally let his eyes meet mine. Did I detect pity there, or was it masked contempt? I addressed him directly.

"Let me guess, Mr. Lasorum. It's Powers, isn't it?"

Jude's tone was smug as he gave me the news. "None other. Plus, she is now Allessandro's direct report. No longer the plate editor. Ion has been promoted to her old position."

Ion had a stupid look on his face and waved to me from across the room when I glanced his way.

I nodded in acknowledgement and covered my mouth with my hand. Everyone came a little bit closer to where I was standing, but nothing was said. As we hovered around the plate I noticed one other thing, but was careful not to say it out loud. *Something* wasn't right in Denmark. Viddie told me all about that expression, and I know it's the right way to use it now.

First off, all the changes were slated to converge simultaneously. That's weird. This was not set up to roll-out like any other product. Clearly, Jude was correct. We were dealing with the restructuring of the organization, refining the mission, and expanding new horizons. Plus, the actual vacations would take place out on the ocean. I continued to scan the verbiage; my heart now racing. Test the waters. Boats, luxury cabins; Graphite hulls, hermetically sealed from the elements. All the words started to blur together.

Zeejay wondered what sort of schedule we'd be working on. He called the design assistants to his desk and looked at me. "This isn't a rush job, is it, Leeya?"

"I will check with Allessandro. I doubt it, Zeejay. There's much to do and we're just starting."

My mind was swimming with information.

So, the interactive element would draw folks out onto the water again. *Hmmm.* They'd be in safe, pressurized cabins, just like they are in our newest models of cars. *Hmmm.* Luxury vacations; expensive; adventure seekers welcome; something for everyone. Wonderful—it's a new age at TLG—but what's not being said? *Hmmmm.* There's something attached to the name. Why call it the X-Initiative, and does it have something to do with the eradication plan Zeejay mentioned to me last week? Was it connected to the memo I saw just a few weeks ago? No matter the connection, the request was there, clear as day, engraved in glass—this X-Initiative—a permanent inscription, identifying it as part of the highest order of mission.

As I examined the specs more closely, Miss hair-flicker herself walked into the station.

"Oh, *Leeya,* what a good thing you are here! Allessandro just sent down these new design protocols and we couldn't reach you with the P/Z. Bad signal, I guess. How *are* you?"

She shoved a clip-glass into my hands and immediately started pointing out the specifications involving the designs.

"We're calling it *True Travel,* and it will be the premier experience in 21st Century vacations; it will set a benchmark for all future travel and double our bottom line within the first 12 months. The maiden voyage will be scheduled as soon as your team produces the style sheets and galleys."

I was fuming, but responded with all the patience I could muster.

"*True Travel?* Yes, it has a ring to it. Of course, I'll have to go over the budget specs with Allessandro and make sure that the project is in compliance with ADMIN and all government safety protocols. Plus, he hasn't given me the timeline yet."

Powers didn't let up and showed no signs of leaving the room, which was the only thing I wanted her to do.

"Oh *Leeya*—{giggle giggle} that's all taken care of. In fact, they've even begun trial runs out on the Atlantic. ADMIN has fast-tracked the X-Initiative and given Alli *carte blanche* to roll it out. It's going well, and he and I have already knocked out all the specs—they're right there."

Her condescending tone was accompanied by a tight-lipped, sickeningly sweet smile. I wanted to smack her face. She wouldn't stop talking.

"If you guys can just get started sketching out the plans I can begin the marketing strategy to launch MaidenX-One—that's what we're calling the first package. You know, to recognize the fact that it's a first voyage and sort of hint at the idea that it's a voyage on the sea. {giggle}"

I nearly laughed, but was far too angry to find humor in any of it. Instead, I addressed her remarkably astute observation. "Hint? You're *hinting* that it's a maiden voyage? Ms. Powers, I thank you for your information. Please leave this glass-board with me and the team. We'll take it from here; thank you."

"Oh, you are most welcome," she quipped. "But . . . there are just a few more details. At first the MX-One will only draw the super rich and super brave, so don't think about the *hoi polloi* when you are designing. Plus, priority seating will be afforded to women between the ages of 18 and 38. {giggle} ADMIN knows that they have been the most neglected demographic in the new economy, and wants to spread the word through mothers and daughters whose words will be taken with the utmost seriousness. Their early adoption of the product will help create a super-sized response from the next bunch of would-be vacationers. {giggle}"

I jumped right in without a moment's hesitation. "Ms. Powers, that makes no sense. Allessandro would never approve that. He has never been interested in limiting our customer base to one group of people. Our mission is . . ."

"No, no . . . you misunderstand the strategy here. This has nothing to do with limitation, Leeya. It has everything to do with marketing. And, for the record, my dear, the new direction is not really a change in mission at all. Allessandro is referring to is as *the Vision.* It's a new vision for a new era, an era of interaction and renewal. We will teach people how to safely access previously closed aspects of nature, all the while remaining safe from the harm that is out there."

My mind swam with conflicting emotions. I swung from terrible and tragic to hopeful and back again in the course of five seconds. *They wanted to re-introduce reality into the VacPacs, but only a measure, still predicated on the lie that the waters were toxic?* I looked at her and puzzled over her words, as well as my own feelings. She barreled on.

"The key to the Vision is to gain their trust, and we will do it through the most productive demographic group. Think of it: women are the ones who are the most cautious and careful so that makes them the ones who are most beneficial to our efforts. Once they experience the safety and fun of a MaidenX-One vacation, they are sure to come back to City Centre and spread the word. Any trepidation that the rest of the populace might have will be washed away with their *bon mot.* {giggle} Washed away, get it? {giggle}"

"Are you finished, now Ms. Powers? Will you kindly allow me to do my work?"

"Not quite. As you are sketching things out, don't hedge away from the fact that the ocean is, in fact, toxic. That's the beauty of this new venture. Even though the water continues to be a poisonous pit of radiation, our Tek is making it possible to overcome the risk and sail into the sunset. It's going to work out just great, accomplishing some of the LAB'S most cherished and long-held goals. Our compression bubble technology will allow vacationers to really get out on the seas and feel the waves. It will be safe and tidy."

Her cold blue eyes sparkled with a luminosity that almost seemed as though they were made of glass.

I wanted to rip them out.

Day 103—The Reflection

Steely clouds covered much of the expanse yesterday afternoon, and as I looked out upon the horizon, a distant rain sheer made it clear a storm was on its way. I wondered how there could be so much light on either side of the foreboding cumulonimbus. Such a strange sort of parallel picture of what was going on in my life.

Staring far past the choppy waters' edge I stroked Russi's back as she lay sleeping on my chest. A twinge of melancholy wandered its way through my heart and a little lump formed in my throat. Viddie stood silently next to me and it was as if he read my thoughts.

"It's shining just as brightly behind the clouds, baby."

I blinked and paused to glance down at the swirls of dark hair that were beginning to grow in on the crown of our precious little girl's head. She was so comfortable on my bosom. I wish I could be that comfortable in my own skin, but every day the situation seems to grow a little darker—like those clouds—and the possibilities for positive change, more dim. I wandered over to our stoop and he followed me.

"City Centre is a dark place, Vidd—much darker than I ever knew or imagined. You get out in the midst of it a couple times a week when you come in to consult, but I am there much more. I see it and frankly, I'm beginning to hate what I see. We may not have certainty about all that's going down, but one thing is clear—there's an agenda that's been launched that involves continuing the noxious earth deception. Oh, and by the way, did I tell you what they're calling it now?"

He tilted his head toward me and kissed the side of my head. "Nope. MaidenX . . . or Oceanliner Something. That's all I know."

"No, that's the project. Here's the latest buzz. It's called *The Vision*. Yup. MaidenX is part of the overarching change that is now being touted as The Vision. The changes in mission, the new direction in VacPacs, the LAB'S new org chart that doesn't make sense—all of it—it's all wrapped up in what

Allessandro is referring to as 'The Vision' and the phrase seems to be on everyone's lips this week. Makes me want to vomit."

I looked down at the sand and tried to shake off the lousy feeling.

A couple of black flies stung my ankles. As I sat on the stoop and slapped at them, the air became dense. Rain was clearly imminent. I closed my eyes and pictured a sunnier day—one of the many we've had this season.

> *Mmmmmm.*
> *Oh how I love spiaggia!*
> *Can I capture your beauty my beachy friend?*
> *Squeeze precious drops of your magical charm*
> *Into a bottle and carry*
> *You with me*
> *Forever?*
> *Please tell me, yes.*
> *Please tell me, yes.*
> *Please tell me.*

Viddie brushed the sand off my legs and squeezed my knee. He leaned in against me and closed his eyes. The rubble of his unshaven face felt good against my ear. The few words of comfort that he whispered, settled on my soul in such a strengthening way. The flies were now coming in twos and threes and he took it upon himself to begin beating them away from me. One landed on my thigh and he slapped it, dead!

"Oww! That hurt!"

I started laughing when I saw his horrified expression and shook my head at his silliness. His apologies tumbled one into the next until he was beside himself for swatting me.

"I am so sorry, *mi amor*. I would never hurt you. That stupid fly! Do you forgive me?"

Composing myself, I flung my arms around him and let him know all was well. I am increasingly comfortable opening up to him, and I find myself doing it more and more these days. Even when he laughs at me, it's not malicious.

"I love it that you can look at those clouds and somehow are still able to see the light. That's so good. I, on the other hand, am just not there. I feel like we're sinking . . . like I'm sinki . . ."

He didn't let me finish, but immediately leaned closer and enfolded me in his arms.

"Emi-girl, I am with you. I repeat . . . we're in this together and we are not sinking. *You* are not sinking. It's just a low time."

I continued to lightly stroke the baby's head and smiled weakly.

An unmoving, waveless ocean appeared as a vast, deep gray carpet, rolling out quietly to the end of the earth. The cluster of clouds covered the last little bit of sun and I felt a slight chill ripple through me. It was getting ready to pour. He glanced down at Russi, who started to stir and make baby noises. She'd be hungry again soon.

Day 104—The Resolve

Viddie had his feet up on the small table in the lounge, balancing a cup of tea on his leg. I was bouncing Russi on my lap. She had just finished eating and was full of energy. As I filled him in on all the recent happenings, he said very little, pondering, the implications, I suppose. Me? I couldn't stop going over the drama of the day.

"*Ugggh*—it's getting worse, not better. How will she cope with this, Viddie? I mean, we can protect her now, but what about when she is old enough to download the archives; what about when the Medic catches up with us for not bringing her in? And what if they completely cut me out of the loop? I mean, Allessandro could ditch me altogether now that he's got Powers. How will we make ends meet? What if . . ."

He broke into my malaise with assurance and gusto.

"You are all over the place, Emi. I know it's upsetting, but when you get going like this it's hard to come to any conclusions—about anything! Let's take it one subject at a time, okay my love?"

Taking a quick breath, my mind had not stopped racing since that lovely encounter with Powers the morning prior.

"I know. I know. You're right—I *am* all over the place, but this is serious stuff, and I can't help it. There are so many strange details in the way this is all unfolding, hon. Even with Jude. Did I tell you he *finally* acknowledged me? When he told me that I had been replaced by the Powers woman, he actually looked right at me. It was insulting, but he spoke directly to me. This was the first time since our blow-up that anything remotely resembling civility existed between us."

I barely let Viddie get a word in between my many concerns and questions, but his wide, inquisitive eyes let me know he was listening to every word.

"So . . . *what do we do?* How do I respond? Should I . . . what? Stop looking at me like that? I mean, should I confront Allessandro about my suspicions—you know, just storm in there in front of his icon and tell him that I don't like the way he has treated me? Or, should I start with a memo, copy ADMIN and state my concerns, demanding that he keep me informed of the upcoming strategies for advancing the mission? Vidd, *I dunno!* I mean, my title hasn't been taken away; I *am* the VP of Marketing at TLG; my office is intact, and . . . and what is she? What *is* Powers? Who is Margene? They're . . . what? *Clerks!?!?!* They are just glorified clerks. None of this makes any sense! Honey, do you think something sinister is going on in Alessandro's office, or is it just change—change that is leaving me in the dust? I need to know what you think. *Really,* hon. I'm afraid I'm not seeing things as clearly as I should."

The deep blue-gray of his eyes became steely as my questions hung in the air. It was just a few seconds of delay, but his furrowed brows struck me as slightly ominous, and his momentary silence didn't help to alter that opinion. Viddie always has a comeback, but he was soaking in my words, and apparently thinking quite seriously about his response.

The tension I felt rise in my shoulders was visceral. I placed Russi in her cradle and rocked it with my foot while looking straight at him. The feeling of being overwhelmed was becoming nearly as strong as it had been before my leave of absence. Finally, he said something.

"What if the sinister thing is not coming from Allessandro's office at all?"

My puzzled look was greeted with more questions from his side of the room.

"I mean, what if he's not the one with the vision for all this new stuff, Emi? Think about it. It could very well be that *ADMIN* has initiated the agenda. I've been thinking about this for weeks now, and it's not outside the realm of possibility. Maybe the government is using its contract with TLG to mask its goals. Maybe he's just following orders?"

This is not something I could really hear and take in. How could it be? I didn't even know how to respond to him so he just rattled on with his terrible theory.

"I . . . I mean, as one of the largest departments at the LAB, TLG is in a prime position to spread the government's propaganda, and Emi—it could be that Allessandro is just a pawn. Remember, I inferred this a while back? I didn't press it, but I haven't been able to shrug it off either. It's just a thought, but hon—I don't have a good feeling about you tangling with them . . . or Allessandro."

Dear Viddie's God have mercy. Could that even be possible? ADMIN would have to be downright immoral if that were true. But *man alive*—Viddie never worries, and he's rarely so definitive as to imply something like that. Stay away from *tangling with them*? I shot back with my own strong opinion.

"No way. First of all, ADMIN has never demeaned me or thrown any signs of malevolence our way. Even when my parents fled, the authority they bucked was coming from the LAB and TLG. It's Allessandro, Viddie. He's the slimy one."

"Fine. I'm just puttin' it out there, babe."

"Vidd, Alessandro runs the LAB and is the Director of all work coming out of TLG. It's true, he has one goal and that's make lots of money. The man's a mercenary. Money and recognition are his two best friends. If anything sinister is going on, my bet is that it's coming from his office, *not the government*. Really, hon. You know what I've told you about ADMIN. It's the high-minded center of the country, working hard all these years to make sure the populace survive and have a decent life. They are true public servants. Anyway, what would be the reason for it? *No*. No, Vidd, I don't think it's possible. They're clueless to the truth, maybe, but not immoral."

I was confident in my estimation. Something may be askew with ADMIN because they are letting Allessandro get away with ridiculous new hires and promotions, but I know my boss only too well. He's gutless, at heart, and all for himself. This new agenda has got his money-grubbing thumbprint all over it!

Viddie said nothing and stared at me with quiet, probing eyes. Even though I didn't agree with him, his thoughts prompted a bit of my own prognostication. I walked into the kitchen to grab a provisio and he followed. The more I thought about what he said the more disturbed I became.

"Wait. You're saying that Allessandro may not even know about the corruption that he *has* been promoting? That he may indeed be in it all for the money, but that he may be in the dark, too? The problem with that idea is that if it's true, then all along he may . . ."

"Then," Viddie cut in sharply, "all along he's been using your team to promote the lie, even if he doesn't know that the earth is truly safe. What I am saying is that you really should consider the possibility that ADMIN has never been about promoting the 3Ps (or whatever they are) and that all along your boss has been a puppet for the government. If that is so, he's simply been used to propagate the deception and advance ADMIN's agenda. It could even be that Powers and her little tag-a-long have been planted there as agents of distraction. You did say you have no idea where they came from, correct?"

Dead silence.

How could I have known what to say . . . or even think? This is preposterous. *Isn't it?* My mind raced in a thousand directions and started to swirl. What if he was right? If it was true, we're all in trouble—*deep* trouble.

My voice eked out a response and I held my hand to my chest. "You've gotta be wrong about this, hon. I hope you're very wrong. If you're not, what good will *any* of these VacaPaks do? What good are all the archived versions? And, and . . . what good are we even doing there, or *were we ever* doing there, simply promoting a corrosive, maniacal agenda? *Oh Vi . . . .*"

My last words choked in my throat and I couldn't quite finish what I wanted to say. The terrible sense that he was right had been nipping at the heels of my heart from the moment he mentioned the word 'control' weeks ago. A thousand times my mind took me toward that possibility, but I always returned to giving ADMIN the benefit of the doubt. The mission, the Principles, the Golden Triangle—it's where we stand, what this society is built upon, and it's been a high honor to be associated with them.

The idea of a possible breech in integrity started making its way up my esophagus until I was two steps away from the toilet. The fear of it was hidden there in my gut, deeper than I imagined, but it was something that I surely did not want to face. However, when have I ever known my savvy husband to be wrong? Probably, he was precisely, disgustingly, right. I mean, *Viddie* was the one who convinced me that the whole toxic earth story was a myth. The day I saw him dive into Grand Lake I realize toxic earth was a big fat lie, but I couldn't bear to frame it that way. I thought it was probably just ignorance on the part of the government, but he has been way ahead of me on this whole horrible plot and I am just, *just* seeing it now. Oh, how truly despicable, the levels of corruption. *Ugh!* I am sick inside.

We stood alongside our little cupboard and just stared at each other, no longer capable of words. I was actually glad Russi's vibra-sensor went off and hustled into her room. I don't think I could have managed one more minute.

There was still so much we didn't know.

Day 108—The Painter

I love love LOVE the salty freshness of the ocean and its playful antics. One day it's a shining sea of turquoise glass, sublime in its solid stillness; the next, it's acting up, roaring thunderously like an angry bear.

> *The Ocean is upset today*
> > *Pitching a fit*
> > > *With waves*
> > > > *Rolling and rocking in*
> > > > > *Opposing direction.*
> *White foam bursting out of the watery green*
> > *Breaking fast*
> > > *This way*
> > > > *And that.*
> *Indecision reigns in the unrelenting flow*
> > *Of forceful waves*
> > > *Kicking up dirt*
> > > > *And shells*
> > > > > *And seaweed.*
> *She paints a peaceful scene standing on the pier*
> > *that once was there*
> > > *But the ocean won't cooperate.*
> > > > *Its demeanor, raging;*
> > > > > *Its beauty*
> > > > > > *Fierce.*

Wow—the ocean and I are in such *simpatico* today. It's like the water is alive and it's having fun mimicking my soul. *HA!* Viddie's word, but so fitting.

###

These weekly alerts from Medic's office are really stressing me! *UGH.* They are a constant heckle. With every reminder, Viddie and I grow in our suspicion that we cannot trust our little one with them, not even for the required injections. It's true, Medic helped me through the pregnancy, making sure my own vitamin supplements were regular, and in spite of the fact that we never made it to the clinic for the delivery, his initial alerts and reminders were quite reassuring. Why is there such urgency for

Russita to come in for her shots? On top of that, the importance of inoculating against diseases that have long been gone from the face of the earth seems uncalled for and—to my mind—even dangerous. What's the pressure?

I don't want them poking my baby.

Day 109—The Nail

Memo 23x action. Halt. In attendance without consequence:
M. Rugor Allessandro
Monica Veslie Powers
Margene Subpowers
Jude Lasorum
Zeejay Katz
Ion Station
Memo 23x abx. Halt. Absent without consequence; final warning: Emilya Hoffman Bowes Florencia.

This was the message waiting in my cache when I diamond-dusted yesterday. Looks like another nail in the coffin of my illustrious career.

Used to be that I was the one sending these memos and there was never a need to get everyone on board. My team was top notch. So disciplined, dedicated, and willing to work hard. And, oh—*we produced such stellar work!* Now, ever since they started micro-managing the department it feels like a hammer's coming down on my head! Every other day or so there's something—some nettling need or requirement that they ask for. It's so aggravating.

I brought him his cup of vanilla chamomile and plopped down on the lounge, not intending to rant about work or even bring it up. That didn't last long.

"*What* on earth is going on with these people? Since when has attendance on First Call become part of the daily protocols? Now ADMIN gets involved in daily corporate culture? This threat of consequences is just absurd! Tell me it's not absurd!"

"You shouldn't let yourself get so worked up, honey. The memo probably doesn't even pertain to you. Like you reminded me the other day, you're still a VP. For goodness sake, they're probably just talking about the staff in the Outer Station. They wouldn't dare come down on you, baby."

Viddie's reaction didn't help much. He still doesn't understand the serious nature of ADMIN protocols. I tried to set him straight.

"*Not me*? My name is right there on the memo. I know you didn't see it, but it was right there under the heading. It read: Absent without consequence; **Final Warning**: Emilya Hoffman Bowes Florencia. *Vidd, they never do that.* Not in all my time at the LAB. NEVER. Now, all of a sudden, they are going to mete out consequences? What is Allessandro thinking? He never used to be this way. I don't think I have a choice, anymore. I'm gonna have to be on First Call every day. Things are getting too crazy at the LAB. I'm gonna have to stay connected when I go to sleep so I don't miss it."

"We'll be okay. It'll be okay, Emi. I'll help with the baby. You'll get used to being up early again and . . . we'll just go to sleep earlier. We'll find a way. You'll see."

Day 110—The Dazzle

Tiny specs of morning light refracted on the water. The ocean was alive, a dancing body of thousands of precious gems! A dazzling display of splendorous light—that's what it looked like to my eyes this morning—a true diamond day, but only if I directed my eyes toward the sun. The scene was so bright I found myself squinting. Mmmm. Diamonds dancing on the water. I'll take that picture with me and remember it forever!

It was almost as if Viddie read my mind—ha—but I know he's not connected through the tek.

"I know you are in your glory here, *mi amor.*"

I looked over at him as he tied his sneakers, and smiled. "Yes, you know me, Mr. Florencia. You certainly do."

Yesterday's high tide and strong wind made it impossible for him to run close to the water, so he did his morning jog up along the promenade instead of on the sand. He gave both Russi and me a quick kiss and once he helped us settle in, he took the stairs behind us two at a time to reach the old boardwalk deck. I got situated quickly and started to write. What a gorgeous day!

The push and pull of a breezy day stirs inside me,
Provoking squalls (and other things),
the least of which is a joy
that reminds me I am alive.
It messes with my hair and coaxes water from my eyes.
It sets my feet on ground that is uneven
and
a bit precarious.
I want to run for cover but choose to stand out in the elements,
Naked and unswerving.

Rain, pelting in on my inner terrain,
Does not let up;

unrelenting.
It's wet, but strangely alluring;
Not uncomfortable, as one might imagine.
In fact, it is somehow refreshing.
Why do I feel more alive than I ever have
Even though everything is crashing down on me?

No more running for cover at the first sign of dark skies.
No more confounding myself with the countless whys.
There may be more options than I currently see
Hey—I could even outrun the rain
Maybe, as long as my heart stays strong enough.

Day 111—The Change

There's a soft breeze coming off the ocean today. It's blowing back my hair and providing some relief from the sticky July heat and the grim awareness of all the change that is in the air. It'll be autumn soon. The season will shift from bright sunshine and sand on my toes to more and more overcast skies and socks on my feet. I don't know why that makes me a little sad, but I do know this: we will not forsake the beach altogether. We'll simply have to bundle up with our jackets and scarves when we come down here. *Spiaggia* will not be the same as the winter months unfold, but then again, I'm not quite the same either. Been thinking a lot about that lately.

Change
I'm not interested in any more change.
I wish it would stay summer.
In fact, just thinking about the coming months
makes me grimace,
shudder.
Life—as close to perfect as it's ever been—is not static.
Just when I can breathe and things seem stable
there's a sign of change.
A brown leaf wafts carelessly to the ground,
reminding us all that things don't stay green forever.
I'd just like to see everything stay
exactly as it is today.
Did I say that already?
Ah—but I digress.
Today, the
Gentle breeze
cooing baby
devoted man
brings me joy.
—what's the plan?
Rolicking seas
Sandy sand.
Dancing waves

Summer jogs
My handsome man.
Breezy beach walks don't evaporate.
Stay.
Wait.

Day 112—The Foreboding

"Holy Cow!" Viddie's voice contained more than a measure of alarm. His bassy intonation ticked up a bit in pitch and mingled with a type of excitement I hadn't heard in him since Liam and Harold hauled that ten point elk into camp last summer.

Plumes of black smoke arose in the distance, emerging, it seemed, from the very edge of the earth. We both looked at each other, utterly befuddled, and watched as dark columns rose steadily on the horizon. Neither of us said a word, but together began walking down the sand to the foot of the water. The smoke was thick—unlike anything I had ever seen. Then, breaking the silence, he grabbed my hand and squeezed it tightly. I detected a note of dread in his voice, something I had never heard in the entire time I have known him.

"In all the months we've been coming down to the beach I've never seen anything like that! There's never any action on the ocean, let alone something like *that.*"

Neither of us had. The smoke looked like neatly symmetric columns of charcoal—rising straight upward, perhaps 75 feet. He held his hand as a visor against his forehead and squinted in the bright morning sun; I looked on with similar awe and clung a bit closer.

"What do you think, Vidd?"

My husband raised his eyebrows and shrugged his shoulders while scanning the breadth of the ocean before us, searching, it seemed, for any other signs of disturbance on the great Atlantic.

"I honestly do not know, Emi. That looks like a forest fire— *nah*—worse than a forest fire, not something that could rise from the ocean. Something's burning out there alright—looks like the fire is right on the surface."

I bundled baby girl in her swaddle and gave a quick check to make sure that she was still breathing. My habit of checking her like this is probably a bit over-the-top, but sometimes she's quiet for so long, I worry. Her papa leaned in and smiled softly as we momentarily looked away from what was happening on the water.

"It's strange, isn't it, that we can have such a sense of joy in the very same moment as worry?" Viddie nodded toward the rising smoke again and continued his thought. "They're both mysteries—that, out there, is a mystery to us but the feelings attached to it are quite different than the feelings we attach to the mystery of creating a brand new human being together, isn't it?"

I could hardly take my eyes from the spectacle and wasn't really focused on what he said, but he continued as my mind considered the possibilities.

"I also find it strange that you've been talking about an oceanliner vacpac at work and now there's . . . this right out there. Too much of a coincidence." He motioned toward the horizon, once again acknowledging the disturbance on the water.

"More than strange, Vidd. It's got to be part of the early trials Powers mentioned, but it looks like something has gone very wrong."

"Yeah. It almost looks like something exploded. Maybe part of the compression equipment? I really don't know." He slipped his arm around me as he spoke, and rested his hand on the small of my back. Neither of us could take our eyes off the spectacle. His gaze continued straight forward, and as he looked toward the water he squeezed my shoulder and made a motion to leave.

"I'll tell you this, Emi, *if it's not* connected to this new vision thing at the LAB, it's a real anomaly. All this talk of MaidenX interactive vacations and now we see some action out on the open sea? It's weird, for sure, and . . . I don't like it. Are you just about ready to go, love?"

"If you are, I guess," I scrunched my chin down on my chest and gave a little peek. "She's still sound asleep on me. You know how this salt air just knocks her out."

"Yeah, but that smoke is bound to waft this way. Do you feel the breeze blowin' off the water?"

I pointed my face upward in attempt to agree, but didn't have a clue what direction it was coming from. "Uh. Not really. It's really subtle, Vidd. You're better than I am at gauging the weather and movement of the air. It's hard to take my eyes away from that mess out there. I mean, it's an ugly sight, but I'm curious, and I don't think that smoke is gonna reach us too soon. But if you're ready to go, let's go."

He squeezed my hand and continued to gaze toward the horizon. "I'm not sure why, but it *is* a bit ominous."

My eyes seemed glued to the plumes of smoke. I acknowledged his comment as we both continued to stare. "*Mmmm*. And a little bit scary, too."

He moved his hand gently and let it rest on the back of my head, and then tilted my gaze toward the old pilings just south of where we were standing.

"So fix your eyes there, *mi amor*. That's the picture you want to take home with you today, eh?"

The tops of the old bulwark poked out of the water, but just barely. They were just outside the sightline of the smoky spectacle, and if I looked that way my gaze was free from the mess on the horizon. As the water undulated it revealed only about six or ten inches of each pole. Sometimes the waves would swell and completely cover them. I wonder how far down into the ocean floor they went, and who installed them. My eyes followed the row of poles out as far as I could see until there were no more. Maybe there were more; maybe they were submerged. I dunno. The two dozen or so of these leftover reminders of summer days gone by intrigued me. They looked almost like they were soldiers, standing guard, making sure the water would not completely engulf the beach, even at high tide.

Motioning toward the horizon, he continued to comfort me with his encouraging perspective, guiding my sight in the other direction toward the spacious open waters of the ocean I have so come to love.

"Whatever's happening out there, this is the picture you fill your mind with and the one you'll share with our little *Bellini* in years to come, yes? C'mon—we'll figure out what the heck's happening out there later. Let's get her home before she wakes up."

Hard to believe our precious Russita Bellini is nearly three months old. Those tender cheeks and tiny pink lips are so very precious.

My goodness, what did I ever do to be so blest?

Day 113—The Denial

The unhurried July breeze brushed lightly against my face yesterday. The sun was soft and welcoming, but the unsightly spew of coal-colored smoke that baffled us continued to be the centerpiece of our conversation. Chock up another anomaly in a whole string of strange, nonsensical happenings these days. I mean, what could be out there burning? The government doesn't allow anyone out on the ocean and hasn't for over forty years. It's got to be part of the expanded vision. It's days like this that I begin to feel rocked in my resolve to stay and make a difference. Especially lately, when I lay my head on the soft pillow I fall into such deep sleep, and I dream of the sweet night jasmine that grows in June outside Grand'Mere's earth shelter. What a difference from black smoke, mysterious agendas and . . . and all the other weirdness we're experiencing here.

Oh, how goaded am I by the need to be with him *here*. Here, in the midst of the city—but, *arrrrgggghhh*—I also have this desire to be free—up there, around family and friends who value what we value, and it's not going away! As much as I trust him, I clearly cannot risk talking with him about it. He'll take my angst as ambivalence and maybe get his hopes up, and well . . . I can't let that happen. Surely it would be too hard for him to know how much I dream of FRANCO, but—*oh-oh-oh*—the memories are so real I can almost smell them!

Then there are days when I wake up and all seems right in the world. I walk around in a rich, deep-seated conviction that there is a purpose for my journey—that my work means much more than just the helpful pay and comfort of convention. Then there are the middle days—days I have no such peace and am balled up in a tangled string of confusion. I feel like my silver necklace; sometimes, when I go to put it on it's in a ridiculous mess at the bottom on my jewelry box. When I finally get the entire tangle out I can wear it, but only until next time when it's all balled-up again! More and more lately, I feel like I'm being pulled back and forth between a rush of competing emotions and desires.

So much of the impetus to stay at the LAB involves the desire to make a difference. Not a name for myself—no—that's not even an issue, but I do want Russita to grow up in a place where she can be proud of her mother—where she can look at the world around her and know that it is a better place when she is an adult than when I was a child. This hope rings through my spirit. And it's maddening, because I have no idea how I even know that I have a spirit, but I know that my soul aches and my soul sings and my soul has its own little personality, but also that there is something deeper than these things—something within me that is alive and full of passion. I know that now. I see it in Viddie. I see it in Russi. I'm not sure how I see it, but I do. It cannot be measured and it is by no means tangible, but I do know this—it is the deepest part of me. I am more than who I thought I was.

The pact that Viddie and I made to keep FRANCO our secret was made before ever walking back into the LAB, but . . . I can't help but wonder if maybe one day the public here will *get it*, and people will branch out beyond the walls of their grey little domiciles. Could they be persuaded to live, breathe, and communicate with one another again outside the walls of their carefully assigned amygdale? *Maybe.* Heck, maybe FRANCO could even become the glowing example of real life and community once folks start to get more familiar with the earth and sea? *It could happen.*

He, of course, believes that it's only in communities of resistance, like FRANCO, that folks find true freedom from the oppression that technology brings. Why? Well, Russa would say (and I know Viddie would agree) that the tek is never neutral—that it is laden with its own values, and these values are not at all favorable to human beings. While I still struggle with that whole idea, I do find moments when my heart is softened to it, because, well . . . *ugh* . . . I've been wrong about so much before, and it's making me think twice about my own hard and fast beliefs.

Man alive, is all of life a struggle?

Work was my life, but now I can feel it slipping away. It's as if there's this big chunk of me that's being set out on the sea, in a lonely boat, never to return. Okay, so I'm being dramatic, but that's how it feels! If they really don't let me function with the autonomy to which I am accustomed, direct the teams, and make the high level decisions that have long been within my purview, well—I just don't know. I don't know how I will go on. I can't imagine how I will be able to function that way.

Yesterday Viddie and I discussed the situation at length and I found myself shaking my head slowly as I listened to his response. He made some good points, and as always he was a good sounding board, but his perspective seems much more conclusive, especially when we moved from the prospect of my continued employment at the LAB to the change in culture there. This all led to grappling anew with the questionable nature of the new mission.

We sat in the lounge for a long time after Russi fell asleep, and our discussion was not only enlightening but more than a little disturbing. As usual, I started up with work stuff.

"Don't you think it's rather odd that TLG is being asked to come up with designs for a new water venture and we just happen to see some subversive-looking action out there . . . on the water?"

My question seemed normal enough to me. I had been thinking about the anomaly we recently observed and have come to the conclusion that the plume of black smoke was definitely no coincidence, especially in the aftermath of the big pow-wow with Ms. Powers at TLG. However, I did not anticipate the ensuing events. Although my question was innocent enough, it seemed to produce a firestorm in my husband. His response seemed like no response at all, and it really threw me.

"You just aren't getting it, Em. I don't understand why you don't get it. There is definitely something aloft that is going to make it very hard for us to continue to invest in that organization. You need to reckon with that. Months ago I made my feelings about your boss clear. I don't trust him, not a bit. And now, we've been dancing around these latest developments for weeks. It's time to reassess."

"Vidd! What are you talking about? I know you have no use for Alessandro, but ADMIN's reach goes far beyond what that man can do. I recognize that there are many things that are wrong about that place, but I'm simply asking about the plume of smoke we saw and the expanded vision at the LAB—the vision that I am still a part of. Hon, I still have hope to make my ideas work, and I am definitely interested in your take on the whole thing, but if there is something subversive going on we can get to the bottom of it and maybe . . . just maybe *TrueTravel* will be the first step toward getting the world back to appreciating nature."

My question seemed innocent enough, but as soon as the words escaped my lips, Viddie just about came out of his skin. I really just wanted to know what he thought.

"Are you nuts?!?! Emilya Hoffman Bowes *Florencia*! The writing is on the wall—this government is up to no good! We just talked about this less than two weeks ago but I don't think you listened to a word I said! Now, I have followed you to this place and fully intended to make a go of it here in spite of the fact that it feels more like an alternative universe to me than just a different part of the country, but I cannot sit by and let our family get sucked into this vortex of oppression and deceit."

Yikes! *Intended*? That's sounds past tense. Where-oh-where is my tender, understanding man when I need him? He continued to give me his unfiltered opinion, and I must say, I'm tempted to call it a rant!

"Emi, let's look at it. First you get threatening memos from the Medic. Then the entire company re-structures itself leaving you outside the loop of the decision-making process. To make matters worse, they have reworked the government's mission statement, which wasn't terribly sturdy to begin with! Then, may I remind you, you caught wind of an eradication strategy that involves an X initiative AND we saw a great billow of black smoke rising from the ocean. *Put it together, babe!* Stuff is going down, and it's not good."

His rant was as close to yelling as one might get without calling it that. His assumptions and assertions were clearly well thought-out, but he may or may not be right . . . I don't know for sure. Neither of us have the entire picture. One thing *I do know* is he is quite perceptive and he's not an alarmist.

I eked out a response, probably more timidly than he's used to, but I was not at all sure that his barking would stop.

"You seem to be quite sure of your conclusions, Vidd. Uh, how are you putting this all together? Is there some connection between these anomalies that I have missed?"

He came and sat down next to me, bringing his voice and his demeanor into greater calm.

"Emi, you are the brightest woman on this planet, and with all due respect, I cannot believe you are not putting these pieces together yourself. Think of it: the MaidenX, Maiden Voyage . . . burning . . . eradication. What does X stand for, anyway?"

"Well, Xtreme Vaca, right? I mean, what else would it be?"

"You know I'm working with even less detail than you are, but have you ever noticed that there are about five guys to every woman around here? Where are they? Where are all the women? And by the way, where are the girls—the little girls? Why aren't there more babies around here? Just what are they trying to eradicate? I mean, maybe it's a longshot, but don't women have an extra x chromosome?"

I opened my mouth, but nothing came out. My tongue went completely dry. I tried to swallow but felt like I couldn't breathe. What was he saying? What does this mean? MaidenX . . . X . . . X . . . chromosome? Is that what he's saying? Oh dear Viddie's God have mercy. My husband continued to expound.

"What I do get is that there is some sort of chromosomal connection between the OLSM and its effectiveness with the public. You yourself said something about it the day we found Cloudland. Remember? The whole way up past the ridge you were explaining how you made the connection between OLSM and your P/Z 1000 because women don't have the Y chromosome; it somehow makes it easier to sequester the various regions of the brain, wasn't that it? Something like . . . the connection worked more easily with women because they have the XX chromosome? Hon, I don't understand it at all, but I do remember you talking about that connection, right?"

"Well, yeah . . . but . . . what does that have to do with the eradication plan? I mean, sure, the 'X' in MaidenX could be a signifier of the extra X chromosome, but I can't see what it would . . . or how it would have anything to do with . . . with the eradication plan."

"How are you *not* getting it? It's time to revisit our decision to live here. There's something heinous going on in the upper ranks of your company and I don't want to stick around to find out where *this vision* is going."

"I'm sorry. I'm not following what you're saying. You are being irrational. This is too outlandish. What you are inferring would never be tolerated by ADMIN. I'm sorry hon. Your imagination is . . . running wild."

Day 115—The Antidote

Poetry helps me breathe.
Poetry lets me stop.
Poetry reminds me there is something more to my life—
More than what I can accomplish in a day.
Why isn't poetry part of our early learning initiative?
Why has it suffered such remarkable defeat?
Why are poets no longer a welcome part of our world?
Poetry helps us live
Poetry helps us breathe
Poetry helps us become
Poetry helps.

Hours—sometimes days—go by before I can return to this journal. I can hardly believe it's been nearly a week. *I miss my writing!* Life with baby girl is so wonderful, but so demanding. I'm lucky if I get to the washroom some days. *It's crazy!* Because of it, I've had to give in and connect my OLSM here at the flat, in spite of the fact that we were going to stay tek-free while at home. I mean, the simplest daily hygiene regiment has become a luxury, let alone finding time to eke out a few words on a page. But this week I am determined to make more regular entries.

The benefit of connecting has made life a tad easier again at the LAB. Now that I am more regularly on First Call, at least I know what's going on and don't have to worry about being left out of the loop. In the meantime, what I heard yesterday almost blew my mind. Just by connecting with my P/Z more I've overheard some of the chatter at the LAB about the new direction, but yesterday was a doozy. Several conversations I tapped into have been peppered with language that defies explanation, unless, of course, you take into consideration the control theory Viddie and I have been agonizing over. They're not talking about it that way, but there are a couple of things that seemed loosely tied together, like the MaidenX One voyage and that new extermination initiative—I'm guessing that's what the X thing is, but I've only caught bits and pieces of it. What's struck me as really strange is that when I tried to discuss it with Allessandro I've gotten nowhere. He has deftly been avoiding my chime, leaving only the acceptable away-message. Even yesterday when I went in to see him, engagement at his icon was impossible. The wall was dark and the shade was pulled. I did catch a glimpse of Margene, however, who was busy at the outer station glass-board, inputting data. I think it may very well be the first time I've ever seen her without Powers by her side.

One of the great things about the public access feature of OSLM is that nothing is really said in private. I've always thought that this is one of the greatest aspects of the Tek. Nothing's secret. Everything's up front. It's common knowledge that anything communicated within the walls of our amygdala can (and will) be heard by everyone . . . that is, by everyone who wants to listen in. Fact is, most of us don't listen in, and I'm convinced that's probably because in order to make it work without catapulting the nervous system into extreme overload, emotions are leveled off by sequestering the neural information that spreads throughout the limbic system.

Unfortunately, now that I see the broader ramifications of this feature of our communication system, I'm concerned. Instead of a real benefit, I think the lack of emotional energy actually hurts more than helps us. While it surely tamps down jealousy, envy, and strife, it also sort of numbs us to love and friendship.

In any case, it was at the precise moment that I queued into Margene's conversation with Queen Powers that the little clone rattled off some figures then sent the information upstairs. Powers herself was nowhere to be seen but I could recognize that tinny, syrupy tone anywhere. I heard the data-strategizer uploading the new configurations to the general archives and listened to the program as it began integrating this X thing through all the old files. Clearly, this is important information; I should know about it already, but truth-be-told, because I have kept myself a bit out of the loop, I have some catching up to do. One thing is clear: It's probably time that I involve myself more fully in the daily communications at the LAB. I might not care quite as much anymore, but I don't want to see things swirling out of control, and that's what it's beginning to feel like.

Day 119—The Quest

The steady, sensuous wind quietly rushes through long, billowy grasses this afternoon. Being here always helps me air out my head. Plus, each time we come I take notes and observe things I can add to the Deep Water/BeachXtreme Vaca, like this maroon-hued seaweed, a tangled mess of wet vegetation. It's shiny and got all sorts of interesting little shells and stones caught up in its mass. I have such fun collecting new images and finding new textures to input into our database. It's sad to think that those new VacPacs may not ever get produced. So much time and thought have already gone into them.

It's hard to write while she is laying on me, but actually it's not a whole lot different than when I was still preggers. She's still right in that spot . . . snuggled tightly, nestled right there between me and my pen. This child sleeps so soundly on my chest, even more so than in her cradle. She has no clue about all the pain and treachery that is swirling around her life. And all I want to do is sit here and drink in the glory of this gorgeous summer day . . . and watch her grow strong and confident of her place in the world.

The sound of the air moving through the dunes is a perfect counterpoint to the rhythmic breakers, sneaking up on the shore, hitting the sand hard with their insistent song of the sea. I am intoxicated by the lavish grandeur of the beach. It never gets old. Ah, and the air! The air is especially fragrant today. Viddie's only on the second leg of his five miles. He just raced off to the water's edge where the hard, wet sand makes jogging a little easier. I'm content to sit here and watch his daily regiment—*ha*—happy just kicking back against the bulkhead with my journal and the baby.

I really thought we would see her frolic through the sand, find her own precious pieces of sea glass, and run into the waves with salt water spraying all over her face . . . one day. I really thought we could make a difference; we could help raise awareness about the beauty of the earth. Inspire change. My strong belief has been that my parents simply had a falling-out with the LAB that the head honchos back then made some very poor decisions and lost my parents' trust in the crossfire. Little did I realize that the corruption was ongoing. Giving them a second chance seemed only right. Sadly, the breach of trust that has been nipping at the edges of my heart for months is something that I must reckon with, but it makes me exceedingly sad.

I did not make room in my head for the possibility that Russita would not be welcome in this world.

Day 120—The Opening

A violent gust of wind struck the side of our building and shook the entire flat. Although it was only 2 p.m., the small slit of a window in our kitchen-space was completely black. The storm was so violent it seemed that the next bolt of lightning might shake the cup right out of my hand. I pattered softly to the lounge, teacup in hand, and sat down gingerly so I would not spill anything. Viddie sat nonplussed in the vertical chair, playing with the small table puzzle that I ordered for him from HQ. He was mesmerized by the puzzle, but I wanted to talk.

"What is going on out there? A couple of weeks ago there was that menacing plume on the water and now today, a mini-hurricane! Vidd?!?!!"

A sudden, screeching-sort-of-sound penetrated the walls of our flat, coming from the bleak weather outside and interrupted my sentence. It didn't sound like anything I had ever heard.

"That's just the thunder and lightning out there, *mi amor.* You've heard it plenty of times; a summer storm, right? I'm sure you have them here, too." He smiled in that semi-mocking way that I've come to know as a regular feature on his face. He does love to tease me, especially when it comes to that growing swath of earthy knowledge that has been so foreign to my life.

"Don't be a smart aleck. Of course we have storms, but this one is particularly violent. Seriously . . . admit it; it's not a regular storm."

"Yeah, you're right. It is more intense than we've seen here, but it happens. That's nature. Sometimes lightning hits a tree or connects with the elements in a way that creates harsh sounds. It's really okay. I've heard plenty of stuff like that back home. I'm gonna get us another cuppa. Do you want chamomile again? You'll see, a storm like this can actually be nice and cozy."

"A second cup of tea sounds great, hon. Thanks!"

As he headed toward the kitchen space, he lifted the cup up from my hand and kissed me on top of the head. I definitely feel rattled today. Not sure what it is, but it's more than the crazy weather out there. Russi's got a low grade temp and she's been coughing, and . . . ugh, there's no sign that the drama swirling around the LAB is gonna stop anytime soon. In fact, I feel so rattled I think I could be persuaded to up and leave today . . . yup—actually pack up for good and go. But that, of course, will never happen. I will not give up on my world and run to the hills and hide like my family. Won't do it. *I can't.*

"Viddie?"

Where is he?

My anxiety level heightened and I called out a bit louder just as he was walking through the door.

"Vidd?!?!?!"

"Honey, I'm right here! What on earth are you yelling about? You want the baby to wake up?"

"She's fine, hon. She's due to wake up anyway. Do you hear what's going on outside?" I made a face at him and accepted the honey chamomile with gusto. "Boy, I needed this. Thanks."

Viddie sat down next to me on the lounge and toasted his mug against my cup with a choppy little *clink!*

"I know. I could tell. Why are you so jittery? You've been in storms before." He leaned over and gave me a quick peck and then plopped back into the sofa beside me. Tea spilled onto my saucer.

"Oh, hon . . ." I exhaled deeply and leaned back against the lounge. "It's just weighing on me—all this."

"Tell me, Baby. I'm here." He took a big gulp of his tea and slurped at the faint residue of honey along the side of the mug. I smiled and shook my head. He wasn't trying to be comical, but uhhhh . . . what a sight. I decided to ignore it and pick up where my heart left off.

"I've got a question that keeps plaguing me lately. It's only one question, but it's a big one. You wanna help me out?"

"I'm ready as ever!"

"Vidd, what are we going to do about the threatening memos from Medic? I know I'm changing gears here, but really not subjects. They are insisting that we bring her in . . . that she is long overdue for her first month's injections. They're saying that immunization is not an option, and lately . . . lately, with all this stuff going on I'm beginning to realize that ADMIN'S agenda may be far worse than simply trying to control the way things run. I think the plot is more pernicious. Yeah, that's what

I see—something ugly is fomenting and . . . and . . . *damn*—I don't want to be a part of it."

I snuggled Russi more tightly and cringed to think about the consequences of non-compliance. I could lose my job. No job, no status. It's shrinking already. I can feel my creds diminish as Powers gets closer to the boss. These concerns have been building up and I am feeling increasingly backed into a corner. Lately I've been feeling that all we have left here is but a vain effort to create something impossible—a subversive undercurrent that can only mean more control is coming to this once-great land. It's difficult to understand . . . heck, even my own transformation is hard for me to understand, but among the many things I do not know, I do know this: There is another way. There is an alternative to the madness being propelled onto all of us here. Yes, it is an alternative life style, but actually it is much more of an alternative consciousness. If they would let us be . . . just be who we are and not push us to conform, I might stay. But today . . . all I need is a feather to come float past me and brush my shoulder—the gentlest of nudges to be on our way.

Day 126—The Protocols

Viddie crossed the room and peeked into Russi's cradle where she continued to sleep soundly and then came back over and sat down next to me. News of the impending nuptials coupled with our invitation to be a part of it all has been the subject of our conversation for days. We have to say yes. If we don't participate we will pay the price, of that I'm sure. What that price actually is remains unknown, but do we want to take the chance?

So much is changing and it's happening right before our eyes. Never before have I felt so powerless to influence them. Every other day or so, there seems to be a new tweak to the protocols or a new strategy or a new *requirement.* The latest thing involves the baby. I mean, she's our child, and now with ADMIN's newly established policy about requiring *au pairs*. Ugh. How on earth will we be able to avoid this intrusion into our lives? I am sick over it!

"Have you thought about using your position to demand entrance into the development meetings?"

"Oh hon, we're so far past that. One would think that I should be part of policy-making, but I seem to have lost so much cache in the events of the last 18 months. Just the very act of marrying and having a child seems to have put me in a lesser position. It's like my credibility has come down a few pegs or something. No, we've got to come up with something else. For starters, how do we counteract the lessening of my role?"

"Should I make a ruckus?"

Day 127—The Pondering

"Vidddddd?" I called to him as the baby rocked back and forth in her little swing. She seemed so content, so utterly unaware of the possible peril we were facing. He didn't answer me. Is it possible he didn't hear me? I mean, I yelled. Where is he? I glanced briefly at our contented little one and breezed into the lounge to find him.

"There you are. Why didn't you respond when I called? Hon?"

Viddie looked up from the paper he was engrossed in and smiled, unaware that I was calling.

"Hey babe—sorry. I was absorbed. Did you take a look at any of the things we found in LJ's attic last time we scavenged? This is incredible. Look, it's an old report from pre-Devastation America from a paper called *The Times*. You've gotta have a look."

I took hold of the yellowed paper and scanned words in courier type that seemed archaic and far out of touch with the culture in which we lived. There was a black and white image at the top of the page with a crowd of people gathered around a giant clock. They were packed into an outside square that had balloons and confetti swirling around their heads and through the air. I looked up at Viddie with a quizzical expression and shrugged my shoulders.

"Yeah, what's this? What am I looking at?"

He came around to view it with me and pointed at the far side of the awkwardly large page. At first I missed it, but there at the right hand corner of a page entitled *Entertainment News* was a headline that read *Central College to Host Winner of Texas Teen Contest*. There was a faded image of a man with a little brown pony tail and an over-sized hat. He was handsome, but I still didn't see what Viddie was pointing out. He looked at me and was smiling from ear to ear.

"Look more closely, Em. Look at his shoulders and his nose and the way he's holding that guitar. And the hat!"

"That's the hat he gave you!!!! I see it, oh my goodness, Vidd. That's LJ!"

The small write-up spoke of him as the young Mr. Moorehouse, winning with a song that charmed the judges and garnered the respect of the whole Texas town. He was awarded 1,500 dollars and a chance to travel to New York for a national competition.

"Oh my, my, my. *Our LJ,* Viddie. Oh my GOODness. How could we have missed this?"

Viddie squeezed my hand and nodded with a chuckle. "I can picture him right now—tattered eye patch, his grayish-white mustache twittering . . . *mmm.* What a guy."

"Truly, what a guy. And that painful amble of his never stopped him from sharing a song or bringing a smile to all of us, did it? That bearish laughter and sweet music is something that will stay with me forever."

What fun reminiscing about our old friend. I was caught up in a reverie, daydreaming about Stone Camp when Viddie broke out in song:

> Love you forever and for-ev-er;
> Love you with all my heart.
> Love you whenever we're together;
> Love you when we're a part.
> And when at last I find you . . . [3]

Day 130—The Information

My hands shook as I ran up the stairs. I don't remember ever feeling as unsteady, not since first finding Grand'Mere's handwritten letters in the upstairs cubby. By the time I reached the door of our flat I was a bit breathless. The tea kettle was whistling and there was an empty mug on the tiny counter space. Viddie walked into the kitchen, took a look at me and immediately came over to hug me hello.

"What's going on, *mi amor*? What's wrong?"

"Not sure, hon. Something about the mission and the Principles." I was still trying to catch my breath.

"She never said Allessandro's name, but I did hear them say 'he' a couple of times. I think she was referring to him, but I can't be sure. I couldn't listen long. It was Margene and she was being careless with her tek. It felt too creepy and I didn't want her to know I was listening. I disconnected immediately."

"Whoa, slow down, Kimosabe. Here, take this tea—it sounds like you need it more than I do. Come sit down."

"I . . . okay. Whew—it's just so off the wall. Hon, what I heard was . . . so weird. I can't put the pieces together. I probably should've just kept listening, but I didn't want her to see my name in the queue."

"I don't blame you for disconnecting, babe. Did you see anyone else while you were there?"

"Ugh—how'd you guess?"

"Uh . . . I'm afraid you have that 'I-had-a-run-in-with-Powers' look on your face, my love. I can see that look comin' for a mile."

"*Ugh.* Well, I guess I can't hide it, but . . . where is baby girl; is she asleep? I'll fill you in after I see Russi. I miss that little angel face."

When I returned to the lounge Viddie was waiting and had placed both mugs on the small table by our sofa.

"She's still asleep. Looks like an angel. Vidd, she's getting so big!"

"I know. She's really growing well. This is her second nap, by the way. She did well this morning. Now, tell me what's up. From the beginning."

"Okay. So, I was still connected and busy reformatting draft 34F of the Nature Package. Totally in the zone. That's when Margene's name flickered. It was just a flicker, but I saw that she was delivering a communiqué and I thought, why not? Nothing wrong with listening in, right? Everything that goes on in the LAB is supposed to be common knowledge."

"Yeah, but we know it's not. There are secrets lurking all around that place."

"That's the thing, Vidd. Margene was talking to Powers through the tek and that's when I heard it. It was the X-Initiative again. Viddie, this 'X' thing—it's being used for some waste elimination project. When I heard the two of them discussing it the word 'women' was uttered in the same sentence as 'waste.' This time there was no encryption involved. I *heard* them. They were in the executive queue—must be a new frequency—which is why I only got bits and pieces. The meaning was muffled but the words I could make out were crystal clear: ocean . . . black plumes . . . dispensable resources. Population explosion. Women. This is getting serious. I know it sounds crazy but I'm beginning to think that your hunch about some sort of plan to thin out the population of . . . of . . . females is not fiction! Viddie, could it really be?"

I put my hands to my head and took a deep breath. A sip of the chamomile was quite necessary because at that moment I could barely keep my thoughts straight.

Viddie drew me to him quickly. His eyes were wide but full of serenity.

"What else did you hear?"

"Beyond what I told you, it was really just the feeling I got from their tone. Couple that with the fact that there are already only about 1 woman to every 10 men left–I just never put two and two together. Even when you were talking about the name of the X-Iniative and made the connection with MaidenX—I didn't see it. I've been blind to it! Hon, I think the X-Initiative has to do with the extra X chromosome!"

"Emi, I don't care about being right; I just want all the details. We can't go on allowing ourselves to be blind. What else did Powers say?"

"Well, not much, at least not of any significance. When I tried to wrangle more info out of her she clearly diverted and started rattling on about her wedding plans and the muslin dresses she ordered, etc., etc., never saying a word about the X-Initiative or anything they're working on. That woman is as fake as a virtual farmer's pet cow! *Oh my God,* what on earth is going on in this place?"

"God has nothing to do with it, Emi—this is vile. Whatever is going on sounds as though it is more fit for hell—not earth! This is what always happens. It has more to do with trying to control things or enact a human ambition or vision. It's definitely serious. I don't like it."

"Me either, but let me ask you this. What did you think of Margene when you saw her yesterday morning? Does she seem really odd to you?"

"Em, I have seen her like five times in total, and honestly, I have not paid much attention to her. She's always around when I see Powers, but she seems fairly innocuous and . . . I don't know, wallflowerish?"

"I dunno. I'm beginning to think there's more to the two of them than just their employment status at the LAB. The whole thing's odd. The new project, their appearance on the scene, her rise to power; For God's sake, her *name* is Powers!!!"

"Stop talking about God as if He's a swear word, would you?"

Day 131—The Pile-On

"I'm on overload. Way too much to think about. I'm so glad there's still a run on diamond dust because I don't think I could manage the glut of information coming at me today if I had to be queued in. But, listen—speaking of diamond dust, I had a thought. Do you remember about two months ago when the sonar alarm sounded?"

"Yeah. What about it?"

"I've been thinking about how the LAB has been able to plan and operationalize this new interactive series all without my knowledge or input, and I imagine there must have been a time when the lines of communication were open and the rest of us were just not privy to it."

"*Yeah?*"

"So, that made me think about the sonar. No diamond dust, no OLSM. Everyone knows that during those rare times when the sonar alarm sounds, communication goes down. Remember, Comm was down for several minutes that day—maybe the better part of an hour—and then throughout that week it was intermittent. Do you think it's too cynical of me to imagine that LAB communications were continuing during that down time on a channel they left open for that precise reason? Oh, Viddie, my mind is just spinning."

In spite of his calming voice, Viddie didn't do much to bring down my anxiety level, but he was kind enough to let me talk it through. He often helps me come to grips with things, but this morning I know I hit a nerve. His eyes grew wide as he bid me to continue.

"Between these new work initiatives and the insecurity I feel about harassment from the Medic, I . . . I . . . I just don't know. There's so much to think about! I keep seeing the Compliance Officers in my mind's eye—they're coming to our doors, ready to call us unfit and snatch Russi away. Tell me that's impossible, Viddie. Please, tell me it could never happen. Oh dear God, my nerves are shot. Do you see how cranky I've been lately? We should make a plan, just in case that does happen. Let's fix up the cooler with provisios and diapenz and leave it next door. If they come, we can just ignore them and hideaway in LJs until they leave. Do you think that will work? Vidd? Viddddd. Are you listening to me?"

When he looked at me he had the strangest expression on his face. I knew he was listening, but I'm not sure I was making enough sense for him to take it in. His response made me chuckle in spite of the stress that was weighing on me.

"Let's take this conversation down to *spiaggia,* yes? You know you do your best thinking down there."

I exhaled through my mouth with an extra long breath and stood up in affirmation.

"Best idea you've had all day! I'll get Russi's things. You'll pull our towels and cooler together, yes?"

Mmmm. *Spiaggia.* Yes. How I need a change of pace. This stealthy stuff at work is really getting to me, but every time I sink my toes into the warm sand the LAB and all its blindingly white tile and slick graphite walls instantly fade away. Oh thank Viddie's God. *Mmmmm.* Yeah, that husband of mine always knows what I need.

Day 133—The Angst

He's jogging and I'm sitting here on my favorite stoop just listening to the lovely sounds filling this space. It's so peaceful here at *spiaggia* that I can almost believe all is right in the world, but then, just as I open my heart to the hope of such harmony, my eyes begin to water and fill nearly to overflowing. Something about the gentleness of this day is stirring my emotions and I'm not sure I can hold back the tears. Am I ready to say goodbye to dreams of making a difference in the world? Can I simply turn off my desire and stop using my talents to create splendid virtual Xtreme vacations? Ugh. My head will not leave me alone. I can't stop thinking about what's going on in my little world.

Maybe if I dwell on all the things I love about Viddie I can offload some of this tiring, wearisome barrage of questions that beat against my brain. Hmmm. The turquoise bowtie he was wearing earlier looked really sweet next to his standard issue white lab coat. I like the fact that he can sport a bit of flair while still looking so masculine. *Ha!* If his father could see him now!

Day 138—The Revelation

"I found out something extremely creepy at work today. Vidd, you're not gonna believe it! Do you know why Margene has always seemed so dull and detached from the team, always tail-gating *her cousin*, Monica Veslie Powers?"

He looked up from his whittling project, chuckling. "Uh, let me see. Uh . . . she's a Power's clone?"

I walked across the car cover, shook his shoulders, and did not join in on the joke. "This is not funny, Belvedere Florencia. Please don't be stupid—*she is not a clone*. This is real! But you'll never believe it. You can't believe what I found out today!"

"Well are you gonna tell me, Emi, or should I keep guessing?"

Just then the vibra-sensor went off and the tiny cries of a waking baby took over.

"Uh—there's Russi! She's up."

I looked at him and quickly turned to run up the stairs and get her. Glancing back, I saw him put down the knife and start to clean up all the messiness that was at his feet. Shavings, shavings, everywhere!

"Turn off the vibra-sensor, wouldja, hon? And c'mon up here as soon as you're done. You have to hear everything!"

Day 139—The Compliance Officer

There's much on the horizon, and clearly it is more than black smoke.

After a couple sips of tea yesterday I decided to keep what I learned about Margene to myself, at least for the time being. As shocking as it was to find out that she is a part of what they're calling 'rebooted Drunge *material*,' I didn't have the emotional fortitude to explain it all to him, at least not then. More pressing was the Medic's new memo. I left it on my private glass board, placed it on the counter while the kettle heated, and waited for his reaction. It was the 12th message we received, one for each week since Russi's birth. The language of this memo went far beyond suggesting that we act. Words like *requirement* and *mandatory* made it clear. There was no mistake about the intention.

"Hon, you've got to see this."

Viddie walked over to the counter and began reading the memo while I fixed our tea. His voice was strong and bold, but as he held the fragile note pad I thought I saw his hand shake.

> This is the final notice requesting infant Florencia's presence at the clinic for federally authorized injections.
> The child must be checked and loaded with required inoculations for the sake of public safety and the order of the Golden Triangle.
> Failure to bring said child to HQ will result in the altered status of Emilya Hoffman-Bowes to NONCOMPLIANCE and may result in forcible entry to the domicile and review of the courts as to the worthiness of parental oversight.

He put down the glass-board and blinked a couple of times. My eyes filled with tears, anger and finally, outrage. Surely, my questions came out like bullets.

"You do realize they are threatening to take her away from us, don't you? 'Worthiness of parental oversight' is just a lame way of saying we're unfit. *You do realize* that they could rightfully burst through our doors at any given moment, don't you?"

Panic threw me into a tirade and I just about lost it as I continued to rant. "Vidd—this is crazy, absolutely crazy! I mean if we could know for sure that the injections didn't include anything more than harmless inoculations I might be willing to bring her in, but after the drama surrounding my parents when they messed with *their* baby, how could we possibly . . . I mean, we'd be nuts to let them . . . Oh, Vidd, how can we possibly take that kind of chance? What on earth are we going to do?"

Never before have I seen my husband move with such conviction. He turned to me, grabbed both my hands and clasped them firmly to his chest, staring into my eyes with earnestness.

"We've got a month before the weather changes up there but much less than that if we want to be sure the Compliance Officers don't come knocking at our door. It's time *mi amor.* No more trying to change this place. You were right last month, but I just tried to help you keep your heart hopeful. You saw the writing on the wall—literally! Your idea of becoming *The Preserver of the Traditions* was a noble one. It brought us both a bit of hope . . . but it is not panning out, my love. We've got to take action before they do."

His words struck my face like a windy blast in the middle of January. I started to weep uncontrollably. Thank God Russi was in her cradle in the next room.

"Shhhhhhh. Listen." He brushed the tear-soaked hair away from my cheek and started rattling off a list of solutions that sounded like bullets to my beleaguered brain. "My mother will have dinner for us every night until we can get settled in and start cooking ourselves. Grand'Mere will set us up with winter supplies. Your father and I will build a new earth shelter. We'll have our own, unfettered, unencumbered space. Don't be afraid. No one will bother us there, Em. It's time."

Every possible scenario of compromise skated through my mind—the options were horribly limited. At that moment I knew I could stand up, rant and rave about the injustice of it all, or fall into his arms in a flood of sobs. The sobs won out.

Moments later I broke away from his embrace and got up to find a tissue. He stood and followed me into the kitchen.

"Oh Vidd . . . it's so unfair. There seems no choice left. I *hate* this! I am feeling completely backed into a corner. Do you see any way out? I mean, honey—her life . . . Russi's life is much too precious to let her grow up in the midst of this . . . this circus. I . . . I am at a loss as to . . . I mean, how did it get so out of hand? We aren't prepared. We have no provisions, no path back, no assurance that we won't be tracked down. We . . ."

"There aren't rations back home, Emi. Think of it: Were you ever limited in what you wanted to eat? There was always enough. We eat whatever is in season or recently caught and we always have enough—a surplus. Here, we've got to live on rationed vegetables and an occasional piece of meat, most of which are grown in a factory or by Drunge workers! You must see now that we don't belong here anymore. Russi has a better chance of growing up straight and strong in FRANCO. She belongs there, Emi. We belong there. Don't cry. It'll be okay—you'll see."

What a deep, deep sense of defeat. How could everything go so wrong? Oh, dear-Viddie's-God-in-heaven! I tumbled back into my husband's arms and let all the fears I had been hiding from come pouring out of my heart. Tears continued to drench his shirt as I wept with quiet resignation. Truth has a way of shrouding itself when the facts belie logic. In my heart of hearts I knew he was right.

"*Shhhh. Shhhh, mi amor*. All is well. All will be well. We are together. God is with us."

His strong arms wrapped around me and I just stayed there without moving, thinking about the prospect of leaving Addison Avenue, *again*. If I really actually left this place, this time would be far different from the last time I left City Centre. I am not confused, nor am I trying to solve a mystery. I'm not going crazy either. I may not have put all the pieces together, but it's clear that the pressure to conform has increased, and now that it is encroaching upon my daughter I have no patience for it. It's also clear that there is a new balance of power here, and I'm not part of it. I whimpered a little and tried hard to completely stop crying. My composure was back, at least long enough to let me whisper a few more things to my Viddie.

"It's not just the thought of icy winters in the mountains that is breaking my heart. Do you understand that, love? I mean, what will come of this place? Who will step in to help show the way back into nature, back into relationships, back into the things that make us human?"

"*Shhhh. Shhhh.* Don't try and figure everything out all at once. God will give us wisdom. We don't have to know where the next ten steps will lead, just the next one. Let's think about what is necessary today and leave tomorrow's troubles for tomorrow."

{Sniffle} "I do miss Grand'Mere and would love to see her again. Plus, uh—it's so hard to say this—every day I am realizing the position my parents were in when they made the decision to leave. I thought they were just disgruntled and . . . and that they didn't know how to fall in line with the protocols, but now I'm thinking it was more than that, possibly this all has a root back then. I dunno."

"And, how much your grandmother would LOVE to meet her great-granddaughter, right?" He kissed my temple and broke out in a broad grin, the likes of which made my eyes start to fill up again. I know how happy this would make him, but did he realize that the whole of my life was being dismantled? Did he know that these developments would not only mean the end of life for us here in City Centre, but also the breaking of my dreams for a better society? The end of my ability to somehow fix the mistakes I made with the P/Z? Did he know that packing a bag to go to FRANCO would mean packing away any hope for the thousands of people who live here? The strength to even explain my heart was ebbing like the limpid water during low tide at Old Bath. I tried, nonetheless.

"It'll be a challenge to live there, but I'm afraid. I guess . . . I *see* that here, the challenge no longer exists. It has evaporated before my own eyes, Vidd. The roads that lead to hope in a flourishing, renewed City Centre are disappearing."

He nodded and took a deep breath, answering me with an unrelenting perspective.

"I'm not sure how much longer we can hold out, Emi. The Compliance Officer is not someone I want to ever meet, and if he (or she?) walks through that door, I am not sure how I will handle it. We may find ourselves on the run, even if we stay."

My head filled with a dizzying array of images—my LAB plate, the skyways, this stupid flat, *Old Bath*! Oh, dear—*the ocean*. The idea of never seeing the ocean again or wiggling my toes through the warm sand brought on another outpouring of water from my eyes. When I stopped crying I realized that there would be other challenges perhaps even greater than learning to weather the elements or cook in a stone pot. I cleared my throat and broached a subject that I never wanted to discuss with him.

"What about your faith, Vidd? Everybody up there believes in your God and you know where I stand with that. You know very well I'm not going to be able to pretend to believe in Jesus Christ."

His reply came after a thoughtful few moments, and it sort of threw me.

"Is there a reason you keep calling upon Him, then?"

"What? I do? I mean . . . no I don't."

"With growing frequency I hear you call on him—in the Name of Viddie's God, or something similar. You acknowledge his Presence. I have heard you."

My voice felt weak—as weak as my knees—and I realized he was right.

"I'm just . . . just . . . well, I guess I don't really know why I've called on Him. I'm just . . . maybe because I hear you speak to Him. I . . . I'm not really sure."

Viddie's tone was tender, as is typical. I looked at him through glassy, tear-streaked eyes as he continued.

"Could it be that somewhere in the deep unknown of your consciousness you have an abiding, resident knowledge that there is a higher power—a Designer who created this . . . all this?"

I shrugged my shoulders while he continued.

"Could it be the same sort of unspoken, unarticulated knowledge as that which propelled you into my life in the first place and let you know that it was safe to love? Think about it. You chose to give your love to me. Before that, you told me you never experienced love, but it was there all the time, wasn't it? It was activated when *you chose* to love me."

"Viddie, I don't know. I . . . I really have no idea. Love? Yes, but . . . I'm not sure. Belief in God is as counterintuitive to me as living off the grid and surviving in the mountains without electricity or provisio bars."

This time, his response was fast and sure.

"Yet, you survived that way for an entire summer."

"Yes, I did,"

"And you loved it."

"Well, *yes* . . . I did."

"Emi-girl, I believe that everyone knows there is more to our existence than just the emergence of a bunch of sexy cells that somehow organized themselves into intelligence and meticulous reproduction. I believe you know that too. Someone designed this incredibly beautiful thing called human life, and for all we don't understand about it, we've got to know at least, that."

I felt completely wrung out. My skin hurt from so many tears. We sat without words for several minutes. I snuggled next to him in my familiar spot. Cozy. Warm. Safe. Then he broke the silence.

"Remember you asked me to quote you something from the Bible that wasn't as dismal and dark as David's psalm?"

I nodded, in tentative agreement.

"I've thought about that more than once and realized that one verse, no matter how positive, would never convince you of a truth that has formed my identity and reigned in my heart since . . . well, since as long as I can remember. You see, my love, contrary to the unspoken consensus here in City Centre, Christians are not clowns. The Bible isn't a magic book; it's not fairy tales, and it's not prescriptive."

"I don't know what you mean by that, Vidd."

He glanced down toward me and kissed the side of my face, thinking for a moment before he responded.

"Prescriptive? *Hmmmm*. For Christians, there's not one, singular way to be or formula for living. We could live here if we had to; it's not like the woods and apple trees and natural surroundings are somehow 'the way'." *Un uh*. Following Christ is really about living in freedom and in hope, the hope of a better life, a *new* life that is beyond this work-a-day world of means and methods, a life that will continue with the Lord beyond physical death. And this hope points us to faith in the Living

God, and Emi, that faith is something that is active in my life every day."

I broke in, not to shut him down, but to make sure he knew I was not mocking him. A tiny aperture seemed to open on the far side of my heart. I realized I no longer thought of people who believed in God as clowns or idiots. Just living among them for several months made it clear. They have a faith that informs how they live, and the values they live by are not only commendable, but . . . well, there's no doubt that they are beautiful. I learned to love through them.

"Vidd, I respect you so much. I love you, hon, and I no longer feel antagonistic to your faith. It's just, well—I don't know how you can be so certain. You stake your life on the reality of God and how . . . well, how can you be so sure?"

"Ah, hon—it's not really about certainty. You may wonder how we can be sure that He is real, that He is there, that His plan and purposes for the world are intentional and good, and I wish I could tell you that there is rock-solid data that could prove it. But, Emi—I can't. In fact, you need to see that uncertainty is not a weakness—it's part of what keeps true Christians from becoming ideological. We don't believe in a set of principles. We believe in *Him*. So, what I can tell you is that certainty grows as we learn to put the little seed of faith that every last one of us has, in Him. Being a Christian is about trusting God in the unknown; Trusting that He is good, that He is leading, that even when our hearts fail us . . . He is there, for God is greater than our hearts."

A slight smile emerged from my lips. "So . . . *do* you have a New Testament verse you know by heart that will . . . what? Speak to this trust?"

"Actually, there are many New Testament scriptures that speak to it, and you may not realize it but sometimes in our conversations I speak them aloud, verbatim. 'Draw near to God and He will draw near to you' is not something I said—it's something from the book of James, chapter 4, verse 8. That's in the New Testament. It's truth. But if you're asking me to pick out a special one, once again I've gotta go back to the Psalms and Proverbs—you know, my section of the Book. It's a passage I've been living by since I was a small boy . . . something that has helped me stay strong even when things look bleakest. Listen to it, *mi amor*:"

"Trust in the Lord with all your heart. Do not lean on your own understanding. In all your ways acknowledge Him, and He will direct your path."

The knot in my throat started to soften and once again my eyes became watery. This man that I love so deeply believes in a God who is real, a God who is alive and cares . . . One who not only created all things, but who is *here*, with us. I didn't speak it aloud, but at that moment I sensed that the next stretch of our road would be completely different from what we've known thus far—that our journey back to the mountains would not resemble the frantic fleeing of the past; that the vacuum once echoing through the emptiness of my soul would no longer ring out in chaotic, reverberation. Instead, somehow I knew we had a way forward that was more real than anything ADMIN could possibly contrive. Instead of fright or panic the words, "Draw near" kept ringing through my being. Draw near, draw near. It was if I could almost hear them.

A peace, nearly visceral in its presence, pervaded every cell in my body. Its chiming echo peeled within me in concentric waves. At that precise moment I knew that I was on the verge of something—or Someone—that would render me changed forever. An assurance that we'd somehow find our way back to the community we both loved, and that once there, we would finally be home, began to wash over my soul.

Tears fell quietly as I slipped my hand into his and smiled.

The End

End Notes:

[1] Day 65 quotes Psalm 88:3-9
    Holy Bible, New International Version®, NIV®
    Copyright ©1973, 1978, 1984, 2011 by Biblica, Inc.®
    Used by permission. All rights reserved worldwide.

[2] Day 65 quotes Proverbs 8:1-3
    Holy Bible, New International Version®, NIV®
    Copyright ©1973, 1978, 1984, 2011 by Biblica, Inc.®
    Used by permission. All rights reserved worldwide.

[3] Day 127 quotes the song I Will—Songwriters Lennon,
    John Winston / McCartney, Paul James, Published by
    Lyrics © Sony/ATV Music Publishing LLC

Questions for Group Discussion

1. What is the significance of the title of this book?

2. How does Emilya's life experience a parallel to the advancement in her writing?

3. What does Emilya learn about herself as she returns to the LAB?

4. What is Viddie's part in her personal development?

5. What is the source of the conflict in her soul, and is it ever resolved?

6. What is the source of Emilya's indecisiveness and why does she spend so much time flip-flopping?

7. How does the conflict present itself as a threat to her identity?

About the Author

Stephanie Bennett, PhD. is a Professor of Communication and Media Ecology in the School of Communication and Media at Palm Beach Atlantic University in Palm Beach, FL. Currently, Dr. Bennett teaches courses in communication ethics, relationship management, digital culture, nonverbal communication, and rhetoric. She is a member of the National Communication Association, the Media Ecology Association, and the International Jacques Ellul Society.

Stephanie has written articles for a host of organizations and ministries such as Focus on the Family, CCM (Contemporary Christian Magazine), and Break Point.

In all that she does, Stephanie brings her love of writing and close-knit community together with a heart to inspire personal growth. Married to her musician/ drummer husband, Earl, she is the mother of three grown children and grandmother of nine. She enjoys playing tennis, writing songs and sharing life with students, family and friends.

You can learn more about Stephanie at:

www.wildflowerpress.biz

Her Facebook author page (Dr. Stephanie Bennett)

Other Books by Stephanie Bennett

Stephanie's books are available in ebook format at Amazon.com, Barnes & Noble, Smashwords, and in the Apple iStore:

Her books are available in paperback through Wild Flower Press, Inc. and soon to be available through other fine retail outlets.

Within the Walls, Book 1, in the *Within the Walls* trilogy.
Breaking the Silence, Book 2 in the *Within the Walls* trilogy.

Stephanie has also written:

Communicating Love, Published by Linus Publishing

Other Books in this Trilogy

Within the Walls, **Book 1**

Within the Walls brings us to the busy world of the character, Emilya, a creator of virtual vacations in the year 2071. What with micro-sleeping, sixteen hour workdays, and her total immersion in virtual relationships (both at work and in her flat), at 29, she hasn't seen much of a need to think about anything beyond the walls of her fast-paced, highly productive life. But the discovery of a mysterious letter sends her world spinning. Enter the inner chambers of Emilya's search for meaning. Take a careful look within the walls; her story may be closer than you think.

Breaking the Silence, **Book 2**

As *Breaking the Silence* unfolds, Emilya is trying to understand the puzzle of these people in the wild—the way they live, and their use of words like "faith" and "soul." Aren't humans just biology and electricity?

How can people co-exist in a place where they can't simply turn off the communications of others or carefully edit responses? Complications pile up for Emilya as she tries to deal with aspects of love and friendship that defy her carefully constructed idea of what it means to be alive.

Other Books by this Publisher

Like fiction with a message?

In addition to Stephanie Bennett's *Within the Walls* trilogy, Wild Flower Press, Inc. also publishes the *Fellowship of the Mystery* trilogy (Apocalyptic Scifi), and Book 1 of a new fiction series by Terry L. Craig, ***Scions of the Aegean C*** (in the "Steampunk" Scifi genre) is available with more to come.

To purchase paperback copies of any of these books or read our articles, visit us on the web at:

www.wildflowerpress.*biz*

CPSIA information can be obtained
at www.ICGtesting.com
Printed in the USA
LVHW040443270922
729373LV00008B/338